It's Not Over

This book is dedicated to
my daughter, Courtney,
who inspires me to keep going
whenever I'm tired and
discouraged and all seems lost.

Also to my Sister, Helene,
she never stopped dreaming.

It's Not Over

by Karen Sloan-Brown

BROWN REFLECTIONS

It's Not Over

Copyright © 2014 by Karen Sloan-Brown

This book is printed on acid-free paper.

ISBN: 978-0-9915517-7-4

Library of Congress Cataloging-in-Publication Data on file.

Editor: Cornelius Brown

IT'S NOT OVER
KAREN SLOAN-BROWN

1
It's Not Over

I'm not hearing voices but something is speaking to every fiber in my being. Today is surely a turning point and my life is about to change. I don't know how but it's coming, and it's about time. Not just because today is my 50th birthday, or that I've pledged to begin working on my bucket list, it's more due to my new found freedom. The last of my three babies is officially grown and on her own, that part of my life is over. I wouldn't give anything for the experience of raising my daughters, but the last 25 years of my life have been devoted to them. The next 25 are going to be devoted to me.

Nelson, my husband of twenty-seven years, and I just got back in town yesterday from the destination wedding in the Bahamas that our youngest daughter, Ebony, insisted on. She's the youngest of our three girls and the last one to move out of the house. It took a ton of organization but the wedding was beautiful and came off without a hitch. Nelson and I caught a late flight that arrived in Nashville after midnight, so scheduling the extra day to be off from work today was a providential decision. Erica, our middle daughter, and her husband, Drew, are spending a few extra days in Nassau for their vacation, and our oldest, Elise, is flying back home to New York early this morning, her company's office is located in Manhattan, New York and she will be present and accounted for in the office today even if it kills her.

"Whose turn is it to make the coffee?" Nelson asked, disturbing my early morning rumination.

"It's whoever gets down there first," I answered, knowing that it would be me as usual.

I swung my feet to the side of the bed and prayed that my knees felt like doing their job today, I'm certain they didn't take kindly to my sitting boxed up on the plane for three hours. I stood up, slid my feet into my slippers, and with the first step I could feel they weren't happy but at least they had decided not to hold a grudge. I put on my robe and made my way down the steps into the kitchen.

"Don't cook anything heavy for me," Nelson shouted from the bathroom, "My stomach is still shaky from all the crazy food we've been eating for three days."

"Are you sure it wasn't all the drinks you had to wash it down," I replied sarcastically, but he probably didn't hear me.

I turned on the small TV mounted under the cabinets to take a look at the news and find out what we had missed over the last four days. Then I reached for the Folgers canister of house blend with one hand while I turned on the water with the other. I was about to grab the handle of the coffee pot when the image of smoke and fire burning out of the side of a tall building stopped me in mid-motion.

"I know that building," I said out loud with my dulled senses becoming keen.

It was the World Trade Center; I had been there several times with Elise. Her office was located in that building.

"Nelson!" I screamed frantically, "Get down here."

I kept my eyes glued on the screen while my hands pat along the counter top for the remote like a blind woman. The remote shook in my hands while I tried to find the volume button. The anchor's voice grew louder as he reported that a commercial jet plane had just crashed into one of the Twin Towers.

"Oh my God," I yelled out in disbelief, pressing the up arrow of the volume over and over.

"What's going on down here?" Nelson demanded, standing

barefoot in the floor holding a towel at his waist.

"The place where Elise works is on fire," I shouted at him above the TV volume, "They say a plane crashed into it this morning.

"What are you talking about, Evelyn?" he asked, looking confused.

"Don't ask me, dammit, look at the TV," I urged impatiently.

"What the hell," he said, seeing the smoke coming out of the building, "Where is Elise?"

That's when I started to hyperventilate. She couldn't be in there. She was scheduled to fly out of Nassau on the first flight of the day. I looked at the corner of the screen and saw that the time said 7:58, surely she couldn't have gotten to the office in that time. Then I remember they are an hour ahead of us.

"I'm going to call Elise on her cell phone," I said, pronouncing my words slowly, I needed to stay calm, but something inside me wanted to panic.

"Hurry up, Evelyn, I need to know that she's not in there," Nelson said with his eyes fastened to the images on the TV screen.

I moved my hands blindly along the wall until I felt the telephone. I took my eyes off the TV only long enough to dial Elise's cell phone number. I listened to the phone ringing in one ear and the interviews with witnesses on the television with the other.

After ten rings I said, "She's not answering."

"What the hell. Oh no, it looks like a second plane just crashed into the other tower," Nelson said, stuttering.

I am witnessing the whole thing but it's hard to believe my own eyes. Thousands of people work in those building. They are in there right now. This can't be real. How could we stand here in our kitchen on a regular morning and watch people die before us on the TV?

"Lord, have mercy, what is happening, Nelson? Maybe I should call the other girls."

"There's no sense in worrying everybody until we find out what's going on. The news just announced that the planes may have been hijacked, and it might be a terrorist attack."

Black and brown clouds of smoke billow out of both towers darkening the sky around them and then the scene is interrupted by a report stating another plane has hit the Pentagon in Washington, DC. I keep standing there in front of the TV horrified by the sights and sounds of sirens and panic. Nelson backed into a seat at the kitchen bar still holding his towel.

"I'm going to try Elise's number again," I said. I hadn't put the phone down from the last call.

"All the lines are probably busy now but go ahead and try," he said slowly, sounding like he was in shock.

I listened for another ten rings and no answer. There was nothing we could do now except wait. I put the phone down and resumed my attempt to make some coffee. I couldn't watch anymore after the news anchor said people were jumping out of windows.

"Jesus Christ," Nelson cried out.

"What is it?" I asked, rushing back over to the screen.

"One of the towers has collapsed down to the ground."

"I can't see anything but swells of smoke," I said, straining my eyes.

"It's gone, Evelyn."

I fell to my knees praying and pleading, "Bless my family, Lord. Bless us in a mighty way, let my girls be safe. Don't let this be an end for us, give us a new beginning. Show us thy mercy and thy grace. Let hope and peace surround us; show us a miracle today, Lord. Grant me this desire of my heart and I will be a vessel to do Thy will. Please, Jesus, hear me. Don't pass over me; I need your presence, God. Put a hedge of protection around my girls. All these things I ask in your precious name. Amen."

I was still kneeling there in the floor when the phone rang,

Nelson answered, "Hello," and then there was quiet while he listened. "It's Erica, honey," he said after a minute, "They're looking at the news in Nassau. She says that she and Drew took Elise to the airport at 4:00 Eastern Standard Time after they hung out and her plane left on time. They want to know if we've heard anything."

I shifted my hips off of my knees and sat on the floor, taking the cordless phone from his hand.

"We haven't heard from her this morning and I've tried dialing her number several times and I haven't gotten an answer."

"This is crazy, Mama, and we don't even know when we'll be able to get a plane back home," Erica said, sounding upset.

"Stay calm and try to catch up with Ebony and Calvin," I told her, hiding my own worry, "I'll call you when I hear from Elise."

I kept sitting there with the phone in my hand, feeling the coolness of the ceramic tiles beneath me, and trying to make sense of what was going on, but it was shear mayhem, no more logical than the random lines scattered in the square of tile I was staring at.

"Get up out of the floor and go sit down in the den, Evelyn, you can watch the news in there and I'll bring your coffee," Nelson said, helping me up with his right hand and still holding the towel around his waist with his left hand.

I put the phone in the base and turned on the TV but the magnitude of the destruction was almost too much to watch on the big screen. Nelson brought me a cup of coffee but I couldn't swallow.

"I'm going to get dressed," he mumbled as he left the room.

I sat there bewildered; everything was perfect just two days ago when Nelson and I held hands and watched Ebony take her vows at the edge of the ocean with the waves playing the sweetest background music I had ever heard.

My girls were my pride and joy. There were two years between them, Elise is 27, Erica is 25, and Ebony is 23 years old. They are all beauties, the same height, but different shades of their father's features. They hadn't given Nelson and me much trouble growing up and we had gotten them all through college somehow, at least Elise and Erica, Ebony had gone as long as it took to find someone else to take care of her. Elise was all about her career and making money, Erica was a teacher but she was all about having a family, Ebony was all about Ebony, we had all spoiled her, but nonetheless, they were all independent strong young women.

Nelson came back into the room dressed in blue jeans and a t-shirt, carrying a lit cigarette in his hand despite the fact that he had quit smoking five years ago. He sat down beside me on the new leather sofa we had just gotten and the added stench of the cigarette smoke and his incessant coughing were on my nerves so bad that the brave façade I had been wearing for the last two and a half hours was starting to crack.

I didn't know if I was about to start yelling at him or screaming to the top of my lungs when the phone rang again. Afraid of any bad news that might be waiting if I responded, I let it ring. Nelson finally figured out after the seventh ring I wasn't going to answer the phone and got up, walked across the room, and picked up the handset. I held my breath.

"Thank God, you're alright," he said, sighing with relief.

It was the answer to my prayer. I was so relieved and grateful that I was too weak to pull myself up. All I could do was look up to the ceiling and say, "Thank you, Lord."

"Give me your hand," Nelson said, helping me on my feet, "Your girls want to talk to you, they're on a three-way."

"I need a minute to take a breath first," I said as I reached for my cup to take a sip of the cold coffee to compose myself before hurrying to the phone

"Hello there, Larry, Curly, and Moe," I said, trying to lighten up the tension from a truly heavy morning.

"Happy Birthday, Mama, they all say together."

"Oh, my goodness, with everything going on I totally forgot."

"It's overwhelming, Mama," Elise said, "I can't believe what's going on; I think I'm in shock. I'm hoping that not many people were hurt."

"Where are you? What happened? I've been trying to call you all morning," I asked, wondering if she had been in or near the World Trade Centers.

"I just got to my apartment. When my plane landed my luggage never showed up. I waited and they looked for it for almost an hour. Then I got delayed filling out the paperwork for lost baggage. Then my cab couldn't even get through Manhattan after the plane crashes, I walked most of the way home, it's a nightmare here."

"This is scary as hell, Elise, you could have been in that building," Erica said.

"If I hadn't checked my bag I probably would have been at work in the North Tower."

"I can't even think about that, baby," I said, "I was worried sick until you called."

"That's an understatement, I stood up in the kitchen with nothing on but a towel for an hour and a half," Nelson yelled loud enough for them to hear.

"Do they know what's going on?" Erica asked, "We don't know whether to come home or stay down here."
"I don't know, sweetie, we'll keep an eye on the news and I'll call you when we know more about it and if it's safe to travel, right now all the flights in the country have been canceled."

"Mama, it's like a bad dream," Ebony said, "I don't know how to feel, I'm supposed to be happy right now, I just got married, but things are crazy."

"Stay cool, don't get yourselves all upset," I said to all of them, "You all are safe and that's all that matters, we'll figure out the rest later. I want you all to stick close together in Nassau until we call you back, so leave your lines open. I love you, girls, I'll call back soon."

When I hung up the phone I realized I was a sweaty mess in my nightgown and robe. I was emotionally and physically drained as I climbed the stairs to get showered and dressed. The water refreshed me and I let the angst of the morning swirl down the drain with the grunge and perspiration I scrubbed away. I slipped into a long comfortable caftan and some slides.

Back down in the kitchen the clock showed it was past noon and we hadn't eaten a bite. I opened up a can of soup since my stomach was still too jittery for a heavy meal. For the rest of the afternoon and evening we were practically glued to our seats in front of the TV screen. We learned that all the events of the day were the result of a terrorist attack assumed to be orchestrated by Osama bin Laden and a group called al-Qaeda. Sitting there I didn't realize that this would begin a new normal for all of our lives.

"I'm sorry that we didn't have the good time I planned for your big day today," Nelson said, rubbing my shoulder during the evening news, "We'll have to pick another day to have your birthday celebration."

"It's not important right now, I've already gotten the best gift I could think of. All of my girls are safe despite all the trouble and the chaos in the world. So many people who weren't as fortunate as us are hurting tonight."

***

"I'm thinking about coming home and chilling down there for a while," Elise said, sounding disturbed on the phone after being in Manhattan for a couple of days. It's hell here now with all the death and disruption. The funerals are never-ending."

Nelson and I listened with concern on two separate receivers, me upstairs in the bedroom and him in the den. The horror and terror in the world and across the country had seeped into all of our lives.

"This is something we've never seen before, baby," Nelson

said compassionately, "Folks don't feel safe anymore and are scared to leave their houses."

"Doing nothing is wracking my nerves, Daddy. I don't have a place to go to work for at least two more weeks and staying in this apartment watching bad news all day is driving me insane."

"I've been watching it too, baby," Nelson said, "It's awful, when you get enough and it starts to bother you, turn it off."

"Being that it will take some time for them to set up a new or temporary office, it will do you some good to get away until things get settled," I interjected.

"With all the commotion and security I bet I can't even get a flight out of here," Elise said, sounding downhearted.

"Don't even sweat that, take the Amtrak to Baltimore or Richmond and then catch a plane from there," Nelson suggested.

"That's sounds like a plan, Daddy," she replied with renewed confidence coming back in her voice. "I'll call you all back when I get it all arranged."

"See you soon, sweetie," I said before she hung up.

Elise is my over-achieving workaholic career-oriented child. She's a math whiz; once she learned her numbers and how to count she has never stopped. Counting money is her favorite. She got the job at Whittington Brothers, the large investment firm right after graduation from Harvard Business School. Wall Street and the investment bank must be her natural habitat because she's only worked there three years but has already been promoted twice. Her career is her first love and up until this disaster she was becoming even more committed. Of my three girls, Elise is the most self-reliant. She has big dreams of running her own firm, so a man, child, dog, or cat would only be a distraction to her reaching her high aspirations.

Erica has some similar qualities to Elise, mainly in being goal-oriented. She is a perfectionist and slight control freak who has planned out every aspect of her life. Unlike her older sister she wants to have it all. Even as a little girl she always wanted to be a teacher, get married, buy a pretty house, and have two children. She met her husband Drew during their freshman year at TSU in a teachers orientation class and they have been together ever since. She's bossy but he's a strong and confident guy, so it's a good match. They live in Franklin, a small town thirty miles outside of the city where he grew up with his parents. Elise teaches 5th grade in middle school and Drew teaches algebra I in high school. They have been married for two years and just closed on the house she wanted a few months ago. Now she's been trying like crazy to get pregnant.

Ebony is my baby girl and she has always lived in a world all her own, a place of romance and happiness where there are no bills, no worries, and plenty of credit cards with available balances. She just quit school in the spring semester, one year short of a degree in Fashion Merchandising. She met Calvin in her sophomore year. He's a couple of years older than her; he did a four-year stint in the military and was just starting school. Ebony wrapped him around her little finger and the next thing we knew they were engaged. As soon as he got a job working at the Nissan plant the wedding was on. He purchased a two bedroom condominium in the Gulch and Ebony had moved in with him just before we left town for the wedding in the Bahamas.

Most of the air space around the world was closed for several days. Nobody knew if there were more planned terrorist attacks waiting to happen. Erica and Drew weren't able to get on a flight until the end of the week and it was in the evening. Ebony and Calvin decided to shorten their honeymoon and were returning early on the same flight. Elise was also flying into Nashville today from Richmond.

New York City was still in a state of pandemonium and Elise doesn't function well in uncontrolled environments. I think we all felt some relief that she was coming home. I got chills every time I looked at the news and saw those building implode with the realization that she could have been in one of them. She was usually pretty tough and unflappable but I could hear in her voice that the magnitude of what happened in the attack was beginning to dawn on her and she wasn't ready to deal with the details of how many of her friends and associates might be among the many casualties.

"Are you riding to the airport with me to pick up the kids?" Nelson asked, jiggling his keys in his hands and coming into the kitchen just after 9:00.

"No, I'll wait here and make something for everybody to eat; they don't feed you much on the plane, besides I don't think we can all fit in the car if I go."

There wasn't anything Nelson wouldn't do for those girls. It didn't matter what time it was or whether they had a husband who could handle it, when they call he answers. That's one of the things I love about him. We had gone through our share of problems and threats of divorce but no matter how shaky things ever got between him and me over the years he never wavered as far as our girls were concerned.

I heard the acceleration of the car through the window as he left for the airport. In the quiet I sat down at the kitchen bar and thanked God again for his faithfulness. All of my family was safe and so many others were grieving. I wanted to be deserving of the favor I had been shown, I wanted to show how thankful I was, maybe volunteer and reach out to the people in New York, but I was so far away and what could I do. It made me feel useless, so I got up, opened up the fridge, and got busy being constructive.

"I don't smell any food cooking," Ebony yelled when they came through the door.

"I'm done cooking for grown women but I did make you all some sandwiches," I said, coming in the foyer to welcome them all back.

"That sounds good, Mama," Erica said giving me a hug, "I'm

going to pack up mine to go, Drew and I are exhausted and we want to sleep in our own bed tonight."

"I hear that," Ebony echoed, "Calvin has to go back to work on Monday. They're working a lot of overtime at Nissan right now and after all we've spent we definitely need the money."

"Okay, sister girls, I see how you do, just desert me after ten minutes. That's all right, go on home and take care of your men folk, I'll be crashing here in my old bed with Mama and Daddy," Elise said, feigning indignation.

"Stop the drama, girl, we just saw you less than a week ago and I'll see you tomorrow," Erica gently scolded, putting her arms around her waist.

"I'll be back over to see you too, even though I'm supposed to be on my honeymoon," Ebony added. "You don't need to go rushing back anyway."

Erica went in the kitchen and quickly wrapped up a care package for her and for Ebony and they were out the door leaving Nelson, Elise, and I sitting in the living room.

"Things are never going to be the same again," Elise said softly, sitting on the edge of the couch with two suitcases beside her.

"They never are, baby," I said, wanting to comfort her, "Things are always changing, most of the time good, but a lot of the times it's bad. That's how life is."

"That doesn't make me feel any better," she said with a voice full of sadness.

"There's nothing I can say right now that would make you feel better. Come on in the kitchen and eat, then at least you can get comfortable," I urged, standing up.

Nelson took her by the hand and pulled her to her feet and put his arms around her as they walked ahead of me. We sat at the table and ate in silence.

"Do you want to stay up and talk for a while?" Nelson asked Elise after they finished their sandwiches.

"Not tonight, Daddy, I'm tired. I'm just happy to get another chance to sleep in my own bed."

"Enjoy it while you can because I've got plans to turn your old room into an office," I said jovially, hoping to lighten the mood. "Your Daddy has already moved into Ebony's room."

"Mama, you and Daddy should be ashamed, there's plenty of space in this house for both of you to live in without taking over our rooms," Elise said, half-joking.

"Those rooms were on loan, baby, and now the leases are up," I said, trailing her upstairs to my bedroom.

We were all tired and Elise was the only one who didn't have to get up and go to work in the morning.

The next afternoon Elise received a call from the representatives for Whittington Brothers with new information. It turned out that her firm was located ten stories below the area where the plane had impacted the North Tower; nevertheless, eight of the members of the company were killed as a result of the fire and smoke inhalation. There was a memorial service scheduled for the 28th of September and employees would be given six weeks of leave while the company struggled to organize and find a new location.

"You don't have to rush back for the memorial service if you need more time," I said, sensing that Elise might be suffering with survivor's guilt.

"I'm good, Mama, I might as well deal with it now. They were my friends as well as colleagues; I have to pay my respects. It could have easily been me. Anyway, I'm just going to go stir-crazy when I'm here by myself after you and Daddy leave for work everyday."

I work as guidance counselor at Cordell Holland High School. I've been employed there for as long as Nelson has been at his insurance company. He's worked for Nation's Trust Insurance Company as a claims adjuster for more than twenty-five years.

"You can come to work with me; I would love for you to give a talk about college life and your career to our juniors and seniors."

"That sounds like fun but not this time, I'm definitely not in the mood."

There was nothing I could do to console her. Healing was going to take all the time it needed and it wouldn't be rushed. I went in the kitchen and put a frozen casserole in the oven and then came back to join her watching the Oprah Show.

"You won't believe it, Evelyn," Nelson said, plopping down on the sofa between us after he had come in. "With all the claims flooding the New York area I've been recruited to travel up there to help the group of adjusters who are servicing the area."

"When is this supposed to happen?" I asked, totally taken aback.

"I have to be up there in four days," he replied.

"Me too, Daddy, I've got to go back for a memorial service."

"Now I'm afraid to ask what's next," I said, leaning back with my eyes on the ceiling.

***

I can't say I was happy but in a way it was a godsend; Nelson would be able to accompany Elise when she went back to the city and support her through her grief over her friends and co-workers while he was there.

"I still don't see why the two of you can't rent a car and drive up there," I said, getting a case of nerves at the airport.

"You don't need to worry, Evelyn," Nelson said, rubbing my back, "There is so much security right now it's the safest way for us to travel. Besides, who would help me drive back?"

"You've heard of Greyhound haven't you?"

"I love you, Mama," Elise said giving me a kiss at the check point for airport security.

"I love you too, sweetie, call me when you get there."

"We will," Nelson said, patting me on the shoulder. I guess

he had too much on his mind to give me a proper hug and kiss goodbye.

I stared through the wall of glass at the aircraft and said a silent prayer asking the Lord to cover the plane and guide the pilot's hands before I went back out to the parking garage. I stood out on the top floor in the open and watched two planes take off and ascend high into the air leaving a thin white trail of smoke behind them. The powerful engines thundered overhead in contrast of the silent bird that shared the sky below it. Suddenly I felt all alone, I got in the car and called my best friend, Macey.

Macey and I had been roommates and running buddies throughout our college days. I was from Chicago and she was from New Jersey. We were both English majors so we took classes together, studied together, and graduated together. We both ended up dating local guys and getting engaged six months apart. Over the years, during our marriages and the births of our children we always stayed close. Her kids, a son, Martin, and daughter, Melissa were grown and gone too and now we were ready to get out lives back and have some more fun again.

"I just took Nelson and Elise to the airport."

"Now what are you going to do with all the time you have to yourself?" she asked.

"I don't know. I definitely don't want to go out of town. I don't know when I'll get on a plane again."

"We haven't even celebrated your birthday yet with all the drama going on and fifty is not the one you let go by unnoticed, Evie. You know I have our tickets to the Prince concert on Saturday. I say we hit the town and party all weekend."

"Now that's what I've been needing to hear. What do you have in mind?"

"I say that we do it up special, happy hour after work, and have a few drinks at Spoken Word to kick things off. On Saturday we hit the malls early and buy ourselves some new outfits to debut at the concert, then we drop into one of the old school clubs, and we finish it off with a nice Sunday dinner out on the town."

"That sounds like a suitable celebration for a fifty and still fabulous woman going into the second part of their life, girlfriend, get me a seat up front. I want this year to be the signal of good things to come."

"All right, Evie, it's on. Do you want me to pick you up at work or at the house?"

"At the house, I want to change into something hot to fit my mood, fifty is on fire."

"I'm scared of you, do your thing, girl."

I woke up feeling great the next morning; our plans for a fun-filled weekend had me energized, so much so, I considered calling in and starting it off early, but I had already been out for the wedding and the aftermath so I got dressed and headed to work. Behind the wheel my mind wandered as I reflected on my life, I had spent half of my years helping young people find a direction for their lives and although I enjoy my work I couldn't help feeling like there was something else out there for me to do. Every since my junior year in college I have been toying with the idea of writing the great American novel.

"Good morning, Evelyn," Dr. Anna Morgan, our principal at the school, greeted me in the hallway on the way to my office, "Have things quieted down for you around the house yet?"

"Yes, Anna, completely, and I can hardly believe it. There's nobody there except for me. I haven't had this much time to myself in all my life."

"Enjoy it while you can," she said, smiling.

"I intend to," I told her going into my office.

I took a quick look at my office calendar and didn't see any appointments or meeting schedules. That's when I decided to write a poem. I was going to do something I had never done before. When they called for open-mic at Spoken Word, I was going to go on stage.

2

"You don't look like you're the big 5-0, old woman. I wouldn't have guessed a day over 49," Macey joked when I came out to the car.

"You know what you can do with all that old shit, I know better. I checked the mirror before I came out and my game is still strong," I said, sliding in the seat and slamming the door. "I'm holding serve and the score is love-love, this is my new beginning and anything can happen."

"Okay, birthday girl, I see I'm not going to be able to tell you anything this weekend," she said pulling away from the curb.

"Come on, Macey, it's just that I know that I'm about to turn a corner. I can see it in my mind's eye, and when I turn this corner it will be dramatic, nothing like I have ever thought in my wildest dreams."

"Like what?" she asked, getting curious.

"I'm not sure but its more than a feeling, it's like I'm being guided."

"Don't go crazy on me," she said, laughing, "Please tell me you're not hearing voices."

"Not like that, I can't explain it, maybe it's more of an urgency that I have to move forward before I run out of time."

"That's just your mortality racking your nerves, Evie, don't let it worry you, we're taking this bitch one day at a time," she said as we pulled into a parking space in front of the Spoken Word Café on Jefferson Street.

"It's a young crowd in here tonight," I remarked when we stepped in the door.

"Exactly where we want to be," she said, walking to a table on the side.

"Can I get you ladies something to drink?" a cute waitress with her hair locked asked, "You can get your food at the front."

"Two glasses of merlot please," I said.

"Hold our table, I'll get us something to eat," Macey said, getting up.

I looked around the room at the mixed crowd of mostly college students; they seemed a bit more mature than teenagers, they were probably upper classmen or graduate students. There were a few guys who I would guess were between 35- and 45-years old who were there trying to catch a young girl, but Macey and I were the oldest ones there, an observable fact that was becoming a more common occurrence.

"This ought to kill any hunger pangs that you're having," Macey said, handing me a plate of pork chops in gravy, rice, pinto beans, and turnip greens. "Surely, somebody's mama is back in the kitchen throwing down."

"I'm not mad at her, this is all good; I thought we were going to have to tear through a plate of fried-hard-to-the-bone chicken wings," I replied, carving into my chop.

A small quartet started to play and they dimmed the lights. The atmosphere was especially mellow and relaxing. I cleaned my plate, sipped on my wine, and let my mind and body unwind. The musicians played a short set and then the emcee moved to the microphone at the center of the small stage and welcomed everybody to the café.

"We're going to start off the evening with open-mic before we get to some special guests we have in the house with us tonight," he said. "Don't be shy, you don't need an invitation, we're all family. I know that everyone in here has something that they have to express. When the urge hits you, come forward and introduce yourself."

The emcee barely had time to leave the stage before a young

man dressed in ripped jeans and wild hair rushed up to the front. He started on a piece about woman who did him wrong after all he had done. It took some effort to keep the grin off my face; young love is so cute and sincere.

"I'm going next," I said.

"Are you kidding?" Macey asked, surprised.

"Watch me," I said, smiling.

Macey just looked at me with her mouth hanging open as I moved toward the stage. I calmly took out the sheet of paper I had written at work today and when the applause for the young man ended I walked up to the front and took my place in front of the microphone.

"Good evening, good people, my name is Evelyn, and I'm celebrating a very special birthday today. Some of you probably think I'm over the hill or even down a mile from it but today I feel brand new. I wrote this poem today when my BFF and I decided to come by, I hope you like it. It's called Brand New."

The band started to play something with a jazzy vibe and I started to speak:

"I'm brand new today,

A little strange some might say.

Yet, I'm coming out better than yesterday.

Don't look for me among the old or the tired,

The antiques, the discarded, or the recycled.

For with each new sun, I wake brand new.

Never seen before, so fresh with flavor.

A mix of unique tastes you'll want to savor.

What bag am I coming out of?

Mama's brand new handbag.

Like fine wine, top shelf, I'm second to none.

Where can you find me?

Pushing forward with the New Year's models,

Because everyday I'm brand new."

I nod my head in thanks and feel the warm applause cover me like a blanket on the way back to my seat and I want to do it all over again. I think back to a month ago when I would not have had the nerve to go up there and I regret all the experiences that I have deprived myself.

"Evie, you are truly brand new, girl, that was fantastic. I don't just mean your poem, it's how you went up there bold as you want to be and did your thing."

"Honey, why should I hold back at this time in my life? It's now or never."

"Get me a copy of that book you're reading, baby, because I'm right behind you."

We sat for about an hour listening to poets and monologues.

"I had a ball, Macey, I can't wait until tomorrow," I told her through the car window after she dropped me off.

"Me neither, you are full of surprises."

"That I am," I replied.

***

I got up early Saturday and Macey and I spent the day shopping like the girls we were before we married and had kids. It felt so good. We didn't have to get back at a certain time, cook a meal, or spend our money on anybody but ourselves.

"What do you think about these shoes, Evie?" Macey asked, strutting back and forth in a pair of pink platform stilettos in the Green Hills' Dillard's, "Are the heels too much?"

"Uh, yeah, at least for me," I answered emphatically. "On the other hand, I don't know about you because you think your feet are twenty-five years old. Granted, I'm not quite ready to sacrifice style for comfort just yet but my years of walking around with my feet hurting are over. Surely we can find a middle ground in here somewhere."

"I'm just trying to follow your lead, Miss Thang."

"Come on, sister, but I advise you to get some shoes you can walk in without having to lean on somebody unless you plan on bringing Richard."

"You're right, girl," she laughed, grabbing the taupe strappy ones with a box heel.

"Now let's go upstairs and check out some sexy dresses," I suggested after we had our shoes rung up. "Under normal circumstances I would not wear a dress to a concert, but since we are seeing his purple majesty I'm going all out."

"I don't blame you, Evie; he's going to be dressed from his head to his feet."

"That's what I love about him, that man has yet to disappointment me."

"That's because you don't know him."

"Even better, that's the key to a long and successful relationship."

"What am I going to do with you, chile?" Macey asked, dropping into a seat amid the racks.

"You can hold all my bags while I take this violet lace number that I know Prince will appreciate to the dressing room."

Usually I can't stand the sight of myself in department store mirrors and lighting, but I'm loving my look in this dress. I take in the full view from all sides.

"I'm still in the game, baby, it's not nearly over," I proclaimed loudly.

"I know you're feeling all renewed right now but hurry up in there," Macey yelled, bringing me back to my senses. "I need a nap before we go to the concert."

"It must be more mental than physical because I've got to get one in too," I laughed, coming out of the dressing room.

We found the nearest sales assistant, swiped our cards, lugged our bags to the car satisfied, and tossed them in the trunk.

"How about we pick up some salads at Jason's Deli, I don't want to eat anything too heavy," I said to Macey."

"Sounds good to me," she said, holding her hand up for a high-five."

"You are so crazy, girl," I chuckled as I slapped her hand.

***

The Gaylord Center Arena was completely sold out and we had to park three blocks away.

"Now aren't you glad you didn't get those high heels for tonight," I reminded Macey.

"That's the truth; I would have been out here walking barefoot by now."

The arena was packed with people, all ages, colors, and genders. Prince was so consistently fantastic that he had three generations of ardent fans.

"Your seats are up the escalator to your right," the attendant said.

"Macey, I hope you didn't get the cheap seats, we didn't bring any binoculars."

"We might have to rent some," she said sheepishly.

We rode the escalator for what felt like two whole minutes. I saw the booth that rented binoculars and plopped down $5. What was the sense in being there if you couldn't even see the man's face. Comfortable in our seats with our binoculars focused on the stage my excitement started to build when the music of Purple Rain started to play. The lights flashed on and we all screamed. It was the small wonder who was bigger than life standing there playing his guitar. He's not my type but I have to give it to him, he's sexy as hell. The Prince performed for almost 90 minutes and I couldn't have asked for more except I would have given the last dollar in my purse to be up front, close and personal.

"The man's still got it," I said raising my hand for a high-five from Macey, "When he did that split and slid across the stage and under the piano and then rose up and started playing it I thought I was going to die."

"Yes, girl, and he changed his outfit three times."

"He brought it tonight. Thank you for getting the tickets, my friend, I would not have wanted to miss this show."

"Let's keep this party rolling, Evie," Macey said, leading the way out of the venue, "The night is young and so are we."

"Okay then. If you say so, Miss PYT, it has got to be the truth."

We headed to a grown folks nightclub on Clarksville Highway not far from our neighborhood.

"I haven't been to a club in almost ten years," I said to Macey after we paid our $5 dollars, were patted down thoroughly, and our purses searched.

"Time to find out if we missed anything," she said, looking around to check out who was in the crowd.

"It looks like we haven't missed much, girl," I answered halfheartedly.

We found a table and sat down. We hadn't been there five minutes when a brother whose face appeared to be scarred from a serious car accident or a fight with someone who wielded a carving knife came over.

"Hello, pretty ladies, I'm Clarence. Can I buy you both a drink?"

"That's very nice of you," I replied.

Then the DJ pumped up the volume on the song, "Where the party at?"

Clarence signaled for a waitress and after she took our order he said, "Oh, that's my jam and purple is my favorite color, would you like to dance?"

"Go on out there and get your groove on, birthday girl," Macey said, smiling.

I gave her our look that says, "I owe you one."

"So where is the party at tonight?" Clarence asked.

"Its right here," I answered, bouncing my hips. I was a dancer from way back.

"No, I mean later. I would like to buy you breakfast."

"There's no need for that, I'll be home with my husband long before breakfast time."

I didn't want to leave any room for confusion. He might need to peddle his drinks at another table. He definitely did not have anything I was looking for.

"I didn't mean any harm," he said, throwing up his hands like he was under arrest.

"None taken," I said at the end of the song, "I enjoyed the dance."

Macey and I took turns fielding off the brothers and shaking our booties to "Independent Women." We made sure we had a good time because it might be 10 more years before we come back. We called it a night around 1:30 am.

"Are you going to church tomorrow?" I asked Macey.

"I doubt it; you are wearing me out this weekend."

"It's not over yet, we still have tomorrow," I told her as I walked in the front door.

***

The house was quiet, a rare incidence in the Winters' household. I decided to skip church to take pleasure in the tranquil Sunday morning all by myself. I turned on the TV but the news was overrun with reports of the terrorist attacks and fears of others yet to come. To escape the fear and paranoia I went out back to sit on the deck and focus on the peace that was in my own small world. The awesomeness of creation was evident all around me, in the sun, the blue sky, the clouds, the trees, and the red bird sitting on the post.

I wouldn't hear a sermon today so I bowed my head and said a short prayer, "Thank you, Lord, for the gift of this earth but we need your presence every hour and every minute of the day.

Grant us your wisdom and the peace that passes all understanding. Help us to love more and not hate. Send us leaders who are compassionate and righteous. Bless us, God, and don't forsake us, take power away from those that misuse it and let good conquer evil. In your wonderful name, Jesus, I pray, Amen."

My peaceful moment was interrupted by the phone ringing. I moved quickly to the kitchen to pick it up. I guess I was still as nervous as everybody else.

"Where have you been, Evelyn?" Nelson asked heatedly. "I've been trying to get you for two days. I was about to catch the next thing rolling out of here to get home."

"What's wrong?" I answered inquisitively.

"Nothing's wrong here; I was thinking something was wrong there."

"Why are you so worried? Everything is fine; I've been out having a good time celebrating my birthday with Macey."

"You must be keeping some late hours; you weren't home after midnight when I tried to call."

"I didn't see any messages on the machine when I got in."

"When I'm calling my wife after a certain time in the night I assume she will be at home. I kept trying and you didn't answer."

"At this age I don't have a curfew, Nelson. You've got me on the phone now and I'm fine. How are things going up there?"

"Elise is going through it; she lost three friends in the World Trade Center, but you know her, she won't let anything keep her down. There's so much damage here I don't know when I'll be home."

"Don't stress it, do what you can and when you get tired come on back. You've got enough seniority at that company to do what you want to do."

"All right, I was just checking in, the football game is about to come on."

"I wouldn't want you to miss a minute of that so I'll let you go."

"Don't be like that, Evelyn, I'll call you back later when the games go off."

"You don't have to; I may be going out for dinner."

There was silence and a short hesitation on the line before Nelson hung up. He's never acted jealous or insecure about our relationship but on the other hand I never went anywhere or gave him any reason to. Now that the girls are out and on their own, I'm not about to be babysitting this house. The phone was still in my hand so I pressed in Macey's number.

"Let's do a late lunch instead of dinner. No sense in waiting, I'm ready to eat now."

"Sounds good, Richard's glued to the TV. Give me forty-five minutes to get changed and we'll meet at the Pinnacle downtown."

I picked out a dress I had bought on sale a year ago but had never worn. I had a closet full of clothes that still had tags on them but that was about to change. I finished my make-up and put on some blinging earrings. It felt good to get dressed up and get out this weekend. I was done with sitting at home and letting my life become predictable and boring.

The elevator at the Sheraton Hotel glided up to the top floor effortlessly. When the glass doors opened I stepped out into the entrance. Behind the podium I could see the circle of the floor that rotated giving a panoramic view of the city.

"Good afternoon, ma'am, do you have a reservation?" the hostess asked.

"Yes, last name, Winters."

"Follow me, Ms. Winters, your party is here," she said, stepping onto the circle moving counterclockwise.

"I can't believe you got here before me," I said when we got to the table. "I feel bad keeping you from Richard all weekend."

"Please, he probably hasn't given it a second thought, we didn't have any plans. Besides, I'm having a ball. It might as well be my birthday too."

A handsome waiter came over to the table and said, "Good afternoon, madam, may I start you off with something to drink?"

"A mimosa please," I answered graciously as he handed me a menu.

"How's that for eye candy?" Macey asked, nodding towards him while he walked away.

"The best, at least Russell Stover quality," I said as I took a second look.

"He's definitely fantasy material," she added lustfully.

"Shame on you, Miss M., I didn't think you looked at anybody else but Richard."

"There's nothing wrong with dreaming. By the way, what are you fantasizing about lately?"

"Are you sure you're ready for it?"

"Oh yeah, tell it all."

"My big fantasy is to finally write my book, it's a bestseller, I go on a nationwide book tour and along the way I meet a young sexy thing and we have a torrid affair. I seriously consider leaving Nelson, who in the meantime realizes that he is losing the queen that I am and suddenly becomes remorseful of all the bad shit he ever did to me over the years and is as reformed as Ebenezer Scrooge. He then becomes the actual man of my dreams, leading me to give a tearful and heartfelt goodbye to the tall, dark, and handsome hunk of a man who was almost the love of my life. I renew my vows to my soul mate and then…"

"Earth to Evelyn, earth to Evelyn, and that's what it is and shall remain, just a fantasy."

"I guess I got carried away up here with this floor spinning."

"Is everything all right with you and Nelson?"

"That's all it is, all right. I remember when he couldn't wait to spend time with me, fired up by his desire to be with me. Now I think he does it out of obligation. There's just a little smoke where the fire used to burn."

"That is so universal that it's a cliché, every woman has to deal with that if her marriage lasts longer than seven years, all these men are brothers."

"That is disheartening; I guess we don't have anything new to show each other."

"None of us do, I'm afraid."

We ordered salads and drank mimosas.

"Let's promise each other that we'll get together at least once a week," Macey said as we rode down the elevator.

"It's a bet," I said, giving her a high five before we parted ways.

I took the long way home to extend my relaxed evening. With the key in the lock I could hear the phone ringing from outside the door.

"Hey, Mama, what's up?" Erica's voice sang through the receiver after I answered.

"I'm good, baby. How are you guys doing?"

"We're cool. Daddy called me and Ebony earlier and said we should check on you since you're at home by yourself."

"Don't pay him any attention; he just thinks I should be here waiting anytime he picks up the phone to call the house. That part of my life is over, I want to enjoy the next fifty years."

"Okay, Mama, sounding all feisty, call us if you get lonely."

"I will, so don't worry."

***

Three weeks have passed, Macey and I talk almost daily but we haven't been out again despite our pledge. Nelson got back in town a week ago and before that I had been feeling a little tired. I guess the excitement of the last two months have finally caught up to me.

"What's going on, running buddy," Macey answered when I called her at lunch.

"Let's start going to the YMCA after work. Everything I eat is sticking to me like glue; I guess it's going to be a championship fight to hold my weight down."

"I'm game, Evie, all the articles I've read say the metabolism slows down with age and the weight shifts to the tummy."

"That's some bad news," I said. "What time can you get there; you know I'm done at 3:00?"

"Make it around 4:30; we can get an hour in before I have to cook dinner."

I went straight home, put a chicken in the crock pot, and changed into some workout clothes. I can barely recognize my body from a month ago. I must be going through the change. They say the only constant in life is change and this is one I wouldn't mind going through already. My cycle usually comes like clockwork but the 28th day passed over two weeks ago, and I'm hoping that I have finally had the last one. I'm tired of the swollen and tender breasts, headaches, and sore joints from the hormonal changes.

"Ooh, look at you, Evie," Macey said when I walked into the gym, "You are getting a little thicker but the rest has done you good. You look fantastic. What are you eating?"

"I'm not doing a lot of cooking; I've been trying to lose some weight. I'm not doing anything different, except I feel a lot less stressed than I have been."

"It looks like your clock must definitely be running back after your birthday."

"I wish."

"So where do you want to start today?" Macey asked, looking at all of the exercise equipment around the room.

"Let's find something that works on the mid-section, every part of my body seems to get more fit except for the tummy. I can't stay looking fine with a middle-aged belly."

"Forget about that waistline, girlfriend, it's the first thing to go and there's nothing we can do about it. It's a sign of menopause in men and women."

"I'm not going to let it go that easy, but it seems like every pound that I lose just relocates in the mid-section. I'm starting to worry that maybe it's a tumor or something."

"Evie, stop talking crazy, but you do need to get your milestone check-up, complete with mammogram and colonoscopy."

"I'm going tomorrow. I made my appointment a month before the wedding. In the meantime, there are two elliptical machines over there with our names on them. Maybe they can work a miracle and I'll weigh less than I did a year ago."

Macey and I worked up a sweat and after forty-five minutes of being out of breath we called it a day.

"That was a good start, Evie," she said while we walked over to get our gym bags.

"I hope we worked up more than just our appetites, I'm starving."

"Do you want to stop and get something?" she asked as we walked out.

"No, I put a chicken on earlier and it's probably ready by now. Not to mention, Nelson has been trying to keep tabs on me every since he got back."

"What's up with that?" she asked, drying the sweat from her neck. "All of us are too old to start playing any games."

"I don't know, he got suspicious when he went up to New York and I'm not about to strain my brain trying to figure it out."

"All right, well, I'll see you tomorrow if you're not too sore," she said as she drove out of the parking lot.

Nelson was already home when I got there. I could hear the local news blasting on the TV.

"Where have you been this late, Evelyn?"

"It's not late," I protested. "It's not even 6:00. I've been working out at the gym with Macey."

"Okay, I was wondering what was so important that dinner had to wait."

"You have two hands and you can cook as well as I can. You didn't have to wait for me. I'll steam some vegetables after I get a shower."

"Take your time; I've already made myself a sandwich."

"I bet you didn't make two," I said on my way up the steps to my neutral corner.

It seems like we got on each other's nerves without even trying lately. Twenty-nine years of marriage is not without a few side effects.

Standing in the shower I realize I should have eaten first. I don't have the strength to soap up my body. I turn off the water and I step out to the floor and reach for my towel but before I can get it in my grasp I drop to my knees. I feel as if I'm going to pass out. I'm too weak to call for Nelson. "I'll have to rest here for a minute," I said out loud. I laid down on my right side and then I felt the small firm lump in my belly. I'm scared and I don't want to think about it. I close my eyes and drift to sleep.

3

I wake up alone the next morning, the same as I went to bed. Nelson must still have his attitude because he left for work again without saying goodbye. He's probably having another relapse of the irritable male syndrome but I have so much on my mind that I can't even think about him right now. I had lain on the bathroom floor knocked out for two hours last night and he never even came up to check on me. Somehow I managed to pull myself together enough to finally get back down the steps to eat something. I sat down at the island in the kitchen and ate a plate full of chicken and a slice of bread with some orange juice. I could hear the TV blaring in the den when I went back up to bed.

I'm feeling much better this morning but my anxiety about this routine check-up at 9:00 is building. After that episode last night I've been praying that I don't have diabetes. It hasn't skipped a generation in my family. Not to mention the lump, we've had our share of the unspeakable 'C' word too.

"I need to get a copy of your insurance card and I need you to fill out these forms," the receptionist at the doctor's office said, taking my card and handing me a clipboard thick with paperwork. "Bring it back up to me when you get done."

"Thank you," I said, grabbing a pen from the glass jar sitting in front of the window.

I chose a seat where I could look out the window and not face the other patients in the waiting room. I methodically worked my way through every question on all the pages, family health history, my medical history, and current complaints.

"I'm done," I said, handing the receptionist the clipboard.

"Your nurse will call you from the door in the rear," she replied with a smile.

Visiting a doctor has to be one of the most humbling of life's experiences. You have to be on time or you won't be seen, then you have to wait long after your scheduled appointment without question, be weighed, undress, and allow yourself to be poked and prodded from head to toe. After all of that you have to trust and rely on their knowledge and expertise without even knowing what kind of grades they made in medical school. It's simply much too much to ask.

I concentrated on the movements of a large black raven that was pillaging for food in a trash receptacle beside the base of a tree while I listened to the different names called by the nurses from the rear door. Twenty minutes later I heard my name called.

"Mrs. Winters, you can come on back," a young woman in abstract printed scrubs said from the door. "How are you today?" she asked, holding the door open for me.

"I'm good. How are you?" I answered politely, both of us dismissing the fact I'm in the doctor's office for a reason.

"Fine, thanks," she answered automatically, "I'm going to get your weight before we go to your examining room."

"Do we have to?" I asked, joking as I took off my jacket and shoes. No sense in adding extra pounds to the situation.

"Nobody wants to get on the scale," she said, adjusting the weights and then writing 176 pounds.

I cringed, that was seven pounds heavier since my last check-up.

The nurse took my blood pressure, temperature, and pulse before she asked, "Do you have any particular concerns today."

"This is a regular check-up, but I would like to have my blood sugar level checked."

"I'll need you to take one of the cups there by the sink to the rest room out to your left and give me a urine sample and leave it in there on the table. Here's a form for you to take to the lab across the hall where you can have your blood drawn. When you come back change into the gown there and Dr. Sutherland will be in to see you soon."

I nodded my head as she walked out. I went through all the motions that she directed and sat down to wait on the examining table. Just as the chilled air of the room had covered my skin with tiny bumps and was seeping in closer to my bones, Dr. Sutherland came in.

"Good morning, Mrs. Winters, how are you doing today?"

"I'm doing fine I think."

"I'm sure you are, I'm just here to confirm that for you," he said with a relaxed chuckle. "Let's start at the top and work our way down."

He looked in my eyes, ears, and my mouth. He listened to my heart, lungs, and cough. I raised my arms and then my legs as he tested my reflexes, muscle strength, and inspected my joints. I lay down and he examined my breasts. I held my breath as he palpated my abdomen.

"Would you like for me to do your pelvic exam or do you prefer to go to your ob-gyn?"

"I might as well get it all done today," I answered with a fake smile.

"All right, hold on while I get my nurse," he said.

I was feeling much calmer than when I first walked into the clinic. Dr. Sutherland hadn't seemed alarmed by anything so far and I was almost done. When he came back in with his nurse she covered my waist with a sheet while he pulled the stirrups out from the table. I put my feet in them and focused on the ceiling while he inspected my most private parts.

"You can get dressed, Mrs. Winters," he said after a few minutes, "I'll be back in shortly to speak with you."

Back in the comfort and security of my clothes I took a seat in one of the chairs against the wall of the room and picked up a copy of *People Magazine*. I had perused my way through more than half of it before Dr. Sutherland came back in.

He sat down on the rolling stool and scooted over in front of me and said, "I don't know if this is anything that you may have suspected but you tested positive for pregnancy."

"Excuse me, Dr., but I don't understand."

"I suspected it from your pelvic exam so we tested your urine, you are pregnant."

"Pregnant, no way, my tubes have been tied for nearly 14 years and I'm fifty years old. That's impossible."

"I can't explain that for you, Mrs. Winters, I can only tell you what the tests say. At your age this is a high-risk geriatric pregnancy so you will need to talk about this with your family and make an appointment to see your ob-gyn as soon as possible."

He stood up and opened the door for me but I couldn't move. I couldn't think. I was in shock. He reached out for my hand to shake and pulled me to my feet and I started to move in slow motion out of the room, down the hall, and out of the office. I sat in the car and dug through my purse for my cell phone. I dialed Macey's number first.

"Hello, Evie, how did your dr.'s appointment go?"

"I'm here in the parking lot at Centennial Women's Clinic; can you come and get me?"

"Sure, I'll be there as soon as I can," she answered without asking why, "Do you want me to stay on the phone with you?"

"No, just come quick."

"All right, sister, I'm on my way."

I sat there in the car trying to clear my head of the daze. Was I in a dream or was this really happening? Everything else looked normal around me. The sky was clear and blue, the sun was shining, and a slow moving breeze tossed the fallen leaves along the sidewalk. The traffic lights were changing and cars passed by in an orderly fashion. Could it be some kind of mistake? What am I supposed to do?

One question after another filled my head until I saw Macey's car pull into the parking lot. I watched her car circle through the aisles of cars powerless to pick up the phone and direct her to where I was. I just kept looking as she weaved through them getting closer to me. I held my hand up when she spotted me. She found a space in the next row and then ran over to my door.

"Evie, are you okay?" she asked, opening my door.

"I don't know what's going on, Macey. I want to lay down in the backseat."

"Come on out," she said, grabbing me by the arm until I was on my feet.

She opened the door and I fell back onto the rear seat and keeled over.

"What tests did you get done today, did they have to sedate you?" she asked, looking at me with a worried expression.

"No, I'm just overwhelmed right now. I need to go home but I didn't call the school."

"Where's your phone? I'll call them and tell them you're not feeling well," she said, climbing into the front seat.

"It's on the front seat by my purse," I said, closing my eyes.

I listened to her speak with the school receptionist, and when she hung up I heard the engine start. The car slowly started to roll.

"Thank you, Macey, for coming, I needed to get away from here."

"You know I'm here for you, girlfriend, whatever. That's how we do."

Laying on the backseat was so soothing; I wanted to ride for a while. I wasn't ready to face my world yet.

"Macey, do you have to go right back to work?" I asked. "Can we ride around for a few minutes before you take me home?"

"Sure we can, I don't have another class until 3:00."

Macey had been teaching freshman English at Nashville Tech since we both got our Master's degrees at Tennessee State fifteen years ago. She had stayed in English and I had changed to psychology.

"What did the doctor say, Evie?" Macey asked as we waited at the stoplight. "You're getting me nervous."

I wasn't sure if my lips could form the words to tell her. Then I felt the car pull away and start rolling again. I lifted my eyelids and looked through the top of the window. My eyes followed the electrical lines strung between the pole and the tree limbs that reached around them. I opened my mouth and waited for the words to travel there from my brain.

"The doctor said I'm pregnant," I said in a low voice.

The car lurched forward as Marcey slammed on the brakes and I was jerked near the edge of the seat. Angry car horns blared as cars sped past us on the left.

"I have to park the car," she said as we slowly drifted to the curb. "Did you say the doctor said you are pregnant?"

"That's what he said," I answered, avoiding her eyes.

"I can't believe it; this is so over the top. Have you called Nelson?"

"No, I haven't said anything to anybody. I just came out and called you."

"Evie, you had your tubes tied a long time ago. I thought you said you were going through the change."

"I thought I was, I don't know what happened."

"If this is true, it is a straight miracle because your tubes have been tied and your ass is fifty years old. I didn't even know you and Nelson were hitting it like that."

Then I found the sense to laugh and my lungs filled up with air again.

"We're not, so I don't know how it happened. I don't think that Nelson even squirts out any juice anymore, much less with sperm in it."

We both hooted and howled at that for a minute relieving the tension that we had been feeling. We sat there for a minute grunting and sighing as the reality of the morning set in.

"Are you ready to go to the house yet?" Macey asked, "It's lunch time and we need to eat."

"I guess so, where am I going to run to?"

"We always have options, we can go down like "Thelma and Louise" if we have to."

"Girl, you are so silly. Take me back to the clinic, I can drive now. You can get your car and trail me home and I'll make you some lunch, and please turn on the radio. You'd think somebody was dying instead of being born."

"She's back," Macey sang in the air.

We picked up Macey's car, drove to the house, and I made us two loaded baked potatoes. We finished them without much conversation.

I was boiling some water for some herb tea when Macey asked, "What do you feel about all of this? I know it's soon but are you thinking about having this baby?"

"I asked God for a lot of things this year but this wasn't one of them. I prayed for a new beginning in my life and I got one. It may not have been what I expected but it's my blessing."

When those planes crashed into those Twin Towers after Ebony's wedding I prayed that my children would be spared from those disasters and they were. So in good conscience, I couldn't take this child's life away after that, not even if I wanted to."

"I just wanted you to know that I have your back either way. So, how are you going to break the news?"

"What do you mean?"

"How are you going to tell them? Are you going to tell Nelson by himself or are you going to tell them all together?"

"I hadn't even thought about it. I guess I'll tell Nelson first and then I'll tell the girls."

"I wish I could be here to see it. Honey, it's going to be better than the Prince show."

"I haven't even thought about calling my mama and daddy."

"One step at a time, Evie, maybe you should have the check-up with your ob-gyn first before you say anything to anybody. You need to know that this is a normal pregnancy and that the baby is healthy."

"That makes sense, no announcements until after I see Dr. Rush."

"Did they make you an appointment?"

"No, I didn't stop at the check-out desk."

"I'll make the call for you while you finish making the tea."

This is about the one hundredth time that I have wondered what I would have done without my friend. When she got off the phone she had me scheduled for an appointment in two days. We sipped on the tea until it was time for her to head back to work.

"You have really raised the bar, Evie," she said on her way out, "There's no way I can top this for my 50th birthday next month."

All I could do was shake my head. The plans I had for the second half of my life were suspended, my future had taken on a life of its own.

***

"Mrs. Winters, I have given you a thorough examination and you are in good health, and as far as I can tell from the ultrasound, so is the fetus," Dr. Rush explained to me in his office.

"I don't know how this could have happened, Dr. Rush, you tied my tubes years ago."

"I have no explanation as to how your tubal ligation was reversed, but you do have options. There are some concerns that you need to be aware of in weighing your decisions. First as far your health, women of your age are three times more likely to experience diabetes and high blood pressure during pregnancy."

"I'm not as concerned about myself as I am about the health of the baby."

"There is a 50 percent higher rate of miscarriage and the preterm births are even higher for women over 50 years of age. The risks to the baby are much greater; the number born with Down's syndrome is 1 in 10.

"You don't need to scare me, Dr. Rush, I'm already terrified."

"It's not that I want to alarm you but I do want you to make an informed decision as to whether you want to continue with this pregnancy."

I thought about the sight of the small fuzzy figure pulsating on the ultrasound screen and the sound of the tiny heart beating through the instrument and told him, "I am going to continue, that much I do know."

"In that case, I would recommend that we schedule you for an amniocentesis to check for any chromosomal or genetic abnormalities. It will give you peace of mind."

"If I had doubts about keeping the baby, Dr. Rush, I would definitely take the test, but there's no need for me to delve into the unknown if I'm not going to do anything to change it. I don't even want to know if it's a boy or a girl."

"All right, Mrs. Winters, that's your choice, but I want to monitor you closely as this is a high-risk pregnancy. Initially I would like to see you every two weeks. My nurse will get you scheduled today."

"Thank you, Dr. Rush," I said as he walked me out to the nurse's station.

Before I left the office I had prescriptions for vitamins and appointments for the next three months. Now all I had to do was pull off a reasonable job of pretending that everything in my life was proceeding along normally at school until I made the monumental announcement to my family. Nelson would probably go ballistic and I couldn't even guess what the response from the girls would be.

On the way to Holland High, I passed by the Hull-Jackson Montessori School. I could see the children outside playing on the playground. Running and laughing, squealing and tumbling, they were moving stores of energy in the flesh. I flashed back to the days when the girls were that age and how much effort it took to care for them. A young mother dressed in blue jean overalls with a sweatshirt over it pushing a toddler in a stroller gave me a big shot of reality, there was a long road before a baby was school age.

Dr. Morgan must have seen me pull in the parking lot because she met me at the entrance.

"Good morning, Evelyn," she said, holding the door for me with a face full of concern, "How are you doing?"

"I'm good, Anna," I answered, putting on a smile, "The doctor thinks it was just a virus or something."

"Is it contagious?" she asked half-jokingly. "You know you have plenty of sick days and the rest of us don't want to catch anything that can run through the whole school."

"You can relax; it wasn't anything transmittable," I said, leaving her at the principal's office door and proceeding around the corner to mine.

"That's good news," she cheered behind me.

It was surely news, although I couldn't think of one person who would feel it was good. There was so much more I hadn't considered. I would have to tell Dr. Morgan and the rest of my colleagues. Then there were my parents, neighbors, and friends. What about my students? It would be uncomfortable counseling one of my pregnant students with my own big belly. I was starting to feel embarrassed and nobody but Macey and I knew about it.

This was one of the few instances when the school day was over that I wasn't eager to go home. I was still trying to grasp the situation for myself but I couldn't put it off any longer. I had to tell Nelson. I stopped at Harris Teeter's on the way home to buy some of his favorite stuffed pork chops, although I doubted that a good meal would make this any easier to digest.

Once I got home I changed into a caftan to be comfortable while I cooked and I almost poured myself a glass of wine to relax before I realized that at my age I needed to take every precaution. Dinner was prepared and the table was set when Nelson walked in.

"It smells good in here," he yelled from the front door.

"Hello, honey bear, it's ready and hot so wash your hands and come on," I shouted back as I placed the food on two plates.

"What's the special occasion?" he asked, coming in the dining room with his hands still wet. "You haven't been in the kitchen for weeks."

"Must you always exaggerate? You haven't missed one meal or lost any weight."

"You must have had a good day today," he said, sitting down and admiring the meal I had prepared.

"I'll tell you about it later. Do you want a beer or some sweet tea?"

"I'll take the tea first," he said, enjoying the service he was getting.

Halfway through the dinner I hadn't found the perfect segue to broach the subject. There just wasn't a gradual or delicate way to drop this bomb. I took the last bite of my pork chops, added a mouthful of mashed potatoes, and washed it down. Then it was time to take cover.

"Nelson, I went to get my check-up and the doctors informed me that by some miracle of medicine I'm pregnant."

"What kind of game are you playing, Evelyn?" he said exasperated, "I'm not in the mood for any of your foolishness this evening."

"I'm not playing any games with you," I replied seriously, "I've been to Dr. Sutherland and Dr. Rush. I've had all the tests and I am pregnant."

"Obviously, there must be some kind of mistake because your tubes were tied years ago."

"That's true but the fact still remains that I am pregnant."

"Now what did the doctor recommend you do about it at your age?" he asked, pushing his chair back from the table.

"From what they can tell I'm healthy and the baby is healthy and the decision on whether I want to continue with the pregnancy is up to me."

"What about me, don't you think this is something we need to discuss together?" he asked dramatically with his fingers pressed against his chest.

"That's exactly what we're doing right now."

"I'm really shocked to shit right now, I can't even think, Evelyn. In two years I'll be 60 years old. This isn't something that I planned. I'm too old to start over raising a baby."

"It's not anything I planned for me either, but all I know is that when that plane hit the World Trade Center I asked God to spare my baby and he did, so there's no way I could do anything to hurt this life inside of me."

"I don't think I can do it, Evelyn. That's a young man's game, and I don't want to come off the bench, I've played my time."

"I've said all those things too but it is what it is."

"How do I even know if I'm the father, you were running wild while I was out of town?"

"I'm not even going to dignify that ridiculousness with a response."

"It's all about you as usual," he said nastily.

"What do you want me to do? I told you I'm not getting an abortion. Do you want me to put it up for adoption?"

"It doesn't seem like I have much choice in this anyway," he said, standing up so forcefully that he knocked his chair onto the floor.

"What else can I do?" I pleaded as he stormed out of the room.

"Don't ask if you don't care," he shouted back.

Nelson and I had gone through our ups and downs like many other couples over the years and there had been many junctures when I even considered divorce once the girls were grown. We had finally reached a point where the distance between us had become comfortable. Now it looks like it's time for me to board the rollercoaster of craziness again and I don't recall standing in line for this. I'm sure there is another middle-aged woman pining away for another chance at motherhood somewhere in this world but I wasn't the one.

4

"What is the scheduled show time for this major drama to premiere?" Macey asked after we got out of the early morning church service.

"I'm thinking we should all talk about it over some brunch."

"I would like to be there to support you but they may need someone to give details on the evening news," she joked.

"Hopefully it won't be that serious where there're no survivors," I said, shaking my head.

It had been two weeks since I had given Nelson the news and he hadn't spoken more than a hand full of words to me. You would have thought I had conspired against him. I had wanted to tell the girls sooner but I wanted them all here in person and Elise couldn't get away on a flight down here before last night. All I had told them was that there is an important family issue that we need to discuss together. I hadn't even called my Mom and Dad to tell them. I figured I'd start in the core of my family and work my way out.

"Okay, Mama, what's all the mystery about?" Erica asked as soon as I stepped inside the rear door of the house next to the kitchen.

"Let's get something to munch on, I'm hungry, some of us went to church this morning."

"I came here to get the word this morning, Mama, so speak the truth. Daddy is tripping; he won't even tell me what's going on. All I know is that y'all are too old to be going through any relationship changes."

"Excuse me, you don't know what we're too old to do so get

busy and make your mother an omelet or something. You'll get the news when everybody else does."

"Well, call Ebony, she always dragging in late and I need to cook dinner at my own house and get my lesson plan ready; Drew is watching one football game after another and he's no help."

"I called her and she's on her way," Elise said, coming into the kitchen.

"Hurry up with my food, Erica; I'm not going to do this on an empty stomach," I complained, feeling slightly dizzy

"Mama, what's the deal?" she asked, frustrated. She couldn't stand not being in charge.

"Hold your questions and grievances, another half hour won't hurt you."

"Throw a couple more eggs in there for me too, Erica, I haven't eaten anything since I left New York," Elise added, taking a seat at the table.

"I'm not the one, people, I don't work here," Erica said annoyed, giving the eggs in the bowl an extra beating.

"Elise, are things getting back to normal at work?" I asked, tossing a sprinkle of grated cheese in the egg mixture.

"Not really, the market is a disaster right now and there are a ton of layoffs at most of the major firms. If I wasn't so damn good I'd probably be out of work too."

"They're laying people off everywhere, things are getting real bad," Erica said, placing a steaming platter of beautiful omelets in the middle of the table.

I grabbed several plates out of the cabinet and place them on the island. I made a plate for myself, poured myself a large glass of orange juice, and sat down to eat.

"We need some toast," Elise said, pushing down four slices of bread in the toaster. "Anybody want some coffee?"

"I do," Ebony squealed, coming into the kitchen with her arms open for a hug.

"Hey, baby sis," Elise said, wrapping her head under her arms in a playful embrace. "How's married life?"

"I'm loving it, except sometimes it feels like I adopted a son to take care of instead of getting a man to take care of me."

"That's why I'm staying single," Elise chuckled, buttering her toast, "I had enough taking care of you two brats."

"You're supposed to take care of each other in a marriage," Erica declared, "Isn't that right, Mama?"

"In a perfect world that's how it's supposed to work out, sometimes it does, other times not so much," I said as I scraped the crumbs from my plate into the trash can.

I took a couple of minutes to enjoy my grown girls as they talked and teased each other while they ate. I was so proud of the women they had become. This was probably going to be the last peaceful moment of the day.

"Ebony, go get your Daddy and tell him to come into the dining room, I don't feel like competing with the TV for his attention."

My glass of juice only had a few ounces left in it but I held onto it to steady my nerves as Elise and Erica followed me into the dining room. Ebony and Nelson were coming in through the other entrance just as we sat down.

"Get me a beer, Erica," he said, sitting down at the head of the table.

"This early, Daddy?" she asked, surprised.

"I didn't ask about the time, I just asked for a beer," he answered irritated.

"Settle down, people," I said after Erica returned, trying to keep things calm for as long as I could. "Your father and I have some family news to share with you."

"I didn't realize I had anything to say about it," he interrupted.

I ignored Nelson's comment and continued, "The reason I asked you all to be here today is to tell you that I'm pregnant."

Nelson slammed his beer down on the table and I focused on

the drops that had splashed out of the top as they soaked into the tablecloth. Elise burst out laughing, Ebony's mouth hung open, and Erica started fussing.

"Mama, have you lost your mind, what are you thinking about at your age?" Erica shouted, "We're supposed to be having the grandchildren for you, not you having them for yourself. I thought this was about you and Daddy getting separated or something."

"Hell, I'm relieved, I thought one of you was seriously ill or something like that," Elise said, holding her chest.

Ebony finally found her voice and asked, "Are you going to go through with it, Mama? It might be dangerous at your age."

"Excuse me but I know how old I am," I said, looking around the room at each of them, "Besides, I had another doctor's appointment on Friday and he said I'm doing fine."

"This doesn't make any sense to me," Ebony said, looking confused.

"Daddy, you don't seem so happy," Erica said, "What do you think about all this?"

"It's not that I'm not happy, sugar," Nelson answered, "It's just that I thought my time of raising babies was over. I'm not sure it's what I want, but if your mama wants to do this I don't have any other choice but to support her."

"How do we know that this baby won't have developmental problems, serious health issues, or Down's syndrome?" Erica asked, still upset.

"For so many reasons this shouldn't have happened but it did," I exclaimed, "I didn't plan it or expect it. I feel like it's a miracle so I'm going to accept the situation no matter what it is."

"It doesn't make any difference to me, Mama," Elise added, "You can have another one after this for me too. If you and Daddy don't want to raise this one, I will."

"This is too ridiculous," Erica commented, shaking her head. "I can't talk about it anymore right now. I have a ton of things to do so I'll call you, Mama. Love you, Daddy," she said, bending down to kiss him on the cheek before she marched out of the door.

"I need to get home too; Calvin and I are going out with some friends to watch the Titans game. I don't know what else to say," Ebony said, shrugging her shoulders.

"It's okay, baby. I know it's a lot to take in at one time; I still haven't wrapped my own head around it. We'll talk later. Give me a hug," I said, standing up.

Ebony put her arms around me loosely like I was a stranger and I wanted to cry. She gave her daddy a hug and left. Nelson got up next and slowly walked out of the room. This was tearing up my family. I had to wonder if I was making the right decision. I looked over at Elise and she smiled at me and then put her arms around me.

"Mama, you know Erica is always trying to run everything and Ebony just wants to keep being the baby. Daddy's just worried that he might have to change some more diapers, he'll get used to the idea. You can count on me for whatever. I think it's fantastic having another member added to the family. You take good care of yourself and everything will be fine. Life ain't over at fifty and don't let anybody tell you something different."

"Thank you, baby, if you hadn't been here, I might have changed my mind."

***

"How was your weekend, Evelyn?" Miss Terry, the school secretary asked as I passed her desk in the reception area.

"It was draining; I probably need two more days off," I said, stopping for a moment, "How was yours?"

"It was the usual, grocery shopping, cleaning, and cooking. Did you do anything special?"

"All the girls were home so it was a blast to say the least."

"Well, Dr. Morgan brought in some bagels this morning if you want one," she said, placing her fingers on the home keys of her computer.

"Thanks, Miss Terry, that sounds good, I could use a snack," I said, proceeding to my office.

I closed the door behind me dreading the days when the conversations would be about my condition, but I had several more missions to complete before we got there. Now that I had told my immediate family it was time to call my Mother and Dad.

She had always insisted I call her, Mother; she thought being called Mama was degrading. I knew it was from her recollections of the white kids in the house where her mother did day work after her daddy died; she hated to hear them call her mother, mama. From eight years old she was determined to marry a college man and become a prim, proper, woman of leisure. She found that man in my daddy. He made all her dreams come true working as a loan originator at Commerce Union Bank for thirty years, buying and renting houses, and when it came to saving money he didn't play around. They had relocated to an upscale condominium in Orlando ten years ago after Dad retired. He said he had enough of cutting grass and shoveling snow. Their golden years were going along just like they'd planned. We were close but the weekly calls had slowly stretched out to maybe twice a month and even longer.

"Good morning, Mother dear, how are you and Dad doing this morning?" I asked, starting with the pleasantries before the real conversation began.

"We're doing great, honey, the weather down here has cooled off and thank God the tourist season is over. How are you all doing, I haven't heard from you since the wedding."

"A lot has been going on and the time has flown by."

"You not getting empty nest syndrome now that Ebony is gone are you?"

"No, Mother, and the nest won't be empty much longer."

"What you talking about, honey?"

"I don't know how it happened but I'm pregnant."

"Have you been to the doctor? It might just be the change."

"I've been to two doctors and I've had an ultrasound."

"Oh my goodness," she murmured. "John, pick up the phone," she yelled out, "Its Evelyn."

"Hello, baby girl," I heard him say after a short pause.

"Hey, Dad, how are you?"

"I'm excellent, what's going on up there?"

"She's pregnant, John," Mother interjected into the conversation.

"What in the world? You mean one of the girls."

"No, Evelyn is the one," Mom emphasized.

"Oh my Lord, baby girl, are you sure you want to start that all over and sign up for another twenty years?" he asked.

"I didn't sign up, Dad, I was drafted."

"I can't believe this," Mother said, "We worried about you getting pregnant when you were a teenager, but we didn't think we'd have to worry about that when you were damn near a senior citizen. I don't even think it's safe for you, Evelyn."

"Hold on now, Earnestine, leave the girl alone. She can have a baby if she wants too."

"There can be complications, John; those things have to be considered," she countered.

"Have your doctors said its okay, baby?" Dad asked.

"So far, things are looking good."

"I know Nelson is not happy about this, he wanted to retire early," Mama chimed back in.

"He's okay with it, and if he wants to retire he can, the house is paid for, Mother dear."

"Well, excuse me, Evelyn; I'm just concerned about you and your health. You've already raised three children and I know how hard that was, I could barely raise one. I wanted you to have some time to enjoy your own life and dream some of your own dreams again."

"I know that, Mother, and I appreciate it. Everything will be fine, don't worry. Anyway, I'm at work so I have to go. I love y'all."

"We love you too," they said in unison.

I sat back in my chair and closed my eyes hoping I could regain my composure after that phone call. I was weary of justifying something that wasn't my fault. I hadn't done anything wrong. Was I supposed to take birth control with my tubes tied? I decided then that I wasn't making any more formal announcements. I was going to let the situation speak for its self.

***

Once I stopped talking about it, things seemed to get back to business as usual. The only difference was my regular scheduled appointments with the doctor. The baby was growing normally and I was feeling great, no signs of diabetes or high blood pressure. We spent the Thanksgiving holiday at Erica's house and all the girls came home for Christmas. January flew by and then it was Valentine's Day, halfway through February.

"Look at you smiling and looking all good this morning," Miss Terry said when I came in.

"Yes, what's going on, Evelyn Winters," Dr. Morgan added, "You are glowing, Nelson must have treated you right this morning."

"Don't even go there you two," I said, "Anna is the one who gets flowers nearly every week."

"That's because I'm dating, not married, that makes them work harder."

"I heard that," Miss Terry chuckled.

"Don't try to change the subject on us, Evelyn; you look like you're going through a second childhood," Anna said, focusing on me again.

"Is there anything else different that you notice about me?" I asked them mischievously.

"Ooh, let me see," Miss Terry exclaimed, looking me up and down and grabbing my hand. Your hair is gorgeous, it has really grown."

"A third of it is probably gray underneath the dye, but who cares," I joked. "Anyway that's not it, keep looking."

"Is it jewelry?" Anna asked, looking at my ears and neck.

"No, not jewelry," I said, "Are you both too polite to mention the weight I've gained."

"What can we say, Evelyn?" Miss Terry laughed, "I put on ten pounds over the holiday myself. I can't get into anything in my closet that's doesn't have elastic. Look at this belly; I look like I'm pregnant."

"I look pregnant too," I said with a straight face.

"Don't let that extra weight bother you, we'll walk it off when the weather breaks," Anna said, trying to make me feel better.

"That sounds like a plan after the baby is born," I said casually.

Dr. Morgan and Miss Terry both stopped in mid-motion and looked at me confused, like they had missed something, but neither one of them dared to ask.

"I might as well tell you before I go into labor, I'm pregnant."

"Evelyn, stop it, this is Valentine's Day not April Fool's Day," Miss Terry said, shaking her head in denial.

"No, jokes, I'm five months," I said.

"I need to sit down," Anna said, "I wasn't ready for that."

"Think about how I felt," I told them, sitting down in one of the office chairs. "I had my tubes tied almost 15 years ago."

"Are you going to sue your doctor?" Miss Terry asked with a hand over her mouth.

"No, they say there's a one percent chance that it fails. There's nobody to blame. I guess I should have gotten Nelson clipped too," I said lightheartedly.

We all laughed at that before Anna stopped and asked seriously, "What does the family think about it?"

"Nelson was upset at first but now he's walking around like he's King Kong. Erica's feels like I robbed her since she and Drew have been trying to get pregnant, Ebony is jealous because she won't be the baby anymore, and Elise is thrilled and wants to adopt it."

"That sounds like a three ring circus, you need to sell tickets, Evelyn," Miss Terry remarked.

"It feels a lot like that I must admit," I sighed.

"Do you know if it's going to be a boy or a girl?" Miss Terry asked, getting excited.

"No, I told them I didn't want to know anything," I answered.

"I don't know how we're going to work after that newsflash," Anna said, gathering up the file she had in her hands. "Good luck, Evelyn, we're behind you, 100 percent."

I retreated to the privacy of my office. Even after the guessing game was over Miss Terry couldn't stop staring at me. I know it's not every day that you see a woman over fifty walking around pregnant, but it wasn't like I was a freak of nature. I tried to stay occupied sending the transcripts of the list of seniors to the colleges beside their names.

After a few hours I felt hungry so I took a break to eat some of the food I brought with me. I had started packing my lunch two months ago. I don't know why but I felt self-conscious about eating in front of people. It was probably because I was getting thick around the middle and didn't want anybody to think I was turning into a pig.

I made it through the rest of the day without seeing Dr. Morgan or Miss Terry. I didn't feel like answering any more questions. I left a voicemail on Macey's phone at work telling her I was coming by after school was out. We hadn't kept our promise to meet once a week and I needed some reassurance that this was all going to be okay.

I made my way through the campus parking lot and walked quickly inside the building to get out of the cold. I climbed the one flight of stairs up to Macey's office to get my blood flowing and surprisingly I feel energized all of sudden, like I could run a mile, correction, maybe the length of a football field.

"Come on in, stranger," Macey said, greeting me at the door with a hug.

"I've been thinking about you, girl," I said, closing the door behind me. "What have you been doing lately? I've been missing you."

"I've been bogged down with the new semester is all, but look at you, you are absolutely beautiful. If I thought my skin would look that good I would even consider giving birth again myself and my uterus is long gone."

"I get compliments on it every day and I must say that it amazes me myself."

"Well, how's my new godchild percolating?" she asked, plopping down in her desk chair.

"My doctor says that my pregnancy is proceeding along as normal as any of his other patients who are half my age," I announced as I sat down on the sofa against the side wall of her office.

"That's good news, Evie."

"Yes, it is, but those were the words that brought me down out of the clouds. I'm not sure I made the right decision. Erica was right; I'm supposed to be preparing to be a grandmother, not having a baby."

"You're just getting nervous as the time goes by. Are you feeling okay?"

"I'm feeling better than I have in years and the occasional fatigue is much less."

"That is a good report, besides, it's too late for you to be having second thoughts, there's no way we can reverse this pregnancy."

"I understand that, I've already told my mom and dad and everybody at work knows."

"That doesn't stop us from having a plan B after the baby is born. You can always take Elise up on her offer."

"Very funny, Macey, my emotions are running like an elevator, from the top floor to the basement."

"That's the hormones, my friend. I have an idea to help you quiet your mind."

"And what might that miracle cure be?"

"I think you should start a journal. It will help you begin writing. Remember we are supposed to be writing the next great American novel."

"I'll do that," I said thoughtfully, "Maybe I should also write my last will and testament while I'm at it, just in case I don't make it through this."

"Don't be morbid; this is supposed to be a time of joy and anticipation."

"All I can tell you is that I've had three babies and this is the first time I don't know what to expect," I said, kicking off my shoes and curling up on the couch.

5

"**D**on't tell me you're finished with all the snacks already?" I asked Nelson when he walked into the kitchen.

He always made himself a huge spread of food, beer, and water whenever he sat down to watch the Memphis Grizzlies. He didn't want to have to get up for anything.

"You're looking sexy, honey," Nelson said suggestively, putting his arm around me and rubbing against my belly.

"It's because its halftime and I look like I have a basketball under my shirt."

"No, it's not that," he chuckled, "You look good pregnant. It takes me back to the time when we were young and having babies. I was crazy about you."

"That was then and this is now, and we're not young."

"I'm still crazy about you."

"Since when, you barely paid any attention to me before I was pregnant. I don't even know how we got this baby."

"I'm getting ready to show you how it happened," he said, kissing my neck.

"Nelson, you are too much for me. If you think you are going to rush me up the steps for fifteen minutes and then rush back down and catch the second half of the game, you are about to get a reality check."

"That is not the plan, honey, I'm thinking about you and me flashing back twenty-five years where you were hot as the Ohio Player's Fire and I was the Funkadelic freak of the week."

I couldn't help but laugh out loud, "All right, honey bear, that's an invitation I can't refuse."

Nelson was a satisfying lover, which was one of the things that kept me with him through the rough times. The problem with our relationship was that as he got older he was rationing out the loving like it was a precious commodity that was close to running out.

I rolled over on my side so we could spoon for a while before I fell asleep, and then I asked him the question that I struggled with, "Are you unhappy about me having this baby, Nelson?"

"No, I'm not, Evelyn, but it's going to be a drastic change for us. I don't even know if I have the energy to go through it all again."

"I know I pushed my decision on you in the beginning, and now I regret it. I let my emotions get the best of me. I felt like it was a debt I needed to pay."

"Let it go, sweetheart, there's no turning back, all we can do is start preparing for a new member of the family. We can use Ebony's room for the nursery."

"That's a good idea; I can't believe that you're thinking ahead of me."

"I always am, you just don't know it. Are you comfortable?" he asked, rising up on his elbow, "Can I get you anything?"

"I'm fine; you're just looking for an excuse to go back downstairs"

"My team is trying to get to the playoffs and I put you first didn't I."

"Go on and enjoy the rest of the game. I'm going to do some writing."

I had taken Macey's suggestion and started writing in a journal everyday and I have to admit that it's helping get my thoughts organized.

Today is March 30, 2002. Tomorrow is Easter Sunday and Erica wants us all to come over her house for dinner. I couldn't be happier; I'm close to seven months now and I need to save my strength. There are days when I feel this new life moving in my belly and I'm excited about the chance to hold my baby in my arms. My curiosity gets the best of me and I want to know everything about the child. I've speculated on all the things I'm going to do differently than I did with the other girls. How I'm going to be more patient and affectionate. Then again, today is one of the days I have doubts about being able to go the distance. This isn't about babysitting for a few weeks, the bible says our years are threescore and ten, or fourscore if we're strong, a baby at my age would be a commitment for the rest of my life.

***

"Something sure smells good in here," Nelson exclaims after Erica answers the door, "I don't know when I've last had a substantial meal."

"Stop, Daddy, you don't look like you've been losing any weight," Erica said, giving him a hug. "I'll take your coats and you all can go into the living room, Drew is watching the game."

"Do you need help with anything?" I asked Erica as I followed her into the kitchen.

"No, Mama, just have a seat, everything is ready and Ebony is bringing the macaroni and cheese. We can eat as soon as they get here."

"Did you all have a good service at your church this morning; you look so happy and uplifted this afternoon?"

"Yes we did, and I am feeling great. I'll tell you about it when we eat."

"Hello, hello, you can all relax now," Ebony said, bursting in the kitchen with her large casserole dish wrapped in foil, "At least one dish on the table will taste like something."

"Please, child, you know I can cook you under the table on any day of the week," Erica replied, taking the hot food out of her hands.

"You wish," Ebony said, giving me a hug, "I still can't get used to seeing you pregnant, Mama, but you look beautiful."

"By the time you get used to it, it'll be over, my dear. Where's Calvin?"

"He went straight to the living room to watch the basketball game.

"Dinner is ready," Erica shouted towards the living room, "Those games are going to be on all day, so you might as well eat now."

"I don't suppose we could take our plates in the den and eat while we watch the game?" Calvin asked, coming into the kitchen to say hello.

"Absolutely not," Erica answered, feeling insulted.

"Drew, I'm glad you took that one off our hands, she was always trying to boss me," Nelson said, following them into the dining room.

"She barks a lot but she's just like a spoiled puppy, you know what they do when you pet them. They roll over on their backs."

"I know you are not talking that crazy talk around my mama and daddy," Erica fussed.

"I'm sorry, baby, I'm just teasing," Drew laughed, trying to give her a kiss on the cheek.

"Stop it," she said, pushing him away, "You're spoiling my special meal."

"Take your seats gentlemen while we get the food on the table," I said.

"We've got this, Mama, you go on and sit down too," Ebony urged.

"I'm not helpless," I responded, "I can put a bowl on the table."

"Nobody said anything about you being helpless, in a couple of months you'll wish you had somebody to wait on you," Nelson chimed in.

I grabbed my napkin and waved it like a white flag in surrender; I knew I had been beaten. The guys chatted for a few minutes about the score and who would win while Ebony helped

Erica bring in the spread. Once it was all arranged, Nelson stood back up to bless the table.

"Just a minute, Daddy, I have an announcement to make before we eat."

"All right, sweetie, but make it quick, the food is getting cold and the game clock is ticking."

"Amen," Calvin added.

"Anyway," Erica said, ignoring their impertinence, "I invited you all here to celebrate Easter Sunday with us but there is also another reason for celebration. We wanted you all here together to tell you that Drew and I are having a baby."

The room went silent for a second. I don't think the family had gotten over the last pregnancy announcement. This was a moment that I had anticipated for many years and this wasn't how I had envisioned it. Then Ebony started clapping.

"That is wonderful news, sweetheart, I'm so happy for you and Drew," I said, suddenly feeling self-conscious. "When did you find out?"

"I went to the doctor a week ago but we suspected it for a few weeks."

"Congratulations, Drew," Nelson said, nudging him, "I guess the Winters women are in the baby making business. Look out Calvin, you're next."

"Hold up, Daddy," Ebony said, raising her hands, "I'm not quite ready to join that family business yet."

"Bless the food, Daddy," Erica said, "Now we can eat."

***

"What do you think about the news?" Nelson asked when we got home that night, "You're about to be a mama and a grandmama at the same time."

"It's a lot to take in. I need to lie down for a while, but I'm happy."

"Go on and rest yourself, I'm going in the den to catch the evening news."

I climbed the stairs up to my bedroom and lay across the bed trying to find a comfortable position and I could feel the baby inside my belly shift positions doing the same. My eyes drifted shut and then the phone rang.

"Happy Easter, my friend," Macey sang in to the phone, "How was the family dinner?"

"Erica gave us a big announcement, she's pregnant."

"When it rains it pours, that's wonderful. Now she can stop being jealous of the baby."

"Stop, Macey, Erica just likes to be the one running things with us at attention."

"She'll learn, the quickest way to lose the spotlight is to have a baby."

"I just never thought I would be pregnant at the same time as one of my daughters. It just feels country or ghetto to me," I said to Macey over the phone.

"You are not country or ghetto; you're a grown woman having a baby. There's nothing wrong with that. You have my respect, Evie, you have done excellent, no health issues or complications and you only have two months to go. Which reminds me, is the nursery ready?"

"Nelson suggested we use Ebony's room but we haven't done anything yet. Dr. Rush has me scheduled to come in for the C-section on June 17, in the afternoon."

"In that case, I think we need to do some heavy shopping this weekend. We're running out of time unless this baby comes out sixteen years old with a driving license."

"Would that be too much to hope for?"

"Absolutely."

6

"You deserve an award too, Evelyn, you have been a trooper," Anna said in the school office after the awards ceremony. "You made it through, it's May 24th, the last day of school."

"I had to be here for my graduating seniors," I said proudly, "I wanted all of their college applications to be complete and to be around to hear where they got accepted."

"You never complained either," Miss Terry added.

"Truthfully, I've never felt better physically, aside from the extra weight," I told them.

"Have you got the baby's room ready?" Miss Terry asked.

"Yes, it's ready and waiting. My college friend and I finished it last month. It was strange buying baby things again after all these years."

"That's a blessing, now you only have three weeks until your due date," Anna remarked.

Have you given any thought as to whether you'll be back after the summer break?"

"I've always been a working mother so I don't expect that to change. Don't go packing up my office yet."

"Well, I've got some errands to run, I'll see you ladies at graduation tonight," Anna said, grabbing her bags and keys.

"I'm right behind you," Miss Terry said, shutting down her computer and pulling her things together. "Good luck to you, Evelyn."

"Thanks and have a good summer, Miss Terry."

Back in my office I looked around the room. Everything was organized and all my papers were properly filed. There was nothing left to do. I pushed my chair neatly under the desk. Then I felt a trickle of wetness, I could barely hold it with the pressure on my bladder. I put down my things and rushed into the restroom. Inside the stall I sat down and felt a gush of water.

"Oh my goodness, I think my water broke," I said, speaking to the empty bathroom.

I didn't feel any pains, and the baby wasn't due for another three weeks. I hadn't gone into labor with my other three girls. Maybe my bladder was really full. I gathered myself together and went back to my office to call Dr Rush.

"Dr. Rush's office, may I help you," the receptionist said cordially.

"Yes, my name is Evelyn Winters, I'm a patient of Dr. Rush's and I think my water broke but I'm not due for another three weeks."

"Are you in any pain or having any contractions?"

"No, I'm not."

"Dr. Rush is with a patient right now, Mrs. Winters, but I'm sure he would like you to come to the hospital to examine you as a precaution. I don't think you should drive, have someone bring you to the emergency entrance."

"I will, thank you," I said, hanging up the phone.

Who was going to take me? There was no one left here besides Mr. Kenneth, the janitor, and there's no telling where he is hiding out. Nelson wasn't due home for at least a couple of hours and the girls were probably still at work. I was only ten minutes away from the hospital; I might as well drive myself.

Pulling out of the parking lot into the intersection I couldn't help but notice that it was a beautiful afternoon. The sky was so blue; there wasn't a cloud to be seen. The sun shone so brightly I reached for my shades to shield my eyes. Two blocks from the hospital at a stop sign, I felt my tummy tightened like a gripped fist, and then I felt two thumps against my lap. I pressed my foot harder against the gas pedal to hurry, something was beginning to happen.

I parked in the emergency room parking lot and took small quick steps to the entrance. I staggered through the automatic double doors and spoke with the attendant behind the glass, telling him that I was in labor.

"Who's your doctor?" he asked nonchalantly.

"Dr. Rush," I answered.

"Fill this out and then bring it back and we'll be right with you," he said, handing me a clipboard full of papers with a pen attached.

I sat down in the row of seats against the wall and dug around in my bag for my cell phone. Then I searched my wallet for my insurance card. Next, I pressed in Nelson's number.

"You finally free for the summer," he said when he picked up.

"I guess I am," I said. "I'm calling to tell you I'm at the hospital. Something's going on but I haven't seen a doctor yet. I'm filling out the papers in the front."

"Is anybody there with you?"

"No, I drove myself from the school. I guess you should call the girls."

"Okay, honey, I'm on my way over there now."

I rushed through the paperwork and handed it back to the attendant.

"Thank you, Mrs. Winters, Dr. Rush wants you transported up to labor and delivery; there will be someone here to pick you up in just a minute."

I feel like I'm having a flashback as the patient transport person rolls me into the elevator up to the 5th floor. Inside a room I followed the instructions of the nurse to change out of my clothes and into a hospital gown. I sat down on the edge of the bed, not resigned to being a patient; this may be a false alarm. The nurse returned a few minutes later and took my vital signs.

"Are you in any discomfort, Mrs. Winters?"

"No, not really," I answered, covering myself with the sheet.

"Dr. Rush will be up to see you very shortly."

I leaned back to relax while I wondered what was taking Nelson so long to get here. I didn't know if I should have asked him to go by the house and pick up the bag we had packed for the hospital. I decided to wait until I saw Dr. Rush. Who knows he might send me back home.

"Hello, Evelyn," Dr. Rush said, blowing in the room like a hurricane, "What's going on with you today?"

"I'm not sure; I think maybe my water broke."

"Let's get you checked out," he replied.

I waited while Dr. Rush listened to the baby's heartbeat and then did a pelvic exam.

"You are in active labor, Evelyn; you've already dilated at least seven centimeters. Take her into the delivery room," he told the nurse.

All of sudden I felt an intense heat envelope my body and beads of sweat popped out all over my body. "Don't panic," I said under my breath as they wheeled me down the hallway. A nagging cramp jumped in my side and settled in my back. I started shaking; I couldn't distinguish if the sweat had turned cold or if I was trembling with fear.

The only familiar face in the delivery room was Dr. Rush. Where was my family? Why is it that Nelson can never be where he's supposed to be? I felt as if my back was about to break.

"You're at nine centimeters," Dr. Rush said, wearing a gown with his head covered.

"Your husband is here, Mrs. Winters," the nurse said, "He's changing into a gown."

"Thank goodness," I said, feeling out of breath. "Is it time for an epidural?"

"There's no time, Evelyn, the baby won't wait," Dr. Rush said.

"Oh no, I don't think I can do it," I hollered out, feeling the intense heat return.

I was close to giving in to insanity when Nelson walked in grinning. Anger replaced the craziness I was feeling. What was there to smile about in all the confusion?

"What took you so long to get here," I asked between the back spasms, "If this isn't an emergency I don't know what one is."

"Calm down, Evelyn, I'm here now; I had to call the girls. Erica and Ebony will be here as soon as they can."

"My back is killing me," I yelled down to Dr. Rush under the sheet they had thrown over me.

"Evelyn, if you'll give me one big push this baby will be out of there. Raise up and brace yourself, and on the count of three, push."

"Come on, Evelyn," Nelson said, supporting my back with his arms.

"One, two, three," Dr. Rush counted and everybody in the room joined in.

I pushed as hard as I could and I felt my back pop. Then my body felt numb. For a second I wondered if I had damaged my spinal cord. Then I felt like I was about to pass out. I heard clapping and my head cleared.

"Good job, Evelyn," Dr. Rush exclaimed, "You have a baby boy."

"Congratulations," the nurse said to Nelson.

"Is he okay, does he look all right," I asked, watching the pediatrician clean him up with the fear of Downs's syndrome present in my mind.

"He looks great," Dr. Rush said, smiling.

"Thank you, God," I whispered.

***

I wake up from a nap and I'm in my hospital room. Nelson is sitting in a chair holding the baby. I look at the card taped on the acrylic baby bed and see the date, time, and weight of the baby. Miracles never cease, I've had three painful c-sections and now I have a natural birth that was virtually painless even though the baby was nine pounds and three ounces.

"You must have been tired, Evelyn, you've been asleep for a long time," Nelson said, seeing I was awake. "I called Elise and your mom and dad to give them the news, and the girls came by and saw the baby; they said they'll be back later."

"Did you call, Macey?"

"Yes I did, she said she'll be by this evening."

"Let me hold him," I said, reaching out my arms.

"You know we have to think of a name," Nelson said, placing him gently on the side of the bed beside me. "He has your eyes."

"I don't know why we haven't given any thought to names. I guess I thought I had more time."

I can't take my eyes off of him; he's copper-colored and glowing like a brand new penny. I search my mind for a name. First I think what about Newcent for my brand new penny, but that won't work because it sounds too much like nuisance, and I definitely don't want to send that out into the universe. I ponder a little longer and then I have it, Newman, his name is Newman Winters, because the fact that he's here means that Nelson is a new man.

"I want to call him Newman," I say to Nelson.

"That's kind of heavy for a baby isn't it?" Nelson asked. "I was thinking about one that started with the letter e, like the girls, like Elijah or Eli from the Bible.

"Okay, his name is Elijah Newman Winters; we can call him Eli for now."

"That's sounds good, honey."

"He's so quiet. Have they run tests on him, I want to know that he is 100 percent healthy."

"Baby, Eli is healthy, stop worrying so much," he said, rubbing the top of his head.

"Don't forget they have a soft spot, Nelson."

"I've raised three babies with you, I know what to do."

A nurse stepped in the door and asked, "Will the baby be nursed or receive formula?"

"I'm not sure," I answered, it was another thing I hadn't thought about.

"You can try and then if you change your mind we can bring formula. There's also a bottle of glucose water under the baby cart," she said with a pleasant smile.

"Thank you," I said as she left.

I looked down at the baby in my arms and his bright copper eyes relaxed me and my heart filled up with love for him. All the anxiety leading up to his birth were gone. I nursed him until he fell asleep. I don't know if he was full or just tired from trying. Nelson laid him in the clear bed on the cart just as the phone rang.

"Mama, I can't believe it, a brother after all these years," Elise said, "Ebony texted me a picture and he looks so cute. I can't wait to get down there for a visit."

"Is your offer still open," I asked playfully as the door opened.

"Sure, Mama, as soon as you get him out of diapers," she giggled.

"Your sisters just walked in, now Erica can get a live preview before her baby gets here."

"Yeah she told me her ultrasound says it's a boy. Now little brother will have somebody to play with."

While we were still talking, Macy walked in the door with flowers and a balloon.

"Since you're on the line and this room is full I can tell everybody at one time. We picked a name earlier, it's Elijah Newman Winters, and we're going to call him Eli."

"All right now, I love it," Macey said, putting the flowers on the window ledge and coming over by the bed to give me a hug.

"I'll call you back when you get home, Mama," Elise said.

"That's a big handsome boy you have there, Nelson," Macey said, giving him a hug, "I didn't know you had it in you. Now at least we know what color baby clothes to buy now." Then she hugged the girls and asked them, "Did you ever think you would have a brother?"

Ebony laughed and said, "Not in my wildest dreams."

"I had given up on that a long time ago," Erica added.

"I'm just grateful that he's healthy," I said, "I didn't expect him to be here for another three weeks."

"It worked out perfectly, Evie," Macey said happily, "You have the whole summer off to get used to a baby in the house again."

"I'm sure I'll need every single day."

"How long will you have to stay in here?" Ebony asked.

"The pediatrician and Dr. Rush say they'll check on both of them sometime tomorrow and if everything checks out, they can get released on Sunday," Nelson told them.

"That's good, get all the rest you can, my friend," Macey said leaving, "I'll see you when you all get home."

The girls stayed for another hour waiting for Eli to wake up so they could hold him. Watching them fuss over him was surreal. I always thought that when the time came and there was a new baby in the family that one of them would have delivered it and I would be the a visitor making a fuss over my grandbaby, but with Erica already four months pregnant I would soon have my chance.

On Sunday morning, Nelson showed up with a baby blue outfit that Erica had bought and he dressed Eli while I packed up my things. My stomach has gone down almost to its normal size and I take it as a reward for hanging in there through this great change in my life. After we had pulled everything together Nelson went down to get the car. A tall heavyset woman from patient transport came into the room and wheeled me out of the hospital with my new son in my arms to the car where Nelson is waiting. Once Eli and I were all buckled and secure in the backseat he slowly drove out of the parking garage. I don't know why but when the sun hits my face I feel invigorated, as if I'm fifteen years younger.

***

The first couple of months flew by. Elise came home for a few days and after she left, my Mom and Dad came and stayed for a week. There were days when I honestly couldn't believe that this precious child belonged to me. He is a breeze to take care of and seldom cries. When he smiles at me it is my greatest joy. It's an infectious smile, and whenever anyone sees it they can't help but smile back at him. Eli is so lovable that even my Mom had to admit she was wrong and take back all of her doubts.

It couldn't all be good, that's not the way real life works, at least not mine anyway. Nelson was so thrilled when we got home, the new life and energy had revitalized him too, but lately he has become moody and withdrawn. He initiates arguments over little things and he sulks about them for days. His attentiveness to Eli has waned, and when he looks at him his eyes are filled with questions. The doubts that he had in the beginning have grown, he's made some rude comments saying that maybe I strayed and this is another man's child.

It was the first week in August and I was sitting in the swing with Eli out in the backyard enjoying a lazy afternoon. I couldn't stop dwelling on the fact that I only had two weeks left before it was time for the new school year. I wasn't ready to leave Eli and turn his care over to someone else but I needed to start searching for a daycare center.

Nelson pulled his car into the driveway and saw us out in the shade. He put down his briefcase and came over to the swing.

"This is the only one of the children that doesn't look like me," he said curiously, putting a halt to the slow rhythm of the swing, "All of our girls had lighter skin when they were born."

"So what, he looks like me, do you have a problem with that?" I responded bitterly.

"I don't know. Is there any reason why I should?" he taunted.

"If you have something on your mind, Nelson, why don't you go on and put it out there?"

"Sometimes I have to wonder why this whole thing didn't happen years ago. For twenty-five years, nothing, then I go out of town for a while and when I come back you're pregnant. Maybe I should swab his mouth and be sure that he's mine."

"Are you doubting me or are you doubting yourself? Either way, it doesn't matter to me. I don't have to prove anything to anybody. If you're having second thoughts it's okay, go on about your business, I can take care of Eli by myself."

"That's not what I mean; I love Eli," he said with his voice full of frustration, "I'm just feeling a lot of pressure right now."

"Pressure from what?" I asked, looking away, refusing to let him upset my day.

"Things are not looking good at work; the company has taken huge losses on claims and investments. They've already started the layoffs and there are going to be deep."

"You've been there for damn near thirty years, don't you have enough seniority where none of this mess will affect you."

"Unfortunately, there is no such thing; this is all about the bottom line. When it comes down to it, I have two choices. I can wait it out and take the chance of a layoff later in the future or even the possibility of the company being sold or accept a buyout. The only secure option I have now is to take an early retirement where at least I will be guaranteed my pension."

"I know you probably haven't had a chance to give it much thought, but I wouldn't gamble with all the years you've put in. It sounds like your best move might be retirement. You can count on that income being there even if you decide to look for another job."

"That's not quite what I had planned out for my life at this stage, Evelyn," he said, taking a seat beside me in the swing.

"What kind of thing is that to say to a fifty year old woman with her newborn baby in her arms?" I chuckled, "Eli definitely wasn't on my to-do list."

Nelson laughed a deep laugh from deep in his belly and the tension was broken. He took Eli out of my arms and held him is his lap. Eli gave him a happy gurgle and I re-started the slow rhythm of the swing. We were enjoying the return of peace in our backyard when I had an idea.

"I know this is going to be definitely to the right of your radar screen but what would you think about taking care of Eli when I go back to work. I know it would be a huge adjustment but it would take a tremendous load off of my mind, and it would save us a ton of money."

"I don't know, Evelyn. If I stop working for too long nobody else is going to hire me. That would mean that my working life is over."

"It's for your son, Nelson. Did you plan on working your entire life?"

"No, I didn't, and I also never thought of myself as a stay-at-home dad. I've always worked and provided for my family."

"You still will be providing, you are going to reap the benefits from all the years you've worked and get the pension and annuity you've paid into. I have twelve more years to work before I can even think about retiring."

We went back and forth three more times in the swing.

"Well, I guess it's going to be me and you and your dirty diapers," he said, raising Eli high up in the air.

"It won't be that bad, honey bear," I said, putting my arm around his shoulder, "I won't expect you to do the cooking and cleaning like you do me when I'm home."

"I refuse to respond to that, anything I say might be used against me in a court of law."

"Smart move, I almost had you."

"No, honey, I'm off the ropes and back on my toes."

"I'm glad to hear it because you are going to need to be able to go the distance with that one," I said pointing my figure at Eli.

7

Once the school year starts, the fall months fly by like shooting stars. The gratification that is generated at the end of the previous year is long forgotten with the responsibility of a fresh onslaught of new students. The summer break is merely a memory.

Nelson adapted well to his new position as full-time father even though I was sure he would rather be working outside of the home. We were wondering how we were going to celebrated Eli's first Halloween when Drew called that evening and said Erica was in labor.

"We don't know how long it'll be before the baby gets here, it may take a while," I said to Nelson as we quickly prepared to go to the hospital.

I was halfway through packing Eli's diaper bag when I realized that a hospital is no place to take a baby.

"Do you think we should take the baby with us?"

"Probably not, you go ahead, Erica will want her mama there. I'll stay home with him and come to the hospital later."

"No, Nelson, I couldn't ask you to do that, I know you want to go too. I'll call Macey and see if we can drop the baby over at her house for a while."

I rushed to the phone while Nelson finished packing the bag. I couldn't believe it but since he had retired, and after three grown girls, he had actually gotten the hang of caring for a baby.

"Hello, Macey," I said, "And before you start telling me off for being a stranger, Erica just went into labor."

"Oh, my goodness," she answered, sounding out of breath,

"What do you need me to do?"

"I was wondering if we could drop Eli off with you on our way to the hospital, I don't want to take him there. You never know how long this birthing thing can take."

"Sure, Evie, I would love it, now that he's sleeping through the night. I don't get much time with my godson."

"Thanks, my friend, we'll be by there in a few minutes."

Nelson pressed his foot firmly on the gas after we left Macey's house, speeding through lights as the yellows blinked red.

"Erica is already at the hospital, honey, we don't have to rush," I said, hoping he would ease off the pedal some.

"You're right, Drew is there," he said, slowing down, "I don't know what I was thinking about."

"I guess you're ready to see your first grandbaby, that's all. I'm excited too, but I think it will be quite different than it would have been if we didn't have Eli. We're all used to having a baby around again."

"Except this one we can take home, Eli isn't going anywhere for a long time."

"Well, at least you don't have to worry about growing old by yourself," I teased.

"No I don't, except I was already old when he got here," Nelson joked

"In that case you can forget about getting any older, honey bear, stop your clock."

"If only I could," he said, pulling into the parking garage of the hospital.

My own experience in the delivery room was still fresh with memories of giving birth to Eli, so I was fine with Erica and Drew wanting it to be just them in the delivery room. Erica was in labor for most of the night but by daybreak of the next morning she had delivered a healthy baby boy that they named Drew Jamison Jr.

The past twelve months had been filled with monumental

changes in our family. Ebony had gotten married, Nelson had retired, and two baby boys were added. When Thanksgiving rolled around we had much to be thankful for even though we all had individual celebrations. We planned a big gathering for Christmas when Elise would be in town for two weeks.

***

"All right, Mama, we have gone to the Christmas Eve church service with you, now let's hit the malls before we go in," Ebony said, "We haven't been out shopping together since before my wedding."

"I don't know if the babies need to be out in this weather," I said, worried about Drew Jr., he wasn't even two months yet.

"D.J. is sleeping, Mama, he drank six ounces in church, he is dressed warmly, and should be out for a while," Erica added, "I've got a few more things I still need to pick up."

"I don't know why you are always waiting until the last minute?" I said, wanting to go home and put my feet up.

"Not everybody has it like you, Mama, I had to go back to work after six weeks and I don't get much help when I get home," Erica complained

"That's why I'm not in any rush to have a baby, I can't be tied down," Ebony said.

"Just in case you all forgot, your daddy wasn't much help around the house when you all were babies."

"Come on, Mama," Elise chimed in, "I've got Eli, besides Daddy probably wants some more time to himself."

"Okay, okay, I don't need all three of you bossing me around," I said, climbing into the back of Erica's mini-van.

"Let's drive to Cool Springs Mall," Ebony suggested from the front seat, "They probably have a better selection than Rivergate."

"You're right, Erica said, pulling onto the interstate, "They have every store you can think of out there."

Halfway to the mall, Drew Jr. woke up started to cry. Eli leaned forward and tried to reach his hand over the side of his car seat to touch Drew Jr. but his arm wasn't quite long enough.

"Ooo, that's so sweet, Eli is trying to help," Elise said.

"He shouldn't be hungry," Erica yelled over her shoulder, "See if he'll take his pacifier."

"Nope, he doesn't want it," Elise replied over his loud wailing. "Maybe he needs changing."

"Just see if he wants some more formula, that boy is so greedy."

Elise rummaged through the diaper bag until she found the thermal bag of formula bottles.

"That's what he wanted, it's so good to him his eyes are closed," Elise said, laughing. "I still can't get over how quiet Eli is, I haven't heard him cry yet. He just grunts when he wants something."

"Now that you mention it, he really doesn't cry much," Ebony said curiously. "Do you think that maybe that's a little unusual, Mama?"

"No, I don't, he just has a quiet disposition, your daddy and I are grateful to have a good baby in our old age."

"Seriously, Mama," Ebony insisted, "Don't you think you should have him tested? He might be autistic or something. He doesn't even try to talk that much."

"Are you insinuating that he has some problems, Ebony, or are you still worried that something might be wrong because of my age? If he was crying too much, then you would think something else was wrong. You can stop your worrying. Eli has had all of his check-ups and the doctors are pleased with his development."

"Don't get yourself worked up, Mama," Elise said, "Ebony doesn't mean anything by it, she's just concerned. Eli is our little brother and we love him."

"It's fine, I understand your concern but Eli's development is normal," I added, trying to hold my temper, "I raised all of you so I should know."

"I am so glad we're here, I can't take anymore of this conversation," Erica said, parking the car. "I need to relax and finish my last minute shopping before you all get on D.J."

An uncomfortable silence surrounded us while Erica got the strollers out of the back of the van. I lifted Eli out of his car seat and he gave me one of his gummy grins and all the stress I was feeling disappeared. We got the boys situated in their wheels and rushed inside of Dillard's to get out of the cold.

We paused in the men's clothing section while Erica looked at some sweaters.

"May I help you?" a short, plump, saleswoman with an accent asked.

"Not yet, I'll look around for a minute," Erica answered.

The woman turned her attention to the babies, "Look here at the two handsome boys. How old are they?"

"He's seven weeks and this one is seven months," I answered proudly.

"Two new grandbabies to celebrate their first Christmas," she said, smiling.

"That one is my grandson, this one is my son," I said, correcting her.

The words stuck in her throat but the look on her face expressed all she couldn't say. She was stunned and embarrassed. She gathered her wits and pulled her cardigan around her belly.

"Well, let me know if you need any help," she said as she hurried away.

"That's a normal reaction, Mama," Ebony said, "With us standing here she assumed he was one of ours."

"That's right, Mama, you don't need to explain that all through the mall," Elise said, reaching for the stroller. "I'll just say Eli is my baby."

"I don't care what they think, I had him. I didn't commit a crime, so be it."

I don't know why I let that get to me. I don't owe anybody in this world an explanation for the things that I have done. The real reason for my irritation was Ebony's question in the car before we got to the mall. She touched a nerve. I had some questions of my own about Eli being mentally challenged. He rarely fussed and he loved to smile. He was very active, crawling about the house, and he was like a bulldozer when we sat him in the walker, but he wasn't babbling or trying to talk. I kept my fears to myself; I was the one to blame. I insisted on going forward with the pregnancy and I had refused to have any prenatal genetic testing.

***

"Get up Mama and Daddy, Eli and I have already made breakfast," Elise yelled from the door with her brother on her hip. "Erica and her crew will be here in a few and Ebony and Calvin are already here."

"Okay, give us a few minutes, we'll be down," Nelson said, rubbing his eyes.

"I don't guess we'll ever get to sleep late on Christmas morning," I said, swinging my legs to the side of the bed.

"It's all your fault, Evelyn; I never told you I wanted a house full of children."

"I don't think I brought them here by myself, you do know how they're made don't you," I said, walking towards the bathroom.

"Yeah, I do, little woman, and since you're parading around here like a spring chicken, I might give you one more," he teased, grabbing me around the waist.

"Don't make me think thoughts about manslaughter on the day Jesus was born."

"Some things are worth dying for," he said, kissing me on the neck.

"I'm going to have to find you another job, you have too much energy."

"I don't know about that, I'm starting to enjoy my retirement."

"On a more serious note," I said, changing the subject and putting on my robe, "Do you think there's anything different about Eli? The girls feel like he isn't vocal enough."

"The boy is only seven months old. What do they want from him? I like the fact he's quiet. Don't let them worry you, honey, because it doesn't matter. If he came here retarded, cripple, or crazy, there's nothing we can do but love him. When I get down there I'm going to tell those girls to leave my only son alone."

"Don't say anything; I don't want to spoil the day."

"Whatever you want, baby," he said, taking my hand and pulling me out the door.

We had a great morning. The girls had put together a delicious breakfast and we exchanged gifts. I couldn't help but notice how the balance had changed. Women had always outnumbered and ruled the Winters' household but now we were outnumber by one.

"The men are trying to take over," I said as we lounged in the living room around the Christmas tree, "Somebody's got to bring us a baby girl."

"Don't look at me, I have to get a husband first," Elise joked, still holding Eli in her lap.

"Well, don't look at me, I just contributed," Erica added.

"We're not even in this, Ebony and I can barely take care of ourselves," Calvin said, "We're still paying bills from the wedding and with this recession, I'm praying I don't get laid-off."

"Hold tight, Calvin," Drew chimed in, "Diapers, formula, and daycare are more than both of our car notes put together."

"It's no joke out here," Nelson said, "If it was this expensive back when these girls were born, the only one sitting here would be Elise, because I would have tied my tube."

Everybody laughed and when we got ourselves together Ebony

and Erica had to leave and go spend some time with the other half of their families.

"Looks like it's just us," Elise said cheerfully.

"I don't know what your plans are but I'm going back to bed," I said, heading towards the stairs after giving Eli a kiss on the cheek.

"You two come with me," Nelson said, "I bet I can find us a bowl game to look at."

I tucked the covers around me as I laid in the bed for the rare minutes to myself. I thought about turning on the TV but I knew that the waves were being bombarded with talk of weapons of mass destruction, pre-emptive strikes against Iraq, and war-mongers. I decided to revel in my private peace. I couldn't help but smile to myself, I was happy. On the see-saw of life it was my chance to be up. I silently thanked God. So much of the world was on the down side.

***

"I can't believe these fake politicians are going to actually do this," Nelson shouted to me as he watched the morning news, "They're going to start this war when they know they don't have any reason to be messing with Iraq. This is all about humongous government kickbacks to companies that supply the military."

"It's nothing we can do, honey bear, I didn't vote for the man and he still got in there," I shouted back from the closet, trying to find something green for St. Patrick's Day to wear to work even though there wasn't an Irish bone in my body.

"Every major nation in the world including the United Nations has said not to do this and they're doing it anyway. Never mind the fact that we're too broke to spend money killing folks who aren't any danger to us. They need to be worrying about how to create some jobs around here."

"You're going to run your pressure up, Nelson," I chided,

putting on my lipstick in the bathroom mirror. "I'll get Eli dressed and maybe you two can go out for a while this morning and calm yourself down."

I walked down the hall and Eli stood up in his bed when I came into the room.

"Good morning, fresh face," I said, picking him up and hugging him close.

Nelson was used to getting up early in the mornings and had already given Eli his bath and a bottle of milk with rice cereal in it. I breathed in his sweet scent while I looked in the dresser for some pants and a sweater. I had bought him his first pair of hard bottom shoes on Saturday and I wanted to put them on him.

"Don't you look like a big boy today?" I said, carrying him down the steps to the kitchen on my hip. "You're almost ready to go to school."

Down in the kitchen I realized I had forgotten to bring his walker down with me. "He'll be all right on the floor for a minute," I thought. As I eased him lower to his feet he clicked one heel against the other intrigued by the solid sound. When I stood him up on the floor he took a step and then another going faster and faster trying to keep his balance until he was running. He ran out of the kitchen and kept going until he reached the end of the hallway where he plopped down on his bottom and laughed with such glee that I laughed too. I took four long strides and lifted him up in my arms.

"Eli, you walked, you ran," I said, looking deep in his sparkling eyes and treasuring this special moment.

"Then he nodded and said, "Yay, Mama."

"Nelson," I shrieked, overwhelmed. "Come down here, Eli is walking and talking."

"What's the matter?" Nelson asked, rushing down the stairs holding the banister to keep from falling, "What's going on?"

"It's Eli, I put him down in his new shoes and he just started walking," I said with tears of joy rolling over the hills of my cheeks.

Nelson took him from me, "My goodness, son, are you ready to walk so soon?" he asked, putting him down to stand on his feet.

Then Eli took one step and nodded again before he said, "Dada."

Nelson and I stood there watching him and crying like two fools. He took two more steps before he plopped back on his bottom. Nelson grabbed him up cheering at the same time and sat down at the kitchen table.

"Baby boy, what's got you walking and talking all on the same day?" Nelson asked, standing him in his lap.

"No, no," Eli said, shaking his head.

"That's it, I'm calling in, I can't work today," I said, reaching for the phone, "I don't know what is going on here today.

"I don't either, Evelyn, but it looks like Eli is going to tell us before the day is out," Nelson said, grinning proudly at the baby.

I called the school and told them something was going on with Eli and it was the truth. As much as I was overjoyed to finally hear his voice and see him take his first step, somehow it was unsettling to me. Something so natural seemed peculiar and I didn't know why. I called all the girls, my mama and daddy, to give them the good news, and then I called Macey.

"Macey, you won't believe it, I put Eli's new hard bottom shoes on and then he started to walk this morning."

"That is amazing, Evie, he's not even a year old yet."

"I know, but then he said his first word, Mama, Dada, and, no."

"Okay, you're right, I can't take all that in at one time."

"That's how I feel too, Macey," I explained, "It all seemed so sudden. I keep wondering what brought it all on."

"Don't start straining you brain, Evie. You were so worried about his development, now there's nothing to worry about. The boy is walking and talking. I can't wait until I finish teaching my last class; I'm coming over to see my godson."

I hung up the phone and found Nelson and Eli in the den. Nelson had turned the TV on and was watching some more of the news about the strike on Iraq. I watched the baby as he cruised around the coffee table.

Suddenly he stopped as if he heard something; he looked at us sitting on the sofa, raised his hand and said, "No war, Mama."

My mouth opened but for a second nothing came out. My baby had said something to me. It was a sentence I think.

When I found my voice I said, "Nelson, now that he's trying to talk I don't think it's good for you to let him hear all that negative mess on the TV."

"He doesn't understand it, Evelyn, but if you're through telling the world that our son is doing what babies do, would you care to join us? I'm taking him out to breakfast to celebrate."

"I might as well, I took the day off."

"Well, grab the diaper bag," he said, holding Eli's hand as they walked across the floor.

8

"For the last time, Nelson, have you got everything now?" I asked, exasperated. "We're not coming back to the house again for anything. Circling back from Murfreesboro has added sixty miles and another hour to the drive."

"I'm sorry, Evelyn, but I couldn't leave without my video camera. With all the babies around here I've got to get my pictures and my movies. Isn't that right, Eli?" he replied, unperturbed.

"Right, Daddy," Eli squealed from the back in his car seat.

"I don't know why we couldn't all just rent a van or something and drive up together," I complained. "With all the mess going on in New Orleans after Hurricane Katrina and the flood, I don't feel right going on a family trip. All those people with no place to go, it doesn't make sense, it's a shame."

"That's why we elect politicians to be leaders and solve problems, Evelyn, there's nothing we can do to help all those people. As hard as it is for everybody in this family to coordinate schedules, all of us getting to spend this weekend in Gatlinburg together is a miracle. I'm just glad Ebony and Calvin are picking up Elise at the airport in Knoxville."

"Those people have to pray, Mama," Eli yelled in the back.

Both Nelson and I were stunned again; Eli was always saying something out of the blue that stopped us in our tracks. Before he was one year old I was worried about him being slow or challenged but from the day he started walking and talking he amazed me with the words that came out of his mouth.

"I told you not to watch so much news on the TV with him around, Nelson, you know he's very sensitive."

"Sounds like he picked that up from you sitting him up in church on Sundays," Nelson said, laughing, "Kids his age always repeat everything they hear."

I leaned my head against the head rest and closed my eyes to relax. I needed every minute I could get before we got to the chalet we had rented. This was the first trip Ebony had taken since she had her baby in May. Amber, the baby girl we hoped for was born two weeks before Eli turned three. Drew Jr. was still in his terrible two's so it was going to be all the way live.

"I want a drink, Mama," a small voice whispered behind me.

"I want one too," Nelson said, "It's a hot one out here today."

"Both of you are in an air conditioned vehicle," I said, reaching in the cooler on the back seat and getting a can of Coke for Nelson, a bottle of tea for myself, and a box of apple juice for Eli. "We've been doing good so far trying to make up the time we lost, if we start having to stop at restrooms it will take us twice the time to get there."

As it turned out, I was right; we stopped nearly every thirty-five minutes. Nelson had to go twice, I had to go once, and Eli went twice and tricked us into stopping two additional times just to get out of the car. By the time we got to the chalet everyone else had already arrived. Eli saw D.J in the back of the cabin with Drew and ran over to play while we unloaded the car.

"What happened, Daddy? We were about to send out an APB to find y'all," Erica said, coming over to the car to help.

"What usually happens, child?" I said, waving to Drew. "Your daddy always forgets something and then he has to make so many stops. The next time I'm riding with you."

"It hot up here, Mama," Ebony said, walking out of the chalet with Amber in her arms. "Why didn't we get a place with a pool?"

"Lord, no," Nelson interjected, "We don't need that drama with these babies running around."

"You're right, Daddy," Ebony agreed, "I didn't think about that."

"Give me my granddaughter," I said, reaching for Amber, "I

didn't get to spend enough time with her, now the summer is over and she's in daycare."

"We both have to work, Mama, the price of everything is going up sky-high including gas. If Calvin didn't have to leave on Sunday we would have rode with y'all."

"Where's Elise?" Nelson asked Erica, carrying the bags inside.

"She's taking a nap; her plane flew out of New York last night with a layover in Charlotte, NC, so she was up most of the night."

"Your daddy was up most of the night too," I said, trailing them inside. "The TV has been on nonstop with the news about New Orleans and Hurricane Katrina."

"We've been watching it too," Ebony said. "I can't believe they haven't gotten any help to the people down there in the Dome yet."

"How do you guys like our home for the weekend?" I asked, trying to change the subject for a minute. "Nelson will have the TV on the news for the whole weekend."

"Calvin has had it on since we got here. There is some big protest going on in D.C. about the war. Maybe we should have gotten a cabin without electricity," Ebony added.

"You all know I wouldn't be going down like that," Elise said, coming into the room. "Hey Mama, hey Daddy," she said, giving us a kiss. "Where's my baby brother?"

"He's outside with Drew and D.J.," I answered, walking towards the kitchen. "This is really nice, I love it. The table is so long we can all sit down together."

"Evelyn, where do you want me to put these bags before I sit down," Nelson shouted.

"I'll show you, Daddy," Erica said, appeasing him as usual, "Yours and Mama's bedroom is down the hall on the right. That way you won't have to go up and down the stairs. Eli can share a room with D.J. upstairs."

"What's the plan for dinner tonight, ladies?" I asked Ebony and Elise.

"Drew and Calvin are going to fry up some catfish; Elise is making a salad, Ebony is boiling some corn and potatoes, and I'm making a peach cobbler," Erica said, returning to the kitchen.

"All right, captain, it seems you have everything under control as usual," I replied happily. "That means I get to sit down and enjoy Amber while you all get busy."

"Yeah, don't forget D.J. and Eli too," Ebony reminded me.

I laid Amber on a blanket in the recreation room while the boys played with some leggo blocks. Nelson was glued to CNN on the 40 inch TV screen. I could hear the anchorman as he described the horrid conditions of the city and all I could do was shake my head. The world was in total chaos. I looked at the babies and prayed the world would be better for them somehow.

Out of the blue, Eli stood up and yelled out, "It's all wrong," and knocked down all the blocks he had stacked up so neatly with one swift swing of his hand.

Erica and Ebony rushed into the room to check on their babies but I waved my hand to let them know everything was fine. Erica went back into the kitchen but Ebony stood in the doorway, protective of her newborn.

"Come here, Eli, what's the matter?" I asked, pulling him close to me by the waistband of his pants. "What were you building, didn't you like it?"

He wouldn't look at me. Nelson called to him but he didn't respond. Ebony came over and tried to pick him up but he pushed her arm away. I stood up and handed Amber to her mama. Then I kneeled down in front of Eli and tried to get his attention.

After a few seconds he looked me in the eye and said, "Mama, it's not right, it's wrong."

"Do you want to go for a walk or do you want to take a nap?" I asked him, standing up.

"I want to go for a walk before it rains," he said, raising his hand to take mine.

Ebony went over and sat on the couch with Nelson and before we were out of the room I heard her ask him, "Why does he act like that, Daddy?"

"He's fine, sweetie," he answered, "Don't worry about him."

We walked hand in hand, silently down to the end of the driveway and into the fresh cut grass that led into a wooded area. I could see his mood begin to change and the bounce in his step return. We heard a rustle in the leaves above us and when a bird flew out up into the sky he looked at me and smiled and I smiled back.

"Why were you upset, baby?" I asked, seeing he had calmed down.

"People shouldn't be suffering in the world; they shouldn't be poor or hungry. They shouldn't have to die for no reason. That's not the way," he said with his eyes searching for the bird.

How could I explain the injustices in the world to a three-year-old, I didn't understand them myself. It bothered me that he was so affected by grown up things. I wanted him to be carefree.

"I love you, Eli," I said, stooping to give him a hug."

"I love you, Mama," he said.

"Are you hungry? I think its dinnertime."

"Okay," he said, running back towards the house.

At the edge of the driveway, I felt the first raindrops hit my shoulder and Eli's words echoed in my head. What made him think it was going to rain? Probably because he's heard so much about the storm in New Orleans I reasoned, pushing any other thoughts out of my mind. Inside the dining room, Eli rushed over to Elise when he saw her sitting at the table.

She lifted him onto her lap and said, "Everybody grab a seat and I'll bless the food. We're ready to eat aren't we, Eli?"

He nodded and she kissed him on the cheek. Then he leaned up and kissed her on the cheek. I felt a tear of happiness burn at the corner of my eye but I pushed it to the side before it got a chance to swell. Erica, Drew, and Calvin brought the food to the table. I took a seat and Nelson sat beside me holding D.J.

"Lord, bless this family gathered around this table, bless these gifts of food we are about to receive for the nourishment of our bodies, may it strengthen us to do thy will, in Jesus' name I pray, amen," Elise prayed with her head bowed.

"Amen," Eli uttered after her with his eyes closed.

"That's all right, little brother-in-law," Drew chuckled, amused at Eli's serious face.

"Don't start," Erica said, "Pass me some fish while it's still hot."

We passed the food around the table at least twice. It was all extra delicious, maybe because I didn't have to cook any of it.

"So what's new around here, everybody? I know there's something, you all don't ever take a break," Elise inquired, taking a sip of the fruit punch Ebony had made.

"As a matter of fact I do have something to report," Nelson said, wiping his mouth with a napkin, "I'm going back to work. The company called me right after Katrina hit and they want me to do some consulting, effective immediately."

"Are you sure you want to do that, Daddy, It's been three years?" Elise asked.

"I'm very sure, I would have found something else to do much earlier but your mama and I decided it would be good for me to spend that time with Eli. Now that he's three, we think it's time for him to go to pre-school."

"It was perfect timing, he and D.J. are going to start their first day together at Andrew Jackson Montessori School," Erica chimed in.

"That will be good," Ebony said, feeding Amber a bottle, "We'll finally get to know if Eli needs any special education before he gets to kindergarten."

"I know we're not going to start all that stuff again," Erica said, throwing down her napkin.

"First of all, don't talk about him like he's not in the room and he doesn't understand," I protested. "Eli is special, very sensitive, but he is by no means slow."

"I'm stuffed," Elise said, getting up from the table with Eli, "D.J., do you want to go to the game room with us."

"Yea," he said, wiggling out of my arms."

Elise gripped his little fingers and they left the room.

"Don't you have enough to think about with Amber? You don't need to concern yourself with Eli. I took care of you girls and I'll take care of him," I said, annoyed with her insinuations.

"That's not what I mean, Mama. He doesn't respond when you talk to him a lot of the time and he doesn't like to be picked up. It's like he's in his own little world sometimes. Those are signs of autism."

"He's an independent child; maybe you can't understand that because you were so spoiled when you were the baby. It seems like you're jealous of your brother. "

"That's not it, Mama."

"Leave it alone, Ebony," Calvin said, taking Amber from her and walking out of the room."

"We're going to have to make an agreement here today," Nelson said, "I going to promise you girls that I won't put my mouth on anything that goes on in your households and how y'all raise your children but I want the same consideration in return."

"I agree, Daddy," Erica said quickly.

"So, we're family but we can't talk," Ebony huffed.

"That's not what I said," Nelson argued, "There are boundaries we need to respect. You wouldn't want me to run down Calvin or Amber here at the table in front of everybody would you?"

"No, I would not."

"Then give Eli some respect."

"I'm sorry; I thought I was trying to help my little brother. My lips are sealed," Ebony said, leaving the table to join Calvin.

"Should we pack up and go back home now?" Drew asked, laughing uncomfortably.

"No, it'll blow over by morning, let's find us a beer and get some air," Nelson said, patting him on the back. "We've been through worse than this."

"Well, Mama, I guess it's left to you and me to clean up the mess as usual," Erica said.

"Some things never change, baby."

Nelson was right, all the fuss did blow over and we had a nice weekend at Gatlinburg. We shopped, took the boys to Dollywood, explored the mountains, and kept our bellies full of good food. We ended up driving home on Labor Day because the boys were going for a half day of orientation on Tuesday, I only had one day before school was starting, and Nelson was headed out of town.

9

The disaster in New Orleans was greater than anyone had imagined. The insurance company wanted to see the extent of the damage as soon as possible. Nelson unpacked the clothes from the weekend and re-packed it with clothes for a week.

"Don't worry about driving me to the airport," Nelson said while I helped Eli with his bath, "I'll park the car in the terminal garage."

He kissed Eli on the forehead and gave me a quick kiss on the lips. He dashed out of the bathroom and it was like the last three years of him being retired were a mere daydream.

Eli was dressed and had just finished his breakfast cereal when the phone rang. I could see on the caller ID that it was Erica calling.

"Good morning, what's the plan?" I asked.

"I'm already driving. I was thinking that we should meet at the school, that way I can go to my school and get my classroom ready for tomorrow."

"That sounds good; I'll be leaving in a little while since I don't have far to drive."

"Okay, Mama. See you in a few minutes."

Erica was already in the parking lot when I pulled in. She had D.J. all dressed up in new jeans and a button down shirt, some of those expensive Jordan sneakers, and a baseball cap. For her I guess her baby was going to school, not the glorified daycare center that stood in front of us. She picked him up for the sake of time as Eli and I strode over to join them.

"Good morning, sweetie," I said, leaning in and giving them

both a hug, "How's my grandboy, today?"

"We'll see once we get inside, he's been used to staying at Miss Ann's house, so he may pitch a fit when he sees me leave."

"If he does, blow him a kiss and wave goodbye and keep moving. I can't handle both of you crying in here."

Inside the lobby there was a man at the desk giving directions to parents bringing in the younger children for orientation.

"Welcome to Andrew Jackson," he said, extending his hand to greet us. "Who do we have here," he asked, giving the boys a questioning look.

"This is Drew and that's Eli," Erica said.

"Two handsome brothers, are they twins?"

"No, they aren't brothers," Erica said with a polite smile.

"They are uncle and nephew, Eli is my son," I said as I watched his eyes shift away embarrassed.

"Pardon me," he said, "The three preschool classrooms are down the hall on the left. The names for each class are listed on the door."

"Don't feel bad," I said, turning to follow Erica, "It's a mistake made quite often."

"It looks like the boys are in the same classroom," Erica said after checking the list of names on the second door.

She hesitated so I moved forward, turned the doorknob, and pulled it open. I knew it was hard taking the next steps as your infant grew from baby to toddler and then starts schools. I had experience it three other times.

"Good morning, come and join us in the circle," a heavy white woman with curly red hair said from a small stool at the top of the circle. "I'm Shirley O'Bryan and Miss LaTonya is our assistant teacher."

I nodded to the young woman sitting just outside the circle and said, "Hello, I'm Evelyn Winters and this is my son Eli."

"I'm Erica Jamison and this is Drew Jr., we call him D.J."

"It's a pleasure to meet you both. April and Jason, slide over so that Eli and Drew can join us in the circle. As you know, today is a half-day so you can pick them up at 11:30."

Eli took D.J.'S hand and led him over to the circle. Eli sat down while D.J. struggled to get comfortable in his new jeans and bulky sneakers. The other children stared in curiosity and Ms. O'Bryan flashed them a warm smile.

"You all have a good day," I said, backing up to leave, but Erica hadn't moved.

"Come on, sweetie, we'll be back in a few hours I whispered behind her."

I could see her shoulders start to move up and down with the emotions that were taking over. She was going to cry. I reached for her elbow just as Eli hopped up from the circle and ran over to her.

"Don't cry Erica, Eli said, pronouncing her name with two syllables, "I'll take care of D.J."

"Thanks, Eli," she said with sincere gratitude, braced herself, and turned around and walked out with me.

For in that moment it was as if he was the big brother and she the little sister.

"That was hard, Mama," she said, peering through the narrow window of the door.

"I know, but it will get easier. They grow up so fast."

***

Eli and D.J. adapted well to going to school in spite of Ms. O'Bryan who was always worrying me about something Eli had said or done in class. I refused to let her make me lose my cool. It was Erica who had a fit when she found out they would have to wear white polo shirts and blue pants as the school uniform every day. She had bought D.J. enough clothes to make fashion statements five days of the week. Having them both at the same school was a help to both of us. I picked them up in the afternoons

Monday through Thursday and Erica picked them up on Fridays and kept Eli until Saturday night.

That was right on time because Nelson was so happy to be back working full-time that he was acting like a new man again. He was out of town most of the week working on claims and testifying in court behind the Hurricane Katrina disaster in New Orleans and Mississippi, but when he came home on Fridays he ran me ragged late into the night and then waking me up early in the morning for sex. I'm not complaining about the attention, except I think it had more to do with his insecurity about me when he was out of town than him getting piping hot for me again.

It was the Thursday morning before the Easter Week break at school, Nelson had been out of town all week and would be home tomorrow evening. The Tom Joyner Morning Show was playing on the radio. I loved to listen to the Thursday Morning Mom segment, hoping to hear my name come across the airwaves one day. I was making some toast and apple butter and a boiled egg for Eli to eat for breakfast, it was his favorite. He hadn't come down yet, he was dressing himself these days. All I had to do for him was tie his shoes. He was one independent child.

"Good job," I said, holding my hand up for a high-five when he appeared in the kitchen. "You are looking very nice this morning."

"You look pretty too, Mama," he said, climbing onto a chair at the kitchen bar.

"Thank you, sir," I replied as I put his plate and a cup of milk in front of him.

"You don't have to worry about me at school today, Mama," he said after he finished his toast and milk.

"That's good, baby. I want you to have a good day and learn something new."

"Did you make a sandwich for your lunch?" he asked with a concerned look.

"Yes sir, do you want me to pack something for you?"

"No, I want to make sure you don't have to go out for lunch; there's going to be a very bad storm today."

"That's right, they did say it's going to rain this afternoon. I guess the April showers are about to begin."

When we finished breakfast, we hurried through the brushing of our teeth and hair and then we headed out the door. I strapped Eli into his car seat, got in the driver's seat, and started the car. I turned off the radio in the car for the short drive to Hull-Jackson. Eli's brain was like a sponge and he soaked up everything in the atmosphere around him. Half of the stuff on the radio was too much for my mature hearing much less for his tender ears. I looked back at him from the rearview mirror and he was staring out of his window as if he was deep in thought. I pulled to the drop-off area to walk him up to the door.

"Hug and kiss," I said once we were inside, squatting down to his height.

He kissed my cheek, put his short arms around me and said, "When it starts, tell Erica to stay at her school too, okay."

"Yes, baby, I will."

On the way back to the car I got a strange feeling, something was going to happen and Eli knew what it was. I wanted to call and share the warning, but to whom and say what? No one would believe my four-year-old son had psychic powers. I turned the radio on loud to drown out my thoughts, my imagination was running amok.

Halfway through the day I started seeing storm warnings on the homepage of my computer. The sky started to get dark as if nightfall had rushed into the day. The winds began to grow more powerful causing our school flag to whip violently at the top of the pole. One gust was so strong I feared the window would break. Then the rainfall began except it wasn't rain, I could hear the pellets as they hit against the windowpane. I stood up to get a closer look and it was hail the size of golf balls dropping out of the sky and pinging on the cars in the parking lot.

Suddenly the school alarm sounded and I heard Dr. Morgan speaking over the PA system, "All staff, personnel, and students are directed to proceed immediately to the gym for safety precautions. No one is to leave the building for any reason. We are under a tornado threat for the next two hours." When her voice stopped I could hear the sound of a far off train. My next thought was Eli and what he said when I dropped him off. I hadn't called Erica like he told me. I grabbed my cell phone and pushed in her number as I ran down the hallway behind the pack of students.

"Mama, I can't talk, there are tornados touching down all over the place," Erica yelled frantically.

"Wait a minute, it's important. Where are you?" I asked quickly before she hung up.

"I'm on my way to pick the boys up; the news says the path of the tornado is going to run through that area."

"Listen to me, sweetie, Eli told me this morning that we didn't have to worry about them and he didn't want you to leave the school," I assured her as I huddled under the bleachers with the eleventh graders.

"I know he can see things sometimes but I can't take a chance on that, I have to get my baby."

I held the phone close to my right ear while the sound of glass breaking, the clanging of metal against cement, and the terrified screams of the students filled my left ear.

"Please, Erica, trust me on this, go back to your school. It's dangerous out there, please."

"Oh no, Mama, the interstate is jammed up, a light pole fell across the lanes and there is a pile-up of cars. The entrance is blocked."

"Turn your car around now. You can't get there in the traffic."

"I can't, there are cars lined up behind me."

"Leave the car there and get off the street," I urged.

For the next few minutes all I could hear in my right ear was Erica's breathing. From the pace of her breaths I assumed she was running. Unconsciously I held my breath to channel her more air to breathe.

"I'm inside a bank," she said finally. "I had to fight through the wind to get here. It was like I didn't weigh anything, I could barely keep my feet on the ground."

"Thank God," I said, hearing the sound of another call beeping on my phone. "Stay there and check on Ebony, your daddy is calling me."

I clicked over and said, "Hello."

"What the hell is going on?" Nelson hollered into my ear. "The news down here is saying twenty-four tornados have touched down in Tennessee."

"It's crazy, we're still at school crouched in the gym and it's dismissal time."

"Where's Eli?" he shouted. "I couldn't get an answer at his school."

"They're probably on lockdown like we are here. I don't know how long the tornado watch is going to last, we don't have access to TV or a computer down here. Anna is communicating with the Department of Education by phone."

"This is too much, I should be there," he said helplessly.

"I'm fine, Nelson, check on Ebony, I haven't spoken to her and my phone battery is just about dead. I'll call you when I get home."

"All right, be safe, honey," he said.

I hung up the phone to preserve whatever minutes I had left. It was another hour before Dr. Morgan received word that we could leave the shelter of the gym walls. At 4:00 quite a few parents had not come to pick up their children.

"You can go on and leave, Evelyn, Miss Terry and I will stay until everybody is gone, I know you need to check on your little one," Dr. Morgan said.

"Thanks, Anna, I'm worried sick, there's still no answer at his school."

The sights outside of the school were mind-blowing. Debris blown from rooftops, broken limbs from trees, and turned over trash receptacles filled the parking lot. My car looked like it had been through a war zone; it was covered with dents and dings from the hood to the trunk. I didn't have time to react; I needed to get to Eli. I turned on my emergency signal and drove through red lights and stop signs. By the time I got to the school my mouth was hanging open in shock. The devastation around the school was unbelievable. Police cars were everywhere.

Even more amazing was the look of the Andrew Jackson school. The building seemed out of place amongst the destruction, it had not been touched. It was as if some type of impenetrable shield had been place around it to protect it from the tornado. Eli knew the school would be spared, but how? I pulled to the side of the street and rushed to the school entrance. Eli and D.J. were sitting in the lobby with Ms. O'Bryan and several other children. For the first time since we met she had nothing to say.

"Hey you two," I said, sighing with relief. "Let's go home."

"Okay, Mama," Eli said, jumping up happily.

I could see D.J. was scared and upset. I took his hand to lead him out. "Where's Mama?" he asked. "I want my daddy."

"They're coming to pick you up at my house," I told him.

Back in the car I tried to call Erica but my cell phone was dead. I turned off my emergency lights but I kept easing through the red lights and stop signs. Who knew what our house would look like. Thankfully, God had been good to me again, there was no visible damage to the house when I pulled up in the driveway, and most of the houses on our street had also been fortunate. I called Erica from the nearest phone in the laundry room.

"I have D.J. here with me and he's fine," I said, "How are you, sweetie."

"I'm still shaking," she said, and I could hear it in her voice. "Drew and I went to pick up my van and it was crushed upside down beside a telephone pole."

"Oh my God," I gasped, covering my mouth.

"Thanks for calling me and telling me to get out of the car, Mama, you saved me."

"Baby, I thank the Lord. If Eli hadn't told me this morning I wouldn't have known. Did you get in touch with Ebony?"

"Yeah, I did, they're good. They didn't get anything except rain on their side of town. We'll be there soon; Drew wants to check on the house first."

"Take your time, we aren't going anywhere."

There was no way I could settle down and cook so I made us some sandwiches to snack on. After that I let them watch Sponge Bob on the Nickelodeon channel while I called Macey.

"Are you all right?" I asked after she said hello.

"I'm fine but half the shutters from my windows are laying in the yard. How are you?"

"We didn't have any damage around here but streets all through town were torn up."

"I didn't have any early classes today and when the warnings came on the news all the afternoon classes were canceled. I haven't even left the house."

"Macey, what really has me shaken up is that Eli warned me this morning. He even told me to tell Erica not to leave her school and her van was totaled."

"I've told you before, Evie, Eli is your good luck charm."

"Something tells me he's more than that," I said.

Erica and Drew came in right after I got off the phone. I trailed her into the den where she grabbed Eli off the floor and held him tight against her chest.

"Thank you, little brother," she said softly.

He didn't say anything back; he just leaned back, smiled, and clapped his hands. Then Erica's stressed face relaxed and she smiled too. We were all too drained to relive the events of the day. Drew scooped up D.J. and they left. Eli went back to watching cartoons. It was all so amazing to me. There was no denying that Eli was special. He was a gift to me but he had other gifts that I was still learning about.

I was upstairs changing my shoes when Nelson called again. "Evelyn, they're showing Andrew Jackson School on the news here. Everything for almost a block around it was damn near leveled and the school wasn't touched. Even the daffodils have their blooms on them. They're saying it was a miracle that no one was hurt."

"It was unbelievable when I saw it myself," I said.

"I'm thinking about renting a car and driving in."

"No, honey bear, relax, it's all over now. Your flight is scheduled to leave before lunchtime; we'll see you in a few hours anyway.

"From now on they're going to have to find somebody else to do all this traveling. Every time I leave the house all hell breaks loose.

10

I can't deal with her right now. Ms. O'Bryan is blowing up my phone again. I've got a long list of transcripts and letters that I need to get e-mailed for our senior class this year. I don't have the time or the patience to deal with her hysterics. I chose a Montessori school for Eli because of the continuity that the students benefit from by having the same teacher for three years, but if I had a dollar for every time Ms. O'Bryan called me I would have enough cash to be able to send Eli to the University School. I picked up my desk phone and dialed Nelson.

"Can you call the school when you get a minute? Ms. O'Bryan just called. Let me know if it's an emergency or another one of her false alarms."

"No problem, honey," he answered in a rare good mood, "Don't let her get to you, she's just a concerned teacher. School will be out in less than a month and he's going to get a new teacher after the summer."

"I know, call me back when you finish talking with her."

Ms. O'Bryan had gotten on my last nerve many times over the years. First she noticed that Eli had an above average vocabulary which she attributed to his obsessive habit of memorizing minute details. She was always observing some behavior characteristic that she believed was abnormal. My mind went over the last conversation we had after the winter break last year.

"Mrs. Winters, I have recommended that Eli be evaluated before the end of the school year. I'm not convinced that this is the correct environment for him."

"What type of evaluation are you talking about?"

"Eli is a special little boy; unlike the other children in the class he is easily preoccupied with facts and memorization. He repeats himself at times, dwelling on events that are past his understanding."

"Why is that a problem, he's a very introspective child."

"I have reasons to suspect that Eli is exhibiting signs of savant syndrome."

"With all due respect, having been a school counselor for more than twenty years, Eli is not a savant. He is very social; he can read beyond his age level, his math skills are good but not exceptional. If I'm not mistaken savants are focused on one subject or area. Eli is well-rounded."

"I can imagine that this is difficult to hear but I'm not able to distinguish what Eli has learned and what he has simply memorized."

"That is a blurred line for all of us; I myself don't know the difference."

"Nevertheless, now that he is nearly six years old he will have to complete the Wechsler IQ test. If a child has a subordinate IQ score and the characteristics that Eli displays then they are considered to be a savant. If his scores are normal, he will be promoted without question."

"Thank you, Ms. O'Bryan," I said, resisting the urge to tell her about herself and what I think about her recommendation.

That had been six months ago and I got mad all over again whenever I thought about it. Why is it when a black boy is smart it's not natural, he's got to be crazy. I was tired of fighting about it and defending my son against personal opinions. He was scheduled to be tested on April 29th and his score would be the judge and sentence him for the rest of his life. The phone ring brought me back out of my reverie.

"Hey, honey, everything is good, Ms. O'Bryan just wanted to remind you that next Tuesday is the date for Eli to be tested."

"I don't understand, with all the craziness going on in the world all she can think about is my child. She needs to get a life."

"You're just over sensitive about anybody being critical about Eli."

"I was the same about all of my children, but none of them have had to endure being put under a microscope like he has."

***

It's the Saturday after the IQ test and the results won't be available until next Friday. Nelson is absorbed in the never-ending news as usual. Between the recession and the election results he can't pull himself away from the television. I took Eli with me to the grocery store this morning and I'm sure they all thought I was out with my grandson. We are rewarding ourselves with fudgesicles and a swing in the backyard. Eli is very close to me and he prefers my company to Nelson's, after three daddy's girls, it feels good to have a mama's boy.

"Mama, we forgot to buy some food for the Second Harvest Food Bank, I saw it on the news, there are a lot of people who are hungry without enough to eat all around us," he said as the swing went back and forward.

"We will, they're taking donations at the church this Sunday," I assured him. "A lot of people have lost their jobs and can't make ends meet."

"It's because some people who have lots of money are really selfish and don't care if they pay their workers fairly. That's why children don't have enough to eat."

"I believe they just don't think about it."

"They have to think about it. If some weren't so greedy there would be enough for the whole world," he said calmly. "It's good that a person can work hard and become rich but that doesn't mean that he is more worthy than another person. The more you have, the more you can share."

"You're right, Eli, I hope things will change for the better soon but we need to choose good men and women to lead us. That is why we have elections."

"It will change this time, Mama."

"I hope so, baby."

We have intellectual conversations like this when we are alone and they always amaze me but today my mind is on his test score. Waiting is torture; I pray that he's not a savant. We swung in the shade until we finished our cool treats.

"Let's go see what you're daddy is doing," I said.

"Okay," he said as he ran ahead and held the door for me.

"Thank you, sir, what a gentleman you are."

"Yes, ma'am," he said with a smile.

We found Nelson in the den with his legs stretched out on the couch with the remote in his hand. Eli sits down on his beanbag and starts playing with his DS game.

"What do you feel like eating for dinner, old man?" I asked, standing over him.

"I don't have much appetite after looking at all the gloom and doom on this TV. It's just one sad story after another, people losing their jobs and their houses. The stock market is going into the toilet and the company will probably be giving me my walking papers for the second time."

"Why don't you just retire once and for all, this house is paid for. We don't have any car notes or big bills to wrestle with," I said, lifting his legs in the air and sitting down.

"That's a luxury I can't afford, Evelyn. Ebony called earlier and said that Calvin got laid-off again at Nissan. There aren't many jobs out there; they may have to move in here with us if he doesn't get called back or find something else soon."

"She didn't mention any of that to me when I talked to her the other day."

"Well, that's the situation. We may have more people to take care of than ourselves."

"I think I just lost my appetite too."

"Since I'm the one who's hungry, can we order a pizza?" Eli asked without looking up.

"Good idea, I don't feel like cooking or going back out. The Kentucky Derby will be on in a few minutes and I don't want to miss it. You know your daddy told me that he was going to take me to see it in person when we first met and I'm still waiting."

"Don't stop waiting because we are still going," Nelson said, changing the channel.

I walked in the kitchen to order the pizza. As soon as I put the phone down it rang again.

"What are you folks up to?" Macey asked cheerily through the receiver.

"Not much, just waiting for the Derby to start," I answered.

"I've been out shopping and I was going to stop by for a minute, I haven't seen you in weeks, my friend."

"I know, it's my fault, come on by, I just ordered a pizza."

Macey knocked on the backdoor ten minutes later with a present in her hand.

"This is for my godson's birthday," she said, handing it to me. "I may be out of town when the semester ends if I can pull it together. I really need a break."

"That sounds wonderful, I could use one myself but I doubt if we'll take a vacation this year. With this recession we're saving everything we can just in case who knows who is out of work."

We spent a couple of minutes in the kitchen catching up. I was telling her about the test the school had insisted that Eli take and then the pizza guy rang the bell. Macey found a ginger ale in the fridge and carried the box into the den. I poured two glasses of juice for me and Eli and grabbed a beer for Nelson. We huddled around the coffee table while the pre-race program gave a rundown on the horses.

"Hey there, Nelson," Macey said, "You got any money on the race?"

"No way, they say don't gamble if you can't stand to lose."

"That's true," she said, kicking off her shoes and sitting on the floor. "Who do you think is going to win?" she asked Eli."

"It's going to be Big Brown," he answered, showing her all his pretty white teeth.

"All right, then that's who I'm betting on," she said, holding her hand up for a high five.

We finished up the pizza and I took the empty box to the recycle bin.

"Hurry up," Nelson yelled out to me, "They're getting into the starting gates."

I rushed back into the den, Nelson put down his beer and we all stood on our feet as the horses got positioned, it was as if we were about to run this race with them. The gun fired and they were off, blasting out of their gates. The horses galloped and my heart thumped to the beat of their hoofs in the dirt. Eli jumped up and down the whole time. I clapped, Nelson shook his fist, and Macy hollered. The race was barely two minutes long and the winner was Big Brown as Eli had predicted. He stopped jumping and grinned at Macey, she gave him another high-five and clapped her hands some more.

"Eli, how did you know Big Brown was going to win?" Macey asked excitedly.

"I heard it in my head, auntie," Eli answered, still smiling.

"Evie, this boy is a genius," Macey said, grabbing her handbag and walking to the door, "Don't let anybody tell you something different."

"I need to take you to the tracks with me, son," Nelson joked, "You might have a talent for picking horses."

Eli went back over to his bean bag and started to play with his DS game again and Nelson turned back to CNN. I was the only one stuck in the moment. I was even more convinced that Eli could see things before they happened. I sat down on the couch and focused on the news.

"It looks like the race is getting tight between Hilary Clinton and Barack Obama," I said, trying to change the subject in my head.

"Typically, I'm not one to subscribe to conspiracy theories, but I think they might use this guy as a spoiler to keep Hilary from winning the primary so they can sweep the presidential election in November," Nelson commented.

"He's going to win," Eli said matter-of-factly.

"He just may do that in the primary, son," Nelson responded, "After that it will be business as usual. They aren't ready for a black man to run things yet."

"Not this time, Daddy, he's going to stop the wars, or else they'll attack Iran and the world will be at war forever."

"From your mouth to God's ears, son," Nelson muttered.

"No way, He speaks to our ears," Eli said, still playing his game.

"Let's go watch a DVD upstairs before it's your bedtime," I called to Eli, unnerved by all the war and politics talk from a six-year-old.

"Yeah," he cheered, "I want to see "*Chicken Little* again.""

"Okay, let's make some popcorn first," I said, thinking about what it will be like to finally have a black president.

***

It was Monday morning, May 12th, the day after Mother's Day that I finally got the gift I had been waiting for.

"Mrs. Winters, Principal Harris would like to speak with you before you leave today," Ms. O'Bryan said cordially after I brought Eli to the classroom.

"Thank you," I replied before I gave Eli a quick hug goodbye.

"The results of the test must be back," I thought as I kept a steady pace to the front office to hear the verdict. The receptionist informed Dr. Harris that I was waiting and then told me I could go on in. I walked through the swinging door of the office barrier and felt as if I was approaching the witness stand.

"Please come in, have a seat," Dr. Harris said, smiling.

I sat down in the chair facing her desk and told myself to relax, my breathing was shallow and I knew my heart rate was rising with my blood pressure.

"I'm assuming that the results of Eli's evaluation have come in," I said, crossing my legs.

"Yes, they have and I am pleased to tell you that Elijah is not challenged in any way. There are no indications of autism or savant syndrome," she said.

"That is great news," I said, hitting the arm of the chair with my fist for all the worry I had gone through. "I'm very glad to hear it; his teacher had some reservations to the point where she suggested he may have to leave the school."

"I'm sure that this is a welcome relief for you, Ms. O'Bryan had voiced her concerns to me on more than one occasion. Actually, from what we have learned this is the ideal place for Elijah.

His score was 137, well above average, which means he qualifies as a gifted student."

I uncrossed my legs and sat up proudly. "I'm not surprised; I've always thought Eli was a special child but because of my age people assume he has developmental issues."

"That is no longer a concern, when he's promoted after the summer he will be in a classroom with children from six to nine years old and he can excel at a faster pace."

"Thank you again, Dr. Harris," I said before I left her office.

Vindication is truly liberating. I felt as free as the breeze that blew through the sunroof and out the back window. The burden of doubts that I allowed others to pile on me were lifted. I sailed through the rest of the day with new vigor. After dinner when Eli was taking his bath I told Nelson what Dr. Harris had informed me.

"I don't want to make an announcement to the girls," I said, "He doesn't need to be treated any differently."

"That's fine with me; I've always said leave the boy alone," he said, getting up from the table.

A couple of weeks later, I was sitting in the den with Nelson having a lazy Saturday afternoon. He was surfing the channels while I held a pen and my journal in hand anticipating a moment of inspiration. Yesterday Hilary Clinton had withdrawn from the Democratic primary and Barack Obama was declared the winner. I flashed back to when Eli had said Barack would win. After the tornado incident I doubted it was a lucky guess.

I glanced over at Eli as he peered out of the window like a detective on surveillance. My own son was still a mystery to me. Erica was coming to pick him up to spend the day with her and D.J. He loved hanging out with his nephew. He grabbed his backpack that held his DS game, a baseball, and other stuff he liked to carry when he saw her car turn in the driveway.

"Which horse is going to win the race in the Preakness today?" Nelson asked him before he rushed out of the door.

"It's gonna be Big Brown again, Daddy," he said nonchalantly just as the screen door shut.

I must have fallen asleep there on the couch after a while because it was about race time when Nelson nudged me and said, "Wake up, it's about to start."

I sat up at attention as the stallions and fillies pranced up to the starting gate. I didn't know where Big Brown was positioned or the number he was wearing, the only thing I was sure of was if I could get there or place a bet, all of my money would be on Big Brown. Less than two minutes later Big Brown crossed the finish line in first place again.

"Eli got it right again," Nelson said, snapping his finger, "I should have made a bet."

"Do you think it might be more than a coincidence that Eli picked the winner?" I asked, wondering if he thought our son might be psychic.

"Naah, he heard the horses name mentioned several times because he was a favorite in both of the races. You know the boy has a good head on his shoulders."

"That makes sense," I said.

Three weeks later it didn't make sense. We were eating a late breakfast and Nelson was reading the paper at the table.

"The Belmont Stakes is today," Nelson said.

"What's that, Daddy?" Eli asked.

"It's the last race of the Triple Crown; they say your horse, Big Brown, is going to win it all today. That hasn't happened in a very long time."

Eli was quiet for a moment before he said, "He's not gonna win today, Daddy. He doesn't feel good. Something is wrong with one of his feet and he can't run."

"I hope not, he's been a real champion," I added.

"We'll just have to watch and see," Nelson said skeptically.

I can't explain it, but I didn't want to see the race. I planned to take Eli and meet up with the girls to shop for Father's Day gifts. Erica lived the closest so we got up early and drove over to her place first. Erica and Drew were sitting out in the yard watching D.J. play with Rover, the puppy they had gotten him on the last day of school.

"I wish we could get a dog, Mama," Eli said, hopping out of his booster seat to play with D.J.

"Your mama and daddy are too old to take care of a dog and take care of you too. When you get a little older we can talk about it."

"Don't do it, Mama, Rover is just like having another baby in the house," Erica complained.

"So what's the plan for today?" I asked.

"Ebony called this morning and she doesn't feel like going today."

"Do you think we should go by and visit for a while? She's been pretty moody since she found out she's pregnant again."

"Not today, she's really having the blues and wants to be left alone. Calvin hasn't been called back to the plant yet."

"I want to stop by for just a minute if you don't mind," I said to Erica, "She can brood for the rest of the weekend."

"Alright," Erica conceded, reaching for her handbag and keys."

"You can leave the boys here if you want," Drew offered, "I'm not going anywhere."

"Let us stay, Mama," Eli pleaded, "I want to play with Rover."

"That's fine with me," I answered.

"Erica," Eli called out, "Count to 31 before you go."

"Why?" she asked.

"Because D.J. was born on October 31st," he answered with a grin, showing her where he had lost his first tooth in the front."

"Okay, one, two, three, four," Erica counted.

Her patience in working with children all day was showing. It was a necessity for anybody who wanted to be a teacher. We got into her SUV, she started the engine, and then she rolled down the window.

"Thirty-one," she shouted in the boys' direction.

Eli looked over and waved. Erica drove down Drakes Branch Rd and we turned left onto Briley Parkway. There was a terrible accident on the interstate blocking two lanes. One car was totally crushed in the front where he had hit into the side of another car that must have lost control and spun around. Smoke and steam lifted into the hot air mixing with the glare of the sun. One driver got out and walked to the other. Erica pulled to the side and grabbed her phone to dial 911 as she got out of the car. I looked out of the back window. Several cars had stopped to help and Erica was coming back.

"The fire department and police are coming and there's an ambulance on the way," she said when she got back in the car. There are enough people with them right now, there's nothing more we can do."

"Was anyone seriously hurt?" I asked.

"Two were in one car and one in the other, it looks like they all need to go to the hospital," she answered, moving the SUV slowly back out on the interstate.

I said a silent prayer for the passengers; we had missed being there by less than thirty seconds. If Erica thought anything about Eli asking her to count, she never said a word.

***

"Ebony, where are you?" I yelled after we went in the open screen door. "Where's Amber?"

"Hey, Mama, what's up, Erica," she answered unenthusiastically, coming into the living room. "Calvin took her to Sevier Park."

"How are you doing, you seem tired," I said

"I'm fine; I just have a lot of things on my mind right now."

"Maybe you need to get away for a while, take a short trip," I suggested, sitting beside her.

"Things are so crazy right now that we can't afford to spend any money. Time you have off being unemployed is not the time for a vacation."

"I'll pay for it, sweetie, if you need some time off. I don't want you to be stressed out. It's not good for the health of the baby."

"It's not a good time, Mama. Calvin is thinking about going to work at another plant out of town and we can't even sell the condo to move, we're upside down on the mortgage. I'm thinking that having a baby right now is only going to cause more problems."

Erica shifted in her chair across from us. I knew she was regretting our coming over. She didn't like to get too deep in other people's personal issues but Ebony was my child too.

"Who are you telling that to?" I fussed, "I've been in your shoes more than once. One thing I can tell you is that you don't choose a permanent solution to a temporary problem. Your daddy and I are here for you. If you need to move in with us for a while do it and don't stress it."

"I'll talk to Calvin and I'll let you know," she said while she stared down at her hands.

Erica stood up and I followed her lead. We headed on to the mall but we weren't really in the mood for shopping. We walked around empty-handed for two hours before we decided to go to Home Depot and buy three gift cards.

"Let's call it a day," Erica said, finally.

"No arguments from me," I sighed.

Back at Erica's, all three of the guys were sacked out in the floor of her recreation room and Rover was watching the TV.

"Don't wake them, get yourself some rest," I said, scooping up Eli and walking back out to my car. "I'll talk to you later."

On the way home I ignored all the questions that fought for space in my mind and wondered what we would have for dinner. Nelson had been home all day but I knew he never considered making something for us to eat when we got back. I went through the drive-thru at Jack's Bar-B-Q and picked up some ribs, potato salad, and green beans.

"Eli was right again," Nelson said when we walked through the door, "Something was wrong with Big Brown and he came in dead last."

"Do you still think it's a coincidence? I didn't think it was before and now I'm almost sure he has some psychic abilities."

"You're not going to worry me with that today, Evelyn. How many times do I have to tell you women to leave my son alone?"

He stomped into the kitchen probably to get a beer. He didn't have to tell me again. I took Eli upstairs to lay him down. From now on I was keeping all my thoughts about our son to myself.

11

Three years had flown by and so much had happened. There were great things that we celebrated and rough patches that we fretted over. Barack Obama won the election just like Eli had predicted but George Bush had already killed the U.S. economy with his wars. The price of a gallon of gas and a gallon of milk were running neck and neck, and the price of meat had me considering life as a vegetarian. Elise was tired of living by the ups and downs of the stock market; she wanted to change firms but she was leery of losing her seniority. Erica had gone back to school and gotten her Master's degree so she could qualify for a pay increase.

Calvin and Ebony had moved in with us before their second baby girl, Azura, was born. Providing for his family had truly tested Calvin's mettle while they were with us. That man worked through temporary services and hustled his ass off to hold on to his dignity but it had taken its toll. I could see the chinks in their marriage that are familiar in any couple when hard times knock on the door. Impatience with the circumstances had them both second-guessing their choices and blame was thrown back and forth. The worst was the harsh cruel words that were spoken, words that would always be remembered even when the good times returned home.

When the Nissan plant called Calvin back six months ago all of us were thankful and relieved.

"I want to thank you two for opening your home to us, your patience, and making us feel so comfortable here. When we came here I never planned for us to be here this long," Calvin said over breakfast.

"We were glad to do it, son," Nelson assured him.

"You all know that you don't have to move right now," I said to both Calvin and Ebony, "It hasn't been any trouble for us."

"We know that, Mama," Ebony answered, "We just want to get the girls settled before the new school year starts.

"Besides, our 10th anniversary is coming up next month and we want to celebrate it in our own place," Calvin said, winking at Ebony.

"A man needs his own, Evelyn," Nelson added, "They've had a tough time but they're on their feet now. If they need us again they know where we are."

"Drew is here with the truck," Eli yelled through the back door, breaking up an emotional moment at the table.

We all stood up and walked through the kitchen to get to the backdoor. I looked at Eli and my grandchildren, D.J, Amber, and Azura as they stood behind the truck and felt a tinge of melancholy. I had enjoyed having my grandgirls here. This was the only home Azura has known and it was like seeing my girls grow up all over again. I thought they were rushing to leave being that they had such a big financial hole to dig out of but I couldn't have put up with my mother for as long as they did. They had found a house to rent just fifteen minutes away in Madison but I was going to miss having them around. Hopefully this would take some strain off of Nelson; his blood pressure was up more than it was normal. Now that Ebony and Calvin were okay I prayed he would slow down and retire.

***

"I could really use some help getting Eli to school," I said between sips of my morning coffee. "I barely have ten minutes to get to work after I drop him off."

"I have to be at work before you, Evelyn."

"You could retire; you've put your years in."

"How am I going to retire, Evelyn," he argued, "I'm still raising a growing boy I have to feed. As much as you complain about your carpal tunnel syndrome, who knows how long you'll be able to work."

"It's not that serious, Nelson," I replied, "You can file for your Social Security."

"These days that's probably not enough for us to live on."

"How do you know, you haven't even looked into it."

"Please don't waste your time worrying me this morning; you have a long day in front of you," he said, changing the subject. "Isn't this the first day of school?"

"Yes it is, and if you would have been a real team player you would have helped me get Eli to Meigs Middle School."

"I don't see any reason for us to drive all the way to East Nashville for the boy to go to school."

"That's the school they recommended he attend after Andrew Jackson Montessori."

"Honey, please, as smart as that boy is it doesn't matter what school he goes to," he said, pouring the rest of his coffee down his throat and walking out.

Nelson was probably right. Eli was only nine years old but he was being promoted to the sixth grade at Rose Park Middle Magnet School. Thank goodness he was a little tall for his age.

"Come on, Eli, we need to get moving or we'll be late," I shouted up the stairs.

"I'm ready, Mama," he said, rushing down in his khakis and a white polo shirt.

"Don't you look handsome this morning," I said proudly. "What do you want to eat?"

"I got up earlier while you were in the shower and ate a bowl of cereal."

I watched him get in the car and I could feel the energy exuding out from him. It was the excitement of youth and the spirit of expectation that comes with it. He wouldn't believe me if I told him that it only lasts a moment.

"You know the kids in your class are going to be a few years older than you and they may give you a hard time," I said to Eli while I drove.

"I'm not worried about that, Mama, I can handle myself."

"Well, if you are worried, you don't have to go there. You can go to another school with kids your own age or we can home school you. Your daddy needs to retire anyway."

"No, Mama, I have things to do and I can't waste time."
"What's the rush, baby, you've got your whole life in front of you, you're so young."

"There are some horrible things going on in the world and I have to make a difference."

I looked at him in the rearview mirror and said, "You are so deep sometimes, child. I believe you've been here before."

He just smiled and said, "Mama, we all have."

I shook my head at the conversation as well as the traffic in the school parking lot. It was typical for the first day with parents unfamiliar with the new routine. I circled around scouting for a space when Eli unbuckled his seatbelt and moved up beside my headrest.

"I'll get out here, Mama," he said, giving me a kiss on the cheek.

"No, I can't let you go in all by yourself; I want to help you find your class."

"Mama, I'm not going to fight in the war, I'm only going to school. There's nothing for me to be afraid of."

"Okay," I said, stopping the car by the side of the entrance.

I watched him walk in the front door with his head held high and confident but he was still my baby. When an empty space opened up, I parked and went inside the school. There was a hall monitor in front answering questions and giving directions.

"On what floor are the sixth grade classes? I asked her.

"They are located on this floor to your right. On the wall outside of the auditorium over there you can find the class lists that are assigned to each teacher."

"Thank you so much," I said, maneuvering my way through the flow of parents and students.

I found Elijah Newman listed under Mr. Filbert's list for room 109. Behind me I saw room 103, so I moved down the hall absorbing the surroundings that would be where my son would be every day. I peeked inside the window of room 109 and saw Eli sitting in the second row from the front. He seemed relaxed with his left hand in his pocket and his right elbow on the desk. He was fine just like he said he would be. I was the one having issues. I backed away from the door and walked out of the school.

"You won't believe it, Macey," I explained after she answered her cell phone. "I just took Eli to school and he didn't want me to walk in with him."

"What's the problem with that, Evie?" Macey asked.

"He's growing up too fast."

"At your age, my friend, he needs to," she said with a chuckle.

"Come on, Macey, I worry about him, he's so serious. I want him to enjoy being a child for as long as he can."

"You know that boy has his own mind, he's been different from the beginning. Plus he sees things, hell, the child can tell the weather better than any weather man. I wish you would let him give me the lotto numbers."

"Leave him alone, he's very intuitive."

"Are you sure he wasn't born with a veil over his face?"

"I'm hanging up on you, Macey," I said before I pushed the end button, I had more questions than I had answers.

***

"How was your first day at the new school?" Nelson asked when he got in.

It was past 7:00 and Eli and I were relaxing in the den.

"It was good, Daddy," Eli answered, "I like that we get to move around and go to different classes with different teachers."

"Any of the big kids give you problems today?"

"No, they just think I'm short, there's another girl who's a little person and she's smaller than I am."

"How about you, Evelyn, how was your day?" Nelson asked, knowing I was upset that he had missed dinner again working late.

"It was long; I spent most of the day on the computer entering data for the new students. My fingers are numb and my wrists and hands are aching. It would be nice if you could help with dinner sometime."

"You know the doctor told you that you might have to have surgery for that carpal tunnel stuff if it gets worse."

"Surgery doesn't always help and I still have to do my job. I was talking about being able to count on you for a little more help around the house."

"Evelyn, I was home for three years after Eli was born and I did whatever was necessary without complaining. You would think I could have some peace when I get home after work."

"Congratulations for doing exactly what you were supposed to, I don't look for awards for all the things I've done around here for thirty-five years."

"I don't feel like arguing," he said, walking out of the room.

I listened to him fumbling around in the kitchen making himself something to eat and a few minutes later I heard his footsteps on the stairs.

"Which hand is hurting you, Mama?" Eli asked.

"Both of them, baby, I'll take some Advil in a minute."

Then Eli kneeled in front of me and put his hands around my right hand and began to massage it. The touch of his hands was so soothing and I could feel the pain subside with each gentle rub. Then he took my left hand and did the same thing and all the swelling and aching deep within my joints was gone.

"That feels so much better. Thank you, baby," I said, looking at my hands.

"You're welcome," he said, smiling as if it was the most natural thing in the world.

"I'm going to go up to bed," I told him, standing up, "I don't want you staying up late. Your daddy will be back down to say goodnight."

"Okay, Mama, see you in the morning."

I stretched out across my bed next to Nelson who was watching TV and wondered what had just happened. The intense pain from my fingers up to my shoulders that had plagued me from early in the afternoon at work had disappeared with his touch. It wasn't an accidental touch, it was deliberate. Did he have healing hands too? I wasn't surprised by anything he did anymore; I had come to terms with the realization that he was a blessed baby, my gift from God, but I felt I wasn't worthy to raise him. I was absolutely sure I done some things that would certainly remove me from consideration.

"Are you still mad?" Nelson asked, nudging me.

"I'm not mad, I was just irritable, my hands and wrist were killing me."

"Did you take something for it?"

"No, I didn't have to, they don't hurt anymore."

"That's good, honey," he said, patting me on my back and getting out of the bed. "I have a taste for something sweet. I'll be back up later after Eli goes to bed. Do you want the TV on?"

"You can turn it off, I going to do some writing in my journal."

***

It was months later before I picked up my journal to write again. It seemed that as soon as I put down the words they were foreign to me. At times they comforted me and other times they filled me with fear. Today was special because Elise was home for the holidays and we were all going over to Ebony's new house for

Christmas dinner.

"Mama, what else are you taking over to Ebony's besides the ham and macaroni and cheese?" Elise asked, looking in the fridge.

"There is some spinach dip in there somewhere and we need to bring the rolls out of the freezer and we'll cook them when we get there," I replied, searching in the pantry, "I need a shopping bag to carry the gifts for my grandbabies."

"The only one who you can call a baby is Azura and she's two years old," Elise remarked. "I've got some things in a big bag upstairs; there should be room in it unless you bought out the stores again."

"You spoil them as much as I do so you don't have room to talk."

"They're my nieces and my nephew, and I have to take care of my brother."

"You know you can still have one or two of your own."

"Mama, I doubt that's going to happen. I haven't found anybody that I can stand to live with much less raise a family with. I guess my attention has always been on my career."

"Speaking of your career, do you miss the excitement of being a stock broker?"

"I don't know if excitement is the word I would use to describe it, but I got tired of fighting Dow Jones. In these days I needed more security since I'm out here by myself. I've discovered that the most secure place to work is as close to the money as you can get. Working as an investment banker, I'm pretty damn close."

"Do your thing, baby, you might have to take care of the rest of us before it's all over."

"Oh no, I have no doubt that Eli is going to do big things. He is so smart. I can't believe it, he's only nine and now they want to promote him to the seventh grade when he comes back after the Christmas break."

"I'm not sure how I feel about it though."

"We are not going to hold the boy back," Nelson bellowed, coming into the kitchen, "If he wants to move up I'm happy for him."

"I'm not about to let you ruin my Christmas spirit," I told Nelson. "Eli come on down we're getting ready to go."

"Okay, I need one more minute to finish charging my Ipod."

"Show me what you want loaded in the car, Evelyn," Nelson said.

"Don't forget I'm driving," Elise added, "The roads are icy and I want to get there in one piece. Southern folks don't know how to drive in this weather."

"Alright, Miss Expert, I'm not going to fight you for the wheel," I said.

Inside the car, Nelson sat up front with Elise and I sat in the back with Eli. He's always loved to look out of the window when he rode in the car, and today the decorations around town made it a scenic drive.

"Did you get everything you wanted for Christmas, Eli?" Elise asked over her shoulder.

"Almost everything," he answered, still gazing out of the window.

"What else did you want, little brother?"

"Christ's birth was supposed to bring love and peace on earth."

"Well, I'm sorry, that's one thing I can't get for you," Elise said with a sigh.

"This 2011 has been a helluva year," Nelson interjected, "I've never seen so much upset in the world in all my life."

"I know, Daddy," Elise said, "There were protests, shootings, and bombings everywhere."

"Don't forget all the tornados, hurricanes, earthquakes, and tsunamis," Nelson added, "At least they killed that Bin Laden and the soldiers are coming home."

"Would you two stop it, I told you I'm trying to stay in the

Christmas spirit and all you all have to talk about is bad news," I complained. I knew Eli was taking it all in and I didn't want all that negativity on his mind. "Why don't y'all turn the radio on to some Christmas music?"

"You're right, Mama, we're back on track," Elise said, turning up the radio where I could hear Nat King Cole singing the Christmas song.

"I'm glad we're here," Nelson said when we got to Ebony and Calvin's house, "I can't open my mouth in the car."

"You are not going to worry me today, Nelson," I said, getting out of the car.

"Help me carry this stuff, Daddy," Elise said, handing him the toys while she got the food.

We hurried up the walkway to escape the bitter wind and I rang the doorbell next to the wreath. Ebony opened the door looking distressed and we could hear the urgent crying that greeted us coming from the girls' room.

"What's the matter, honey bun?" Nelson asked, reaching for her hand.

She stepped to the side to let us in just as Drew, Erica, and D.J. came up the walkway.

"What is it?" I asked as the contagious worry spread among us.

"It's Azura, she's been crying all day and running a fever," Ebony answered with tears forming in her own eyes. "She won't eat anything, and she's been scratching her face and pulling her hair.

"Have you asked her where it hurts?" Erica asked, going towards the baby's room. "It may be an ear infection."

"Did you give her some Tylenol to bring down her temperature?" I asked, following Erica and leaving the guys in the living room.

"Calvin gave her some but it hasn't given her much relief," Ebony said inside her room.

"Let's take her temperature again, she's burning up," Erica said, running her hand over Azura's head and neck.

Erica held the ear thermometer inside of Azura's ear until it beeped despite her screams and protests. "We may have to take her to emergency," Erica said, "Her temp is 104 degrees."

"When was the last time Calvin gave her some Tylenol?" I asked.

"It's was around 1:00," Ebony replied.

I looked at my watch, that was about two hours ago. We all stood there around the bed contemplating what to do for a moment when Amber walked in the room pulling Eli by the hand.

"Come on," Amber urged him, "Help her, please."

"Sure," Eli said nonchalantly, putting down his new Ipod.

He put both of his hands over each of Azura's ears while Ebony stood there stunned into silence. He held them there and gave her a kiss on her forehead. Her crying turned into a whimper and when she stopped he took his hands away.

"Eli, come look," D.J. called out from the other room, "I got a new PS2 game."

"I'm coming," Eli said excitedly, rushing from the room to see the new toy.

Erica trailed him out of the room without saying a word. Azura stood up in her baby bed holding the railings and glanced around the room. Ebony snapped out of her daze and hurried over to the bed and picked her up.

"Take her temperature," Calvin insisted.

"You don't have to," I said from the doorway, "She's fine now."

"What did he do, Mama?" Ebony asked with her baby calm in her arms.

"Eli has a gift, he has healing hands."

"How did Amber know?" she asked.

"I don't know. It is what it is. I don't want you to mention it again, let him be."

"I want to thank him for doing it," Ebony said.

"He knows you're grateful. Now let's get the food ready, we're all hungry and ready to celebrate," I said, putting my arm around her waist.

Ebony handed the baby to Calvin in the living room while the guys watched a bowl game on the TV. Eli and D.J. were playing the PS2 game. The upset of the day had dissipated.

"That's right, get your butts in here," Elise said when we walked into the kitchen, "Always trying to leave all the work to me and Erica."

"Mama, I'm really sorry about giving you and Eli a hard time for so long," Ebony whispered to me while we set the table. "I guess I was feeling some kind of way about him taking my place as the baby in the family."

"Forget it, baby, no harm was done, and you're still the most spoiled of all of my children," I said with a laugh.

12

The New Year had come in with Nelson and me babysitting while Erica and Drew and Calvin and Ebony took Elise out to remind her of what it's like to party all night in Nashville. I laid blankets, sleeping bags, and pillows all over the carpet in the den and we camped out watching movies and eating popcorn. Nelson was asleep before midnight and I gave it up once I saw the ball drop in Times Square.

Three days after we put Elise on a plane back to New York, my mother called to tell us that they were going on a seven-day cruise in the Mediterranean and were coming to stay with us for a few days before they flew to Civitavecchia, Rome. I was glad they were coming; it was just the timing that had me bummed. The holidays had been busy and tiring and we would have more company in less than a week. Mother was very particular and I wouldn't have time to properly clean up the house to her specifications.

I took the day off on Monday to meet her and Dad at the airport. I couldn't help but smile at the sight of Mother strutting through the security point leading the way as usual. I moved toward the escalator to the baggage area to join them on the way down.

"Hello, daughter dear, there you are, it's good to see you," she said, giving me a church hug and then checking my clothes to see what I had come out in. She was a stickler for coming out dressed to the 'T' no matter where you were going.

"Hello, Mother dear, hi Daddy," I said, basking in his soothing embrace.

His had been the warm shoulder I could lean on when I grew up and I guess some things will never change.

"Hello, my sweet girl," he said, giving me a soft kiss on the corner of my eye.

"We've got a lot of luggage, but most of it we can leave in the car, it's for the cruise," Mother said as we approached the baggage carousel for their flight.

"When did you all decide to take this cruise?" I asked, making conversation.

"It's been something I always wanted to do," she answered. "Now seems as good a time as any, plus I want to be back home to work the polls for President Obama's re-election. At least there won't be any funny business in my precinct."

With me rolling two of their suitcases we were able to make it out to the car. The most effort was spent trying to arrange everything in the trunk to close the door.

"I see you all have a little snow on the ground," Daddy remarked after I paid for parking and got out on the interstate.

"Yeah, we get a couple of inches every now and then."

"I don't know what possessed me to come up here in all this cold weather," Mother dear said, "I just hadn't seen you in so long and we're going half way around the world. I figured we should at least drop in. I have to come and see my only child since she won't take the time to come and see me."

"Mother, you know I'm still working and I have a child still at home in school."

"Whose fault is that?" she asked.

"Leave it be, Ernestine," Daddy said sternly.

The car was quiet for the rest of the ride home. I parked in the garage and Mother directed Daddy on the bags he needed to bring inside. Once I unlocked the door, Mother stormed in like she owned the place with Dad following behind her as usual.

"I'll hang up your coats," I said, holding out my arms.

"We're about to starve, what do you have in here that our sensitive systems can eat?" Mother asked, walking around me.

Daddy put down their bags and followed me into the kitchen where Mother dear was foraging through my refrigerator. She swore she was the queen of politeness and good manners but she never respected my space or privacy for as long as I could remember.

"So where's everybody?" she asked, opening up a can of clam chowder soup. "We're only going to be here for a couple of days. Is this how family acts these days?"

"It's Monday, Mother, they are all at work," I answered. "You did call on short notice."

"I guess I should thank God they still have jobs, half the folks at home are out of work and they're foreclosing on homes left and right," she said.

"So where is my grandson?" Daddy asked, changing the subject.

"Erica picked him up from school, she'll bring him home in a little while," I replied while I got the crackers from the pantry and made a fresh pot of coffee.

Mother talked nonstop between the spoonful's of her soup. We were sitting at the dinette sipping coffee when Erica came in with Eli and D.J.

"Grandmother and Grandpop, how are you?" she asked, leaning over and giving Mother a kiss while both boys stood there watching

"We're good," Daddy said, standing up to hug her before he turned his attention to Eli and D.J. "Good afternoon, gentlemen."

Eli stuck out his hand and said, "Hello, sir," and D.J. did the same.

"How long are you going to be in town?" Erica asked.

"We'll be out of here day after Wednesday," Mother chimed in.

"We should plan a big dinner for you tomorrow," Erica said, "I've got to rush home today."

"That sounds nice," Daddy said, "I want to see everybody

before we go."

Erica and D.J. hurried out and Mother and Daddy went in the den to relax. Eli was doing his homework and I was cooking dinner when Nelson called to say he had a ton of work to do and wouldn't be home until late. Ebony called to say that she couldn't come by today but that she would be over for the dinner tomorrow.

"I guess it's just us," I said, announcing that dinner was ready.

Daddy said grace and Mother started talking about how fabulous the ship was and all the cities they were going to visit on their cruise.

That's when Eli pushed away his half-eaten plate, stood up and said, "Don't go on that cruise, Grandmother and Grandpop. Stay here and visit with us, you can always go later."

"I wish we could," Daddy said, "We'll do it another time; your grandmother has already made the plans. There's no way she's changing her mind."

"That's right, Eli," she added, "I waited my whole life to go to Europe. I've wanted to go to France since I was a little girl."

"It's not going to be good, something is going to go wrong," he said anxiously, "The ship won't make it to France."

A knot grew in the pit of my stomach and shot to the top of my head. My temples starting throbbing as my blood pressure rose. Experience had taught me that Eli's warnings weren't to be taken for granted. How could I convince Mother and Daddy not to go?

"Oh, I'll get there all right," Mother insisted, "The ship isn't the thing worrying me, it's the thirteen hours I have to sit on a plane before I get there."

"That's enough of that negative talk," Daddy said, "I was happy sitting at home in Florida in my own living room, but if going makes your mother happy then that's what I'm going to do. She's made me happy for sixty three years."

"Why don't we let it go for now, everybody's tired," I said, "We can talk about it tomorrow."

We basically finished dinner in silence after that. Eli went to his room and we watched a couple of *Law and Order* re-runs until they were ready to go to bed. Once they were settled in I went to my room and closed the door behind me but I couldn't lie down. I paced across the bedroom deliberating with myself. It didn't take me ten minutes to decide that I had to tell my parents about Eli and his gift. It was the only way I could get them to cancel their trip.

"Mother and Dad," I whispered, knocking softly on the guestroom door at the end of the hallway. "I need to talk to you for a minute."

"Come on in, sweet girl," Daddy said.

"I'm concerned about you two taking this trip," I said, standing in front of the bed. "Eli is very intuitive, he can sense things. He tells the weather better than any meteorologist on the TV. If he says you shouldn't go, I don't want you to go. I trust in his gift."

"Daughter, I put my trust in the Lord when I was twelve years old and that is where it has stayed," Mother declared. "I don't want to hear any more of that mumbo jumbo mess. You need to go on down the hall and get yourself some sleep because you are so tired you have started talking crazy."

"We'll be all right," Daddy said, taking my hand and steering me out of the room.

All I could do was pray. I prayed that Eli was mistaken. I prayed that Mother was right. I prayed that I was being irrational. I prayed that Daddy knew best. When Nelson came home just before 10:00, I pretended I was asleep. He was the last person I could confide in. They say girls marry their father but I had married a man like my mother.

In the morning we went about our regular schedule. Nelson left early. Eli and I had our breakfast as usual but he was quiet and moody. I didn't have much to say either. I dropped him off at school and went through my day as if I didn't have a worry in the world. Mother and Dad called and said they were going to look up some friends but they would be home for dinner. Then I called Erica and asked her to pick Eli up from school. I needed to stop at Harris Teeter's; I wanted to prepare a special meal.

I bought a Cornish hen for each of us, golden potatoes, asparagus, and Italian bread to bake. I bought lettuce and parmesan cheese for a Caesar salad. I couldn't make up my mind whether to get a cake or pie so I bought one of each. I even bought some wine. I put the television on a music channel to listen to while I cooked. I set the table with my best table cloth and china. At around 5:30, the family started coming in one after another, first Nelson, then Erica and Drew with D.J. and Eli, Calvin and Ebony with Amber and Azura, and lastly Mother and Daddy.

"Honey, you went all out," Nelson said when he saw the spread.

We ate and enjoyed ourselves like it was Thanksgiving, Christmas, and Easter dinner all at one time. Drew took pictures all through the meal. Eli took the other kids in the den after they finished eating while we stayed at the table drinking wine and toasting whatever came to mind. Heartfelt goodbyes were said around 9:30 and we all went to bed. It was a good evening.

It was still pitch black dark in the morning when Daddy called a taxi to take them to the airport since their plane left at 6:00 am. We all stood inside the doorway while the cabbie loaded up their bags.

I hugged Daddy's neck tight not wanting to let go until Mother said, "Save some for your mama."

"I love you," I said in her ear while she held me close.

"I love you the most, daughter," she said, pulling my arms down.

Nelson shook Daddy's hand and gave Mother a hug.

"Take care of yourselves," Nelson said as they went out of the door.

Mother stopped and turned around. "Although I didn't approve of Evelyn's decision to go on with the pregnancy, I've got to tell you that you have a fine young man up there." she said, pointing at the stairs.

Nelson closed the door and I swallowed a scream that sat at the back of my throat.

"Come on back to bed, honey, we might be able to get another hour of sleep before the alarm rings," Nelson said, guiding me up the steps with his hand on the small of my back.

***

It was two days later on Friday the thirteenth that I saw the news I had been dreading. The Costa Concordia, the cruise ship my mother and daddy had boarded, had capsized in Tuscany after striking against rock on the floor of the sea. They had only sailed for two hours. I watched the TV news horrified at the boat leaning over on its side. Emergency crews had been evacuating passengers for hours. I sat in agony waiting for a phone call saying they were rescued but none came. Unable to bear the torture another minute I went up to Eli's room. He was sitting on the floor with his laptop

"Baby, are they alive?" I asked.

"No, mama, they've gone to heaven."

13

It was hard to believe but at the end of the 2013 school year Eli was being promoted to the ninth grade and the child was only eleven years old. I was having mixed feelings about him going to high school at such a young age but we reached a compromise with him attending Cordell Holland High where I worked as a guidance counselor. I had been considering retiring myself but with Eli coming to the school I decided to hang on in there for another four years. He seemed to be moving through this life too fast and I was helpless to slow it down. All the worries we had about him being slow had vaporized as though they had never existed.

The two of us sat alone on the church pew during the early service on Mother's Day and I thought about all the mysteries of my son who sat next to me, most of which I had kept to myself. Nelson didn't want to come with us, his job had recently forced him to retire, again, and he was pissed about it. He wanted to keep working. You would think a man almost sixty-seven years old would be ready to accept his status as a senior citizen and enjoy whatever years he had left. He spent most of his time brooding in his favorite lounge chair under a tree in the backyard.

I refocused my attention on the sermon and tried to get something from the message. Why my pastor was preaching on the last days and the perils of life, strife, greed, and wickedness on the day for mothers was beyond me. I was more than relieved when he concluded and came to the invitation to Christ.

"Pray women of God, because your prayers won't go unanswered." our pastor implored, "Never forget that it was a woman who was instrumental in the saving of our sins through her birthing of Jesus Christ. The bible says, 'Blessed art thou among women because God hath blessed the fruit of thy womb.' Jesus is coming again."

That's when Eli took my hand and moved towards the front of the sanctuary to join the church. He stood tall, his head just above my shoulder, and gripped my hand tightly and I heard a few claps as we marched up the aisle. It took me back to the three times, years ago; that his sisters had each asked me to walk with them down this same path when they made their professions of faith. I stood beside him as members of the congregation came up to give him a hug and the right hand of Christian fellowship. It was as if he glowed there beside me and I felt a warmth come over me and it wasn't just pride, it was spiritual. I felt as if I wanted to cry.

"Sit up front with me," I said as we got into the car after the church service.

He fastened his seatbelt and I started to drive. I didn't have any particular destination in mind; I was merely cruising around trying to find the right words to say what I needed to say. I didn't want to sound 'crazy or deranged' as Martin Lawrence often referred to in his comedy act but there was no avoiding it.

"How about a milkshake before we go home?" I asked, wanting to stop the car.

"That's a plan, Mama," he said tapping his hand on his leg to the gospel music on the radio.

I drove down to Sonic and ordered through the intercom speaker, "Can I get a strawberry and vanilla shake mixed and an Oreo shake."

We sat listening to the radio until the carhop brought our shakes. I took sips of the mixed one and place it in the cup holder and handed him his favorite, the Oreo.

"I want to talk to you about something serious, baby, and there's no graceful way to approach it. This is going to sound crazy, Eli, but I have to ask."

"This is not about girls and stuff is it, Mama?" he interrupted.

"No, it's not, I'm saving that conversation for when schools starts after the summer," I said, taking another sip of the cool milkshake.

"Is it about me joining church today?"

"Not really, but it is related," I answered, searching for words in the styrofoam cup.

"Whatever it is, hurry up and tell me," he said restlessly, "D.J. is coming over when they get out of church and Drew might take us to a movie."

"It's something I have been thinking about for quite a while. In church for most of my life, I have always been told that the Messiah would come again and be amongst us and we might not recognize him. You have always been such a special child and you have so many extraordinary gifts. I've been wondering if this is the second coming, and if you are the Messiah?"

I had finally said the words. I leaned back in my seat and waited for the laughter that I thought would soon follow and I could put these ridiculous notions out of my head.

"No, Mama," he responded evenly, "It's not over yet, I'm a messenger. There have been many sent here to be guiding lights. There are others here now."

I rubbed the skin on my hand and felt the coolness that still lingered on my fingers from the milkshake. Surely I was awake and not dreaming. Eli's answer repeated in my inner ears. I felt some relief at first and then I felt the weight of what he had said to me. It was more than I could fathom. I wanted my child to live a normal life. I wanted him to go to college, get married, have a family of his own, and be happy. Notwithstanding the fact, if anyone of authority at Child Protective Services would have overheard our 'out this world' conversation they would have taken him out of my care and put both of us into psychotherapy.

"What does this mean?" I asked him.

"Don't start stressing, Mama; I'm not that different from

anybody else except I know what my purpose is, and if we stay here much longer I'm going to miss the movie."

"All right, we're going," I said, backing out of the space at Sonic's and wishing I hadn't opened my big mouth.

I turned off the air conditioning and opened the windows to get some air. Eli changed the radio station and nodded to the old school music coming out of the speakers and I did my best to pretend that I wasn't in a state of shock.

"Breakfast is ready," Nelson shouted as soon as we walked in the door.

Erica's truck was parked in front of the house so I knew they were probably in the dining room waiting for us to get back from church. Eli ran ahead of me to find D.J. I wasn't in the mood for company, I really wanted about an hour to lie down and pull myself back together, but that wasn't on the agenda.

"I'm in the kitchen, Mama," Erica said cheerfully.

"Happy Mother's Day," I said, walking into the kitchen and putting on a happy face.

"Happy Mother's Day to you too, Mama," she replied, drying her hands to give me a hug and a kiss on the cheek. "Elise called just before you got home; she said she'll call back later."

"All right, have you heard from Ebony this morning?"

"Yeah, she said she'll stop by this evening, they're going over to see Calvin's mom and she's going to watch the girls so he can take her out to a nice dinner."

"That sounds good, that girl needs a break. She's following in my footsteps having number three. Having a baby every two years is no joke."

"I'm good with one; anybody else can do whatever makes them happy," Erica added, pouring the orange juice in a glass pitcher.

"I'm going to take off these shoes real quick," I said, "I'll be right back."

"Okay, I don't want the food to get cold.

I took my shoes off at the bottom of the stairs and hopped up the stairs as quick as my tender knees would let me. Inside our bedroom I slipped out of my Sunday dress and into a loose fitting knit dress. I wanted to stop and pray for Eli but I didn't know what to say. I thought about calling Macey, she was the only one I could tell this too but I didn't have enough time to talk. With no other options, I stuck my feet into my slippers and went back down the stairs.

"Happy Mother's Day, honey," Nelson said sweetly, trying to make up for his sour mood earlier in the morning.

"Happy Mom's Day from me and D.J.," Drew added.

"Thank you," I answered, taking my seat at the table. "Everything smells so good. I hope you two gentleman didn't leave all the work to Erica, it's her day too."

"No, ma'am," Drew said emphatically, "All she did was clean out the skillet."

"I hope you don't mind if the sinner who didn't make it to church blesses the food, Evelyn," Nelson said with sarcasm.

"Go ahead, but be careful what you say."

Everybody laughed and most of the drama in the air dissipated. Nelson said a short prayer and we enjoyed the breakfast of pancakes, eggs, and sausage. By the end of the meal I had made peace with what Eli had told me and decided to let things be. Besides, none of it was in my control anyway.

"What are you going to do with yourself this summer, Eli?" Erica asked. "I know you don't want to hang around the house with Mama and Daddy every day."

"I'm going to be in a track and field program at the YMCA," he answered, much to my and Nelson's surprise.

"This is the first I've heard of it," Nelson commented.

"They told us about it at school and I decided I wanted to do it, since I'm going to try out for the track team when I start high school."

"I like that," Drew said, nodding, "The boy can run."

"We'll have to see if you have to be a certain age to participate," I said cautiously.

"I already know," Eli said confidently, "The coach who came to our school said that if we are students at the school then we can try out. He's going to help me train at the Y."

"You sure you don't want to play baseball, that's what I grew up playing?" Nelson asked.

"No, Daddy, I like running," Eli said.

"He's a natural athlete but he doesn't want to play on a sports team," Drew said in his defense, "He loves to run, it may be one of his passions."

"I heard they were teaching music at the Centennial Arts in the park," I interjected, "I always wanted to be able to play an instrument. I thought it might be a good experience for Eli."

"I like listening to music but I don't want to play it," Eli said in objection. "I know what I want to do."

"The boy needs to get some air instead of having his head stuck in a book all the time, the track thing will be good for him," Nelson said, putting the subject to rest.

"Well if we're going to make it to the first movie we need to get rolling," Drew said, "Are you all coming with us?"

"What are you going to see?" I asked, knowing I didn't want to go.

"Iron Man 3," he answered.

"I'm going," Erica said, raising her hand.

"I'll pass, I think I might take myself a nap," I said.

"You all go ahead; I'm going to talk my wife into going out to the mall," Nelson said, patting me on the arm, "I feel like buying her something pretty."

"Alright, Daddy, you're still a player," Erica joked as they left for the movies.

"What are you talking about, Nelson?"

"You just seem a little on edge and I want to cheer you up."

"Is that right? I'm going up to put some shoes on. You go get your cash and credit card and I'll be ready to go."

"No problem, I'll meet you in the garage," he said boldly.

I ran a comb through my hair and put on some lipstick and blush. I remembered the days that I wouldn't have cared, but now I was too old to be going out of the house without checking with the mirror. It seemed the older I got the more I wanted to hold onto the remnants of my youth.

"Where to, Mrs. Winters?" Nelson asked with a poor excuse for an English accent as he opened the car door.

"To Green Hills, Mr. Winters," I answered, trying to sound like Queen Elizabeth.

He drove humming to the radio still on 92Q while I gazed out of the car window. I thought about my conversation with Eli earlier as he sat where I was sitting. He's barely eleven years old, what does he know about the world? Granted, he had special gifts, but that didn't make him the chosen one. It's possible that he had let his imagination run away with him in the same direction that mine had. Being the youngest in a neighborhood where all the children had grown up left him with too much time alone. I smiled as I recalled some of the fantasies I had growing up, I used to imagine myself as a famous singer despite the fact I never even had the nerve to join a choir. Running track in the summer would be just the thing to give him something else to focus on.

"Let's walk through Nordstrom's, big spender," I said to Nelson in the parking garage.

"Your wish is my command," he said, locking the car.

He opened the heavy glass door at the entrance and held it for me. I walked through brushing against him as I passed. Inside he took my hand and we walked like we did when we first met. Here I was damn near sixty-two years old but I felt no different from the young woman I was forty years ago. It never ceased to amaze me how many times I had fallen in and out of love with this man. We looked and walked for about twenty minutes before Nelson suggested we go to the Cheesecake Factory.

"It'll be a long wait," I warned.

"There's no rush, besides there's something on my mind that I want to run by you."

"Now I'm starting to get scared."

"It's nothing like that," he said after we gave our name to the hostess and found a bench to sit and wait for the gizmo to buzz.

"I think we should take a trip together this summer, just the two of us, we haven't gone anywhere by ourselves since Eli was born and he's not a baby anymore."

"Where would you like to go and for how long?" I asked, surprised at his suggestion.

"I was thinking about a trip to Florida for a week or two, Disney World and then the beach in Ft. Lauderdale."

"Disney World, isn't that a trip for the kids? What brought this on?"

"I've been thinking about it since your mama and daddy passed. I want to have some fun, make more memories for us before I get too old or too sick to enjoy myself."

"I don't think we can plan that trip without the girls wanting to come and bring their families with us."

"In that case we won't give them all the details until we get back."

"How will we look, two old folks standing in line to get on a ride?"

"Who cares? Who said we have to stop living this life to the fullest?

"I think it was our low energy levels and achy joints."

"You're right about that, Evelyn," Nelson said, laughing, "But that's what I want to do for my birthday, right before I file for my Social Security."

"That's a date, honey bear; it'll do us some good to get away. Eli can stay with Erica and Drew."

The little gizmo lit up and vibrated, our table was ready.

***

I love watching Eli run. I started coming to the track a little earlier each day to see his practice. Watching him I can feel the freedom he gets from pushing his legs to go farther and faster, the rush from his heart beating at a high level, and his lung filling with air. This is the way I want him to be, carefree as the wind, like the deer that run through our backyard every now and then. I didn't want him burdened down with the troubles of this world.

"Mrs. Winters, I'd like to speak with you for a minute," Coach Templeton bellowed, getting my attention as he stepped up on the bleachers where I waited.

"Hello, how are things going?" I asked when he reached my row.

"Great, I'm really pleased with the group we have this year, particularly Eli."

"Oh really," I responded, wondering if my son had done something out of the ordinary.

"Yes, he's really got talent. I have a small group of kids that I work with all year long and I'd like for Eli to train with us."

"That's something for us to talk about; I know he's been looking forward to joining the track team at the high school in the fall."

"That won't interfere with my program and I'd seriously like to work with him."

"I appreciate that but he doesn't seem to be the fastest out there from what I can see."

"That's true," he admitted with a grin, "What I see in him is more rare, it's the temperament and discipline to be a tremendous long distance runner. Furthermore, he's got the stamina that's needed for long hours of training."

"That child has been the captain of his own ship since birth; if he wants to do it I don't have a problem with it."

"All right, thanks, we'll see how it goes then," he said as he moved quickly down the bleachers.

The more I ran the coach's proposition in my head the more I was against it. Eli was already separated enough. Going to the high school he was already separated from kids his own age. Something was always setting him apart. Why wouldn't they just let him fit in?

When the practice was over I went down to the lowest bleacher to wait. He looked so happy as he trotted over to meet me. It must be that thing they call the runner's high.

"Your coach seems impressed with you," I said as soon as he was in earshot.

"Yeah, he wants me to join his track team."

"I was thinking that might be too much until you get used to being at your new school. You are going to have to focus on your studies more."

"I got this, Mama; you can't stand in the way of me doing the things I need to do."

"He's talking about you running long distance. That isn't a quick run around the track," I said with my eyes following one of the girls as she made the large loop.

"Running doesn't take anything out of me, it makes me stronger. I get in the rhythm of everything in nature and I can feel God's power."

"You know when you say things like that it leaves me speechless."

"Sorry," he laughed, "It's just that when I'm running everything is peaceful."

"I know, son, I wish I could run again myself but if I dare step on that track my knees would scream bloody murder. When I see young people running I know some probably take it for granted but they shouldn't because I discovered that for most of us our running years are short."

"Mama, if you want, I can fix your legs so you can run."

It scared me when he said that because I knew he might actually have the ability to do it.

"Not now, son," I said, "I just enjoy seeing you run."

***

It was a week before Nelson and I were scheduled to leave for Disney World. Macey stopped by the house unannounced, something that she never does. Her eyes were swollen red and full of fear. Something terrible had happened.

"What is it Macey, what's wrong?"

She shook her head from side to side, despondent. Nelson and Eli were in the den eating leftovers from the 4th of July cookout. I took her right hand and led her upstairs where we could talk privately. We sat down at the foot of the bed still holding hands. I started to panic before she spoke one word. She was the only sister I had ever had and I couldn't stand to see her hurting.

"Richard was having some problems and we got the test results back today," she said in a low voice. "The doctor says he has prostate cancer."

"Oh no, I'm sorry to hear that."

"They referred him to a specialist and we have an appointment for next week."

"I know you're still in shock from the test results but my uncle Jimmy was diagnosed ten years ago and he's doing fine, I don't think you need to get yourself worked up until you've gotten a second opinion and decide how you're going to proceed."

"I don't think I can go through this, Evie. I didn't even know I still cared this much about the man anymore until I realized that I could lose him."

"You're not going to lose him; you have to stay positive in situations like this. I truly believe that prayer changes things."

"That's easy for you to say. What would you do if you were in my position?"

"I would do everything I just told you."

"Are you sure that's all you would do?" she asked, looking me in the eye.

"What's on your mind, Macey?" I asked bluntly.

"Eli has the gift of healing; I need him to come over to the house. He can heal Richard and we can go on living the rest of our lives without this cancer bullshit."

"That's not a decision for me to make. I can't use my son like a genie to grant me all my wishes or those for the people close to me. I can't put that kind of pressure on him, he's just a boy. My conscience won't let me do that."

"Evie, we've been best friends for over forty years. I've had your back and you've had mine. I need your help right now. You have a blessing and you don't want to share it."

"Macey, it's not mine to share. It wasn't given to me."

"He's your son; he would do it if you asked him."

"There would be no end if we started down that path."

"I'm only asking this one time."

"I've still got your back, girl friend, and I'm here for you, but you have to leave Eli out of it. I have to put his needs above my own and anybody else's. He's not responsible for all of us."

Macey jumped up abruptly and headed to the bedroom door. Her fears had switched to anger directed towards me. She stopped in the doorway and turned around.

"If anything happens to Richard, I'll never forgive you, Evie."

I was stunned. How could a gift that was supposed to be a blessing have cost me my closest friend? A week later Macey still ignored my calls and texts. We dropped Eli over to Erica and Drew's house and boarded a plane to Florida leaving Nashville physically and mentally.

The villa we rented in Orlando was gorgeous. A big discovery was made in the Epcot Center, I saw the smile I had fallen in love with on Nelson's face. In Disney World we giggled on the rides, oohed and aahed at the Universal Studios, and sighed with satisfaction on the beach in Ft. Lauderdale. It was only a week, but by the time we left I understood how our relationship had lasted forty-one years. Time would tell if my oldest friendship had run its course.

14

I still haven't gotten used to having another man in the house and that's what Eli is becoming. I'm sixty-five years old so having a fifteen year old has its plus and minuses. I don't know how it's possible but he keeps me young and ages me at the same time. When I'm not looking at him I don't even recognize his voice. He looks me straight in the eyes and I'm every inch of five-foot-eight. The cross-country training with the light circuit lifting that he does every other day keep him lean but muscular.

He won the All-City Championship in the 1600m and 3200 meter race. The high school years have been good for him. He's pretty tight with some of the guys on the track team and the freshman and sophomore girls are practically running circles around him. He keeps his cell phone on vibrate but I can see the light flash every time he gets a call or a text which means it goes on continually like the emergency lights of a car.

"Eli, you know you need to come to my office at school, all seniors have to go through me," I repeated for the tenth time when he came down for breakfast. "We need to talk about your plan of study and narrow down the list of schools you're going to apply to."

"Mama, I keep telling you I've got this. My grades are good and my SAT score was right where I wanted it to be. Coach Templeton is going to help me find the school with the best cross country team; he thinks I can make it to the 2020 Olympics. He says I'll get a scholarship, no problem."

"That's not the issue, I don't doubt that, but we still need to go through the process and put the applications in."

"Okay, Mama," he said, grabbing the gallon of milk out of the fridge and a handful of protein bars, "I'll come at lunch time."

"I can scramble you some eggs and make some sausage if you like?" I asked, watching him chug down a big glass of milk.

"No thanks, where's Daddy?"

"He's outside in the yard trimming the hedges."

"Did you all remember that I'm running the Music City Half Marathon this weekend?"

"Of course, we haven't missed any of your races yet have we?"

"I know, but I'm going to win it this year," he said, rushing out the backdoor.

Through the window I watched him speak to Nelson for a minute before he slipped his arms in his backpack and jogged down the street. I reached for my cell phone to text the girls; I wanted them to be at the race on Sunday when Eli crossed the finish line in first place. I wanted to call Macey; she was still his godmother even though we barely spoke to each other. Richard was doing well, but she still blamed me for the misery he suffered on chemo.

I finished a bowl of cold cereal before I headed off to work. This is my last year, at the end of the semester I retire. Backing out of the driveway I waved at Nelson across the yard. He needed so much time by himself; I hoped the house would be big enough for both of us to have our space when the school year ended.

"Good morning, Miss Terry," I said, walking into the school office.

"Good morning, Mrs. Winters, Mr. Hardin was here to see you a few minutes ago. He went to get a cup of coffee and should be right back."

"Thanks, Miss Terry, I better turn my monitor on real quick," I replied moving a little faster through the inner office.

Mr. Hardin was our physics teacher and all the seniors heading to college had to pass his class. I barely had time to set my bags down before he knocked on the inside of the open door.

"Hello, Mr. Hardin, what can I do for you this morning?" I asked as I turned on my monitor.

"I've been meaning to come by and talk to you about Eli and his plans for the future."

"Sure, why don't you sit down and tell me what's on your mind," I said with my curiosity and my guard going up at the same time.

"I've never had a student like your son," he said, sitting his mug cup on the edge of my desk. "He's a brilliant young man, and he absorbs information like a sponge but I can't get a feel of his future interests or what he wants to do."

"Well, he's younger than the other seniors and he may need a little more time to figure out what field he'd like to study in college."

"I can understand that, however, I wanted to come by and suggest that engineering would be a fantastic field for Eli. He has such an analytical mind for problem solving."

"He's supposed to come by at lunch; I'll try to pin him down then."

"Let me know what he decides, I believe he can really do something that might make a difference and I want to help if I can," he said, picking up his mug of coffee on the way out.

That was a reality check. Eli was really going to graduate from high school at the end of the year and my baby was most likely going to leave home. He had reached his first fork in the road and he wasn't even old enough to drive. I organized my thoughts for a serious conversation to have with him when he came by and then a message popped on the screen of my monitor. I touched the message and watched him speak on the screen while some of his friends joked and laughed in the background.

"Mama, I can't get by there for lunch today, we'll talk when I get home after practice."

No need for a reply, it would probably be easier to talk about at home. I heated up some soup for lunch and spent the afternoon processing the college applications for other students and then I did a search for the top engineering schools in the state. I couldn't think about Eli being too far away from home.

On my way home the phone buzzed saying it was Ebony calling, I pushed the button on the steering wheel to answer, "Hello, baby, how are you?"

"I'm good. Do you and Daddy have plans after dinner? I wanted to stop by and talk for a minute."

"No, sweetie, come earlier and you can eat with us."

"I might, but don't wait for me."

"Okay, we'll see you later."

I didn't want to guess what might be going on. I could only pray that it wasn't anything serious. The last three years had been tough on Calvin and Ebony. Financial pressures on them may have been the cause of her suffering a miscarriage. The economy had been up and down, but mostly down, and the car industry had practically priced itself out of the consumer market. Calvin was already a year into his last lay-off and things weren't getting any better. It was hard to watch them struggle while Erica and Drew moved into their dream house.

The hedges were shaped in a neat row when I pulled into the driveway but there was no sight of Nelson in the yard. That might be a good sign. On days when he was in a bad mood he stayed out in the yard and refused to come in the house. I went in through the backdoor and inhaled but there wasn't a scent of anything cooking. I hung up my jacket and put my work bags away.

"Nelson," I called out, looking in the freezer for some tilapia to thaw out for dinner.

"What's the emergency," he yelled back from the den.

I put enough fish for four of us in the sink before I went to see what kept him from getting up and greeting his wife after her day at work.

"What's going on, old man?" I asked, sitting beside his legs stretched out on the couch.

"I'm resting and relaxing like you said I should," he answered sarcastically. "Is there a problem?"

"No, I'm about to cook us something to eat. Ebony called and said she wanted to come by and talk this evening, so prepare yourself."

"If Calvin is giving her anymore problems I'm already prepared to whip some ass. He's not the only man struggling out here right now."

"It's not easy, Nelson, especially if you have the demands of raising a family."

"Who are you telling, I raised four and I live in the same world he does. There ain't no way I'm going to let him take out his frustration on my baby."

"Before you come out of your corner fighting we just need to listen. I'll call you when dinner is ready."

It didn't take long to pan-fry the tilapia in olive oil and microwave a bag of creamed spinach. I threw a couple of sweet potatoes in the microwave to add a little more color. Looking out of the kitchen window under the sound of the microwave hum I let my mind drift back to my college days. The sight of Eli running across the yard toward the door brought me back to the present.

"You have time for a quick shower before we eat," I said as soon as he stepped in the door.

"Okay, Mama," he said, dashing up the stairs without stopping.

"Was that Eli coming in?" Nelson asked, coming into the kitchen.

"Yeah, it was, he's taking a shower. By the time you help me set the table he'll be back down. There are some things we all need to talk about for his college applications."

"Lord, I don't guess there's any rest for an old man."

"Nope, not as long as you're still breathing," I added, handing him the plates.

We got everything ready and the food was on the table when Eli came down. I said a quick grace before Nelson got his fork to his mouth. We ate without speaking for a few minutes before Nelson slowed down to talk.

"How was your practice, son, are you ready for the long race on Sunday?"

"Yeah, Dad, Coach says I'm ready for even longer distances. He says I can probably try to qualify for a marathon next year."

"That's pretty ambitious. Let's just get through this one first," Nelson said, shifting his attention back to his plate.

"Mr. Hardin came by the office to see me today and he thought that your skills might be ideal for the engineering field," I said to Eli.

"He mentioned it to me a couple of times but that's not what I want to do."

"You're so smart, baby, I believe you can make a real contribution to mankind," I added.

"Engineers make a good living, son, and there's lots of room for advancement in that area," Nelson added, "There's no end to new technologies. There's nanotechnology, genomic engineering, and 3-D printing. Hell, they have those lights-out factories where robots are doing all the work.

"Medicine might also be something interesting for you, you already have healing hands," I suggested, trying to release some of the pressure Nelson was exerting.

"I've been thinking about what I want to study and I'm looking at something focused on the humanities, maybe starting in philosophy."

"Really," Nelson remarked sarcastically, "Okay, well I guess money isn't everything cause you won't get rich with that degree."

"My purpose is not to make a ton of money, Dad, it's deeper than that. Chasing the dollars hasn't made this world any better. I have to follow my own way, I'm not worried, and I have faith that I'll have all I need."

"The days of manna falling from the sky are behind us, son," Nelson argued, "You have no idea what it takes to make it in this world. Sure, the Lord will provide, provide you with the opportunity to get an education and a job to go to where you can collect a paycheck. I'm damn near seventy years old and nothing has changed, it's still dog-eat-dog out here."

"My eyes are open to the truths of the world, I know I'm about to go in the lion's den. I intend to impart peace and love all over the globe."

"Do you mean peace of mind or peace between enemies?" I asked, confused.

"I mean the peace that passeth all man's understanding," he answered frankly.

"Eli, are you saying that you are called to preach God's word and that you're going into the ministry?" I asked.

"No, Mama, I'm speaking metaphorically. I can't only wait for those who seek out God's message; I have to position myself to influence those who hearts are closed to the love of God. That means subcommittees, board rooms, and politics. Those are the places where the decisions that affect all of our lives are made. I want to apply to Carnegie-Mellon University; they have a major in International Relations and Politics."

"That is a tall task, Eli, politics is a treacherous business, more evil is done in its name than good from what I've seen," I said.

"The time has come for that to change, Mama. This country's enemies lead it into conflict to weaken us. We siphon off critical resources that should be used for nation building. Strength is in peace, agriculture, preserving the ecosystem, education, and the uplift of all people."

"It's your life, do what you want to do with it," Nelson said, irritated. "Just remember I won't always be around to pick up the pieces for this family."

"There's something else I need to say since we're here talking and you probably won't like it but I can't put it off anymore."

"This sounds serious, Evelyn, can you get me a beer?"

"What is it, Eli?" I asked, ignoring Nelson.

"It's about my name. I going to drop our last name and go by Eli Newman. In the direction I'm going I don't want to compromise the safety or well-being of my family in the future."

"What in the hell are you telling me, boy? You're my only son and you don't want to carry my name."

"That's not what I'm saying, Dad. I want my actions and the consequences of them to be on my name and not the name of my family. I don't want anything I do to bring harm to you all."

"You don't even know if you'll ever amount to anything where that might even matter," Nelson argued.

"I don't have any doubts that the way will be made clear."

"I'm tired of listening to this bullshit right now, why don't you go run around the block and let grown folks talk for a minute. I ain't never heard of anything like this in my life."

"We'll talk some more later, Eli, give us a chance to digest this for a while," I said as Eli got up from the table.

There was so much that Nelson didn't know about his own son. To him this was a personal affront to him as a man and as a father but I knew that it was out of love. How could I express in words that which had to be seen to be believed.

"What about that beer, Evelyn?"

I felt bad for Nelson so I got up to get him a beer without any comment. I popped the cap and put it on the table in front of him and sat back down.

"Nelson, I want you to think back to the time before Eli was born, after Ebony's wedding. The 9-11 terrorist attack was that weekend. We didn't know if Elise was on one of the planes or at work in the World Trade Center. I prayed so hard that morning, and I said I would do whatever the Lord asked of me if He would spare my child's life. Elise was safe and the next thing I know I was pregnant at fifty years old. Having Eli was a gift but he was also recompense for God's grace to our family. He's our son but he doesn't belong to us. We have to understand and respect whatever he feels he needs to do with his life."

"Evelyn, if you want to believe that go on ahead and do that, but I have never turned my back on any of our children and I never expected that they would turn their back on me."

"That's not what he's doing, honey. He loves you, it's only a name."

"That name is my name. I'm through with it. It is what it is. He's always been a mama's boy anyway."

"Hey, Mama, hey Daddy," Ebony said, walking into the dining room.

"Hi sweetie, I didn't hear you come in," I said, standing to give her a hug. "Did you have dinner yet? I can fix you a plate if you're hungry."

"No thanks, Mama; I just came to talk to you and Daddy about some things."

"Sit on down, baby," Nelson said, "It can't be worse than what I've already heard today."

"Calvin got a letter that says his job will be permanently phased out. His position on the assembly line at Nissan has been totally computerized."

"We could all see that coming, sweetheart, pretty soon machines will be doing all of our jobs," Nelson said. "Has he thought about what his next move will be?"

"He wants to go back to school but I can't carry the mortgage by myself. I'm thinking maybe we should let the house go and rent a condo."

"Have you thought about selling the house and using anything you can get out of it for his tuition?" I asked. "The market is still soft but that's a good location out there."

"That sounds good, Evelyn, but the man needs some income, they can't live on air," Nelson barks. "You can do what you want Ebony but I think you and the girls need to come and stay here with us for a while."

"Nelson, you're upset right now. Sweetie, we don't want to encourage you to break up your family. We're here to help you guys get through this together. You're all welcome to stay here, Calvin too."

"I'll talk to him about it, but we really might need a break from each other, Mama. I don't know how long we can make it under this pressure. Every time I think we're about to get on our feet, his job messes us up, and he takes it out on me. He acts like we're a burden on his back, but I'm the one carrying him."

"You have to remember that you two are a team. Sometimes one of you gets in a slump, that's when the other has to be stronger. If you still love each other none of what you're going through is worth quitting over."

"A little time apart might help him to appreciate what he's got," Nelson said angrily.

"That's a gamble, it might not work the way you expect," I warned her, "Take your time and don't make any decisions while you're mad."

"I won't," Ebony said, getting up from the table to leave.

"Don't forget that Eli is running in the Music City Marathon on Sunday, I want all of us to be there," I said, walking out with her. "And don't be discouraged, baby, these men are not easy creatures to live with."

"Thanks, Mama," she said, hugging me around the neck before she left.

For a moment I thought about going back to talk to Nelson but I knew it would be a waste of time. He refused to hear anything until he was ready. For him everything is black or white, up or down, there was no in between. I went up to the office I had made out of Erica's old room, logged on to the computer and looked up Carnegie-Mellon University, if that's where Eli was headed I needed to know what it was all about.

15

It's a beautiful morning, close to 70 degrees even though it's halfway through October. It's only 7:30 but we've been at the Titans football stadium for at least an hour. The runners are crowded down on the field waiting for the 8:00 start. I'm sitting in the stands between Erica and Ebony, Drew is standing down at the gate with D.J, Amber, and Azura. Eli is wearing a bright neon green shirt I bought him to wear so I can see him among all the other participants but they are all hovered together at the starting line and I can only see a blur of the tops of their heads. I could kick myself for not remembering to bring my binoculars.

"I wish I could get D.J. to do something like this, all he wants to do is play video games," Erica said looking down at all the commotion.

"Can you see where he is, Mama?" Ebony asked, looking across the sea of runners.

"I'm still looking," I answered, "I should have reminded him to wear his wrist phone, and then we could just call him."

"He probably wouldn't have worn it anyway; he can't see or hear anything when he's running, he stays so focused," Erica responded.

I didn't bother telling them but I knew it was because he received his directions from God with complete clarity when he runs.

"Drew is going to drive around with the kids and try to make a video of Eli running at two of the checkpoints along the way," Erica said.

"I'd love to go with Drew and see him in action but I promised

Eli I would be waiting here at the finish line when he comes in and I don't want to miss it," I told them.

"Mama, do you really think that Daddy won't change his mind and show up here?" Ebony asked. "I can't believe him."

"Probably not, you both know how stubborn he is. He sees Eli dropping our last name as a rejection of him and so he's refusing to support anything he does as some kind of punishment."

"I think both of them are being extra, it's not that serious," Ebony said, "It's just a name, it doesn't change who you are."

"If you think Calvin is giving you a headache now, I guarantee you that the wedding would not have even happened if you told him you weren't going to take his last name," Erica said.

"You're right about that, and Mama, if it's okay with you and Daddy; I'd like to bring the girls and stay at the house for a while. Calvin is running my pressure up. I'm not going to solve his money problems for him by stroking out and letting him cash in my life insurance," Ebony announced.

"The door is always open, you know that," I said.

"Let me know when you get ready to move," Erica said, "You don't need to be there by yourself with the girls if he decides to have one of his temper tantrums."

"I will, but it's not necessary," Ebony said, "He makes a lot of noise but he's never done anything to hurt me or the girls."

"You never left him before either," Erica said, giving her a serious look.

Then we heard the shot, the race had begun. The frontrunners dashed out of the stadium and the bottleneck of racers fanned out like the sand in an hourglass. They empty out without me getting a chance to wave to Eli.

"It sure didn't take long for them all to get out of here," Ebony remarks, shaking her head.

"Most of them will slow down," Erica reminded her, "It doesn't take much energy to run a block or two but we're talking

13 miles to the end."

"Anybody else feeling hungry?" Ebony asked, "I didn't have time to eat any breakfast."

"You two can go get something to snack on, I don't need a babysitter," I told them.

"Are you sure?" Erica asked.

"It's not raining and I'm comfortable, just be back in 45 minutes, the race isn't that long," I answered."

"Okay, call us if you need anything," Erica said.

I relaxed there for a few minutes watching all the spectators sitting in the bleachers. It was amazing how you can be alone in the midst of more than 10 thousand people. This is the way most of my time will be spent after my retirement from the school system at the end of the year. Maybe I'll finally write that book or some poetry I talked about years ago. Eli will be going off to college and Nelson has already joined the club of 'grumpy old men.' Macey and I had so many plans before Eli was born and now 15 years later I can't even remember what they were. She would have been the one to remind me but we haven't spoken for almost two years. I don't guess she'll ever truly forgive me.

Thinking about the friendship I lost with Macey brings me down and this is not the day for that. I reach into my purse for my DS game to play Sudoku. Since I turned 65 years old I need all the brain stimulation I can get. I'm making good progress and then I hear the uproar. I look behind me and it's Erica and Ebony screaming and rushing down the stairs in the aisle.

"Mama, Drew just called," Erica said breathlessly, "He says the first runners have gone through the halfway checkpoint and are headed back here. He says he saw Eli running with the leaders ahead of the pack. It's about seven of them, and Eli looks real good."

"I wish your Daddy and Elise could be here," I said, getting energized.

"Drew said he's on his way back here so he can video Eli when he runs in," Erica said, sitting down beside me.

My leg starts to bounce up and down faster and faster as my excitement builds, but the time seems to pass slower and slower.

"They're almost here," I hear D.J. shout as he, Drew and the girls come in to join us, "Eli was ready for them today."

A few more minutes pass before we here an announcement broadcast through the stadium, "The first runners are now approaching the stadium." The crowd starts cheering. The jumbotron which had been flashing advertisements now switches to the route of the marathon and there's my baby running in front with the number 34 pinned to his chest. Drew turns on his camera, I'm so proud I could bust.

"Eli is gonna win, Mama," Azura yells, jumping up and down.

From the screen we can see him running through a path of onlookers towards the entrance of the stadium. There are two other runners not far behind him. I stand up and turn my head from the big screen and wait for him to come through the passage onto the field.

"There he is, Mama," Ebony screams in my ear.

"I see him," I said quietly as he runs through the victory tape and drops to his knees.

His time of 65 minutes and 57 seconds flashes on the jumbotron. We are screaming and waving so much that Eli sees us and he waves. Other runners flow onto the field. There's a man on the field who moves toward Eli with a microphone.

"That was a phenomenal race. How do you feel?"

"I feel great. It's a blessing."

We clapped louder than the rest of the people in all the stands.

"Come on let's go," Drew said, turning to leave, "We can pick Eli up and go to the award ceremony; it's going to be at Papa John's at 11:00."

"Yeah, Daddy," D.J. shouted, "Eli is going to be on the news."

We hurried down onto the area off the field near the concessions and found Eli surrounded by a group of people congratulating him. I don't know how he had space to breathe but he somehow managed to put on his warm-up suit.

"You did it, man," D.J. hollered, breaking through the crowd and giving him a high-five.

I followed through the slim path behind. "I'm so proud of you, Eli," I said, giving him a hug.

"Where's Dad?" he asked, looking past us.

"He wasn't feeling well, baby, so he didn't come," I said, trying to smooth it over, "Drew made a video so he can see it when we get home."

"The van is in the parking lot across the street, champ," Drew said as the crowd drifted away. "Do you want to go home and take a quick shower? We don't have much time before they're giving the awards at the ceremony at Papa John's."

"That's okay, let's go ahead to the ceremony, you all just have to smell my sweat."

"I'm sitting way in the back," Amber said, laughing.

"Me too," Azura added.

The small restaurant was packed to capacity but there were tables reserved for the three top winners. Eli joined the other top two winners at the front and received a check for $2500.

"I can't believe you're just fifteen," the reporter from WZTN remarked, "What is your motivation for the long hours of training necessary to run this race?"

"I've always loved to run," Eli answered.

"What inspires you as such a young person to do this?" the reporter asked.

"When I'm training I feel like I'm running towards my future, but my family inspires me, and I want to dedicate this race to my Mom and my Dad. They haven't had much time to rest or relax raising me."

"You are certainly a determined young man; I have no doubt that you will achieve whatever you set your mind to, that was a great performance," the reporter said.

"Thank you, sir," Eli said, finishing the short interview.

I was sorry that Nelson wasn't here to hear him say those words. Eli sat at the head of the table and our food was on the house. We had eaten three extra large pizzas before the excitement of the day, together with rising so early, caught up to all of us and we just wanted to go to the house and kickback for a while.

It was a short drive home. The streets that were so crowded with detoured traffic that morning had cleared quickly and Drew got us back in no time. Eli burst through the front door; he couldn't wait to show Nelson his trophy and his check.

"I came in first, Dad. These are for you," he said, holding his awards high in his hands.

"I don't know why," Nelson said, unimpressed. Then he turned and walked away leaving the rest of us standing there dumbfounded and brokenhearted.

Eli's arms slowly fell down to his sides with disappointment. I knew he had wanted to please his Dad with the news but it was to no avail. My heart hurt for Nelson as much as it did for Eli, why couldn't he see what he was giving up shutting out his own child.

"Don't worry about it, baby, he'll come around," I whispered to Eli, "You're on your way."

"Yeah, Mama, it's only the beginning," he replied, "I've got a long way to go."

***

Nelson only got more sullen as the months went on. I had to wonder how he could sit on the pew on Sunday mornings and act so ugly to his own son. Even Elise coming home for the holidays didn't change his disposition. The consolation was that Ebony and the girls had moved in and with their presence in the house the discord between Nelson and Eli wasn't as noticeable amongst the daily clamor.

Eli became more focused than ever. He ran for miles early every morning, trained more in the afternoons, and studied till late in the evenings. Coach Templeton said Eli was ready to run a full marathon. He had him registered in the Albany Marathon in Georgia that was during the first Saturday in March. It was one of the fastest long distance races in the country and a USATF-certified course. If he did well in that race he could qualify to run in the Boston Marathon.

"That's the week before your interview at Carnegie-Mellon in Pittsburgh," I reminded him.

I thought he was pushing himself too hard. He was still just a kid.

"I got this, Mama," he said confidently.

True to his word, Eli did have it. Drew drove us all down, minus Nelson, to Albany for the 26 mile marathon. Eli didn't win but he came in the top 20 percent of the runners cementing his qualification for the Boston Marathon next year. The following weekend I flew up to Pittsburgh with Eli for his college interview. He had already received his acceptance letter offering him a full scholarship but I needed to check out the campus. I was still having difficulty wrapping my head around my fifteen year old son being that far away from home. The compromise was that Eli would not live on campus with the other freshman; he would be staying off-campus with a family that lived nearby.

Pittsburgh was as cold as Alaska and walking down the streets felt like we were mountain climbing. The city could probably challenge San Francisco in the most steep hill category.

"I don't know how you're going to run around here," I said during the tour around the campus.

"That's the best part, Mama, the inclines will help me train harder and my legs will get stronger."

Eli wowed the university admissions committee in his interview as I knew he would, he still wowed me and I've known him all of his life. We met Mrs. Parrish, the woman that he would be rooming with, and she reminded me of my mother.

"Don't worry, honey," she said, smiling through her bifocals, "I'll look after him."

On the way back to the airport Eli said, "This is the place for me, Mama, Coach has arranged it where I can train with the University of Pittsburgh Panthers on their men's cross country team. Now I won't have to train by myself. That's real big, that's the ECAC."

"What's that?" I asked, totally oblivious.

"That the Eastern College Athletic Conference, there're the best in the country."

***

The last months of the school year were a blur. I pulled my certificates off the walls, packed up my mementos, and removed the pictures of former students that had yellowed around the edges from the years they were sitting on the windowsill. You always look forward to the day when you won't have to go to work every day but you never really think it will happen, and now I don't know if I'm ready to leave what has been such a big part of my life. I've watched several principals and teachers come and go over my 35 years here, the only person who has been here longer than I have is Miss Denise in the cafeteria. Nevertheless, it was because of Eli that I had worked another five years.

"Now you have officially joined the ranks of the unemployed," Nelson said when I stepped through the door with all my working life stacked in a box.

"We're not unemployed, we're retired," I retorted, "There's a difference."

"I've been at this a little longer than you have and there's no difference."

"You're not supposed to work until your dying day. We have

pensions and money in the bank, and thank the Lord, the house and cars are paid for. I'm going to enjoy the rest of my life."

"I'll check back and see what you're saying six months from now."

"Be my guest," I said, carrying the box upstairs.

I laid the box on the floor in the closet and pushed it to the back with my foot. I started to sift through my dresses for something special to wear to Eli's graduation. It had been a while since I watched a high school graduation with one of my children getting a diploma. I chose a white dress flowered with red and yellow blooms. It's three hours before the ceremony so I have time to have a snack before I get dressed, it'll be a long time before I get to eat again.

"Where's everybody?" I yelled out to Nelson in the den while I looked through the fridge.

"Drew picked up Eli to go the barbershop and Ebony and Elise are at the beauty shop, Calvin has the girls this weekend," he yelled back.

"Do you know if he's going to bring them to the graduation?" I asked, taking out some leftover pasta to re-warm.

"I don't know, but Ebony said she's riding with you and Elise."

"She's riding with all of us, Nelson."

I didn't hear a response so I walked into the den.

"If somewhere in your stubborn mind you have the idea that you are not going to your son's graduation, you need not even think about it, because you are going."

"Why should I go if I'm not wanted there?"

"I don't know why you can't see that nothing changed between you and Eli except he said he wanted to drop his last name. He didn't stop loving you or wanting you in his life, you are the one nursing bad feelings and I'm tired of it."

"I can't help it if I have a problem with my son not wanting to be connected to me."

"I don't have time to go through this with you today and I'm not about to let you spoil this day for Eli. If you don't get dressed and put a smile on your face you're going to have more problems with me than you can ever imagine."

"All right, Evelyn, don't have a hissy fit. I'll be the bigger person."

"It's not about that, Nelson, be the boy's father."

The exchange between us made me lose my appetite and I stormed up the steps to get dressed, I had enough time to relax in my Jacuzzi and get my head back together for the evening. I was putting on my earrings when I heard Elise calling out downstairs.

"Let's go people; we need some extra time to find a parking space," she said.

"You look really nice today, Ebony," I said, coming down the steps to join her in the foyer. "It's good to see you smiling."

"I'm feeling much better about myself, because of the classes I've been taking I'm up for a big promotion at work."

"That's good, baby," Nelson said, coming into the room, "Now we have something else to celebrate tonight."

"That'll hold, tonight is Eli's night," Elise said, leading us out of the front door.

Ebony drove and let us off in front of the Belmont University Auditorium where the commencement exercises were taking place. Erica was standing there to meet us.

"Come on sister, Mama and Daddy, Drew is saving some seats for you, Calvin and the girls are here too," she said, ushering us through the huge double doors.

We made our way halfway to the front where the rest of the family was seated. The graduates were seated in the first twelve rows. I looked for Eli near the last four rows of cap and gowns where I thought he would be seated. He had tied with another student, Marjorie Thompson for highest GPA but he yielded to her to give the valedictorian speech. Ebony came in and found us just as the program was beginning.

"Congratulations Cordell Holland High School Class of 2017," Dr. Morgan announced above the cheers and applause that rose above the mass of people in the auditorium.

The program moved quickly after the welcome to the farewell speech from Marjorie. The words of her speech mixed with the murmurs of a multitude of conversations going on and my mind drifted into my own thoughts. This was the first fork in the road along the course of life, where the child becomes an adult. Eli was younger than the rest of them, he couldn't drive a car or vote, but he would be making decisions for himself from now on. All the graduates stood on their feet and moved towards the stage.

"Jennifer Abrams," Dr. Morgan called, and the awarding of the diplomas began. We listened to the proud families whistle and shout as each name was called. When she finally got to the names that started with 'W' Drew moved closer to the front to take a video.

"Eli Newman Winters," Dr. Morgan called, even though the diploma said Eli Newman. I asked her to do that for Nelson and Eli agreed.

I stood on my feet and clapped earnestly for my son and he smiled and waved in our direction when he heard the clamoring from D.J., Amber, and Azura. I sat back down and grabbed Nelson's hand in my exhilaration and noticed the tears in his eyes.

We met up with Eli in the lobby.

"I'm so proud of you, Eli," I said, folding him in my arms close to my chest.

"Thanks, Mama," he said quietly.

"Yeah, baby bro, you did good, I wouldn't have missed it," Elise said, hugging him next.

I gave Nelson a sharp elbow to his side and then he reached out his hand towards Eli to shake. Eli moved past it and put his arms around his Daddy's neck. That's when the tears rose up in my eyes.

One by one everybody gave our graduate a hug, a pat on the back, and a hit to the back of the head by D.J."

"Come on y'all we've got reservations at Maggianos," Erica said, bringing us back on schedule. "Who are you riding with, Eli?"

"I'm going in the big ride with you," he told her.

It was a special evening.

"It's not often that I get to have all my family together so I just want to say how happy I am and how much I love you all," I said after we were seated at our table.

"Speech from the valedictorian," Elise shouted from the other side of the table.

Eli stood up and said, "I just want to say I love y'all and I'm glad everybody is here to celebrate with me."

The tables next to us clapped too. We spent the next hour eating, laughing, and even Nelson got out of his self-imposed funk for a while.

"If you paid us half the attention that you've given Eli maybe we could have done better," Ebony said low enough where he couldn't hear.

"Don't even try that," I told her, "I had you girls when I was young, energetic, and committed to winning mother of the decade. Eli practically raised himself."

"I know, but sometimes I wish I was where he is, starting out, I would do things so differently."

"There's nobody in this world who wouldn't do something differently if they could do it all over again, the good thing is that it's not over, you can still do whatever you put your mind to."

"Really, Mama."

"Yes really, I believe that."

16

Nelson refused to ride with us up to Pittsburgh to take Eli to school. I stood in the doorway early that morning while Eli went over to his side of the bed to say goodbye. I couldn't hear his response but it wasn't more than a few words and he never raised his head up from the pillow. Why was he being this hateful over just a name, the boy hadn't given us a minutes trouble. There wasn't much I could do, it wasn't my battle. It had taken me several decades but I had finally learned you can't make another person do what you want or feel what you want.

We hadn't been on a road trip in years and we had a ball. I taught them some road songs they thought were totally ridiculous but they got a kick out of the 'that's my car' game. We got Eli settled in at Mrs. Parrish's house and she cooked us a nice dinner. We checked into the Residence Inn a little over a mile away for the night. Erica and Drew and D.J. had a suite and I shared mine with Ebony and the girls.

Amber and Azura went into one of the bedrooms where they could watch TV, play games, and skype with their friends. I was tired but I was wound up from the nervous tension of the whole day so I sat up talking with Ebony.

We had barely been chatting for five minutes before she said, "I've been wanting to talk with you about something, Mama, but we never seem to get to spend a private moment together anymore."

"You sound so serious. What's on your mind?" I asked, putting my feet up on the ottoman.

"I've met someone that I have become close to, somebody I

could see a future with."

"Have you forgotten that you have a husband already?" I asked in a hushed voice, putting my feet back on the floor.

"I don't think I'm in love with Calvin anymore, things haven't been the same between us for a long time."

"That's marriage, baby, you're not in love all the time."

"Maybe not, but I want to be. I'm about to turn 40, I don't have time to keep waiting for Calvin to get his shit together."

"Look at you, this new man has you cursing in front of your mother," I said, feigning insult.

"I'm serious; this man is established and can take care of me and the girls."

"I can't tell anybody how to live their life, I still trying to finish the puzzle on my own but I don't think that's something that you can rush into. It's almost impossible to bring another man around your teenage girls and not have a problem."

"I believe I can trust him."

"Personally, I'd rather you stay by yourself than take that risk. You don't have to have any man for a while. Since I'm retired I can help you with the girls."

"I know that but I have a right to go on with my life."

"Yes you do but you made a big investment in your life with Calvin. You can't let money or the lack of it make your decisions for you. The only time you two had problems were when he was out of work.

"That's true, but it seemed like that was a lot of the time. I did what I could to be there financially, ride or die through the hard times; he's the one who couldn't hold up his end mentally or emotionally. I walked on eggshells for years worrying about him so much that I forgot about me."

"Believe me, I know marriage is tough, but you all are a family. You dated him for three years before you got married; give him at least half that time before you think about getting a divorce."

"I can do that, but I'm not promising not to see anybody else."

I couldn't do anything but shake my head. It's amazing to hear my baby all grown up saying the same things I said when I turned the big 4-0. It must be a phase, it'll pass.

"The grass isn't always greener," I said standing up, "I'm going to bed; you kids take more out of me now than you did when you all were babies."

"Goodnight, Mama, and thanks for not judging me."

"Who am I to judge anybody, I'm flesh and blood too," I said, going into the other bedroom.

The muffled voices, sirens, and sounds of gunshots from the TV on the other side of the door served as background music to my own thoughts as I tossed and turned the whole night stressing over one child of mine and then another, it was probably just as well that Ebony never did come to bed. Neither of us would have gotten any sleep. I was worried sick about driving off and leaving Eli the next morning and I don't know why; I knew he would be okay. I believed him whole-heartedly when he said he had been sent by God, but history tells me that the devil is always busy. I couldn't help feeling guilty about him being all the way up here by himself at such a young age. For more than a minute I considered getting an apartment in town so he could stay with me and still go on with his plans.

There wasn't much time to say a long goodbye before the early morning freshman orientation.

"You know I'll move up here if you need me to," I told him, standing in Mrs. Parrish's front yard.

"I know, but I'm ready for this. If you or Daddy need me for anything at anytime hit my number. I love you, Mama."

"I love you even more, son."

I hugged him to my neck and kissed him on the side of his face. What I really wanted to do was pull him into the van and speed away but I knew I had to let him go. He walked me to the car, opened the door and helped me in, and closed it. I sat there in the second row seat and closed my eyes. I couldn't bear the sight of him standing there as we pulled off. I slept most of the way back home just like Amber and Azura. I didn't want them all to see me crying like a fool over leaving Eli in another state by himself.

"Did you miss us, Grandpa?" Azura asked as soon as we walked into the door.

"I sure did, baby girl," he said, wrapping her up in a warm hug.

"You should have come too," Amber added, walking by him up the stairs like she was grown.

Azura ran behind her big sister up the steps and Ebony stepped outside for privacy before she answered her ringing phone.

"Did you get your golden boy settled in?" Nelson asked.

"I'm not going there with you today, Nelson," I answered with much attitude. "You are not going to make your problem one of mine."

"Fine with me, I was only asking a question."

"If you really care we did get him settled in and he seemed to be very happy, probably because he won't have to be around your evil ass every day."

"I'm sorry, Evelyn. I can't help how I feel but I'm glad you all are back safely," he said, trying to get back in my good graces.

"Maybe you just wanted somebody to cook you a decent meal," I said, letting the bad feelings go to keep the peace.

"Elise called earlier; she wants to hear about the trip."

"Why didn't she just message me on my iPad, I'll call her right back."

I sat down at the kitchen table and fished my tablet out of my bag. I pushed Elise's picture and her face filled the screen.

"Hey Mama, you don't look like you've been crying," Elise said jokingly.

"I'm still in shock; the tears will be in the next phase."

"How did Eli do when you guys were leaving?"

"You know your little brother; he takes it all in stride. This is simply the next step in his master plan."

"I envy that, I wish I had something to be excited about again."

"What's the matter? You sound like you need a vacation."

"Maybe so, I'm getting tired, Mama, I don't even know why I work so hard. I don't have a family to support. What is it all for?"

"Don't tell me you wanting to get married at this late date?"

"Hell no, all these years of being by myself, I couldn't stand to live with anybody and they probably couldn't stand me either. I just want to switch gears, slow down, and do something different, I'm getting old."

"Well you're not alone in that, baby. You've got plenty of company."

"So what is Eli going to be studying?"

"He's majoring in Public Policy and Decision Science, he says it analytical social science."

"All right then, I'll have to go and see him; the SuperTrain can get there in less than four hours."

"It would really make me feel better if you did that from time to time, I guarantee you spending time with him will make you feel energized."

"I'll do that, at least once a month."

"Also, you might need to touch base with your baby sister too. She's got a lot on her mind."

"Uh-oh, I will. Take care, Mama, we'll talk soon."

I nodded as her face blinked off of the screen.

***

"How are you, baby?" I said when Eli's picture bounced on my phone.

"I'm good, Mama. Through our skull sessions in class I'm discovering the direction I need to go to make meaningful changes. It's basic economics. The greater amount of the United States' wealth is spent on wars and weapons."

"You might have something there; this country is definitely out of cash."

"Don't believe it, Mama. The ones that have it just don't want to share it. America has always wanted free labor, that's what it was built on. The largest employers are still getting away with it paying low unfair wages. When management eliminates unions and the power of workers to negotiate, it's sharecropping in its purest form."

"I can't argue that, baby, I've been one of those sharecroppers all of my life. My question is are you having any fun? Too much thinking will give you ulcers. You're young; these are the years for you to enjoy yourself."

"It's all good, Mama. I'm training with the track team and I've taken five full minutes off of my marathon time. This is going to be my year to run a marathon.

"Well, if you're happy I'm happy."

"Cool, I'll see you on the holiday break," he said, hanging up.

I said a quick prayer for my child in hopes that he would also see the great things that the world has to offer and have some fun. Even though I had no idea what a kid his age would do for fun at college.

17

"Where's the large suitcase, Nelson?" I shrieked in a futile effort to stay calm.

He looked down around our feet on the carpeted floors of the airport and then I could see him mentally tracing back to the house as his facial expression changed.

"We may have left it back home on the bed," he answered, uncertain.

"What do you mean we, I asked you to bring all the bags down and put them at the door when Drew called to say he was on his way."

"I thought I did, I guess I forgot."

"That bag has most of our clothes in it, Nelson. What are we going to wear?"

"We'll just have to call Ebony or Elise to bring it to the airport."

"There's not enough time, our plane leaves in less than a half hour."

"I'm sorry, Evelyn, I told you I didn't want to come in the first place. We can either catch a later flight or just buy some clothes when we get there. That's all I can tell you."

"We're getting on that plane," I insisted, throwing the two other bags on the scale to be checked by the Northeast attendant. "You are not going to spoil this trip for me."

One bag had our underwear, toiletries, and medications in it and the other had a couple of pairs of shoes for each of us.

"Terminal B, gate 23, and you'll need to hurry; the plane will be boarding in ten minutes," the attendant said, handing me our ID's back with a nervous smile.

"Thank you, we will," I assured her, rushing towards the security area.

He had better not have any change or keys in his pockets to slow us down because as much as I wanted him to be there for his son, I wasn't going to miss that plane. We got through security without incident and I was about to make Nelson start running for his life when a young man with an electric cart drove up beside us.

"Would you like to ride?" he asked in a foreign accent I couldn't distinguish.

"Absolutely," I answered, hopping onto the first seat beside him, "Gate 23, please."

He got us to our gate in less than three minutes.

"Thank you so much," I said sincerely as I placed a ten dollar bill in his hand.

We fell in at the end of the line and cool relief began to circulate around my hot head. Three flight attendants welcomed us aboard, two females and one male. I eased into the second row window seat of first-class and leaned back against the cushioned leather and closed my eyes. I could feel Nelson fumbling around in the seat next to me but I had no interest in what he was doing. The only thing on my mind was getting to Boston to see Eli run in the Marathon. He had been training so hard that he hadn't even come home for Christmas; I hadn't been able to touch my boy in almost five months.

Last year Coach Templeton had registered him the New York Marathon because he was too young for the Boston Marathon and he had come in the top 5 percent of the finishers. This year he had gotten special approval since he was classified as a junior in college and had run with the Eastern Conference for two years. I couldn't believe how many big companies wanted to sponsor Eli in the race. They were providing for additional training and all of his running clothes and shoes. Eli had even gotten them to pay for our first-class travel expenses.

"What do these sponsors get out of the deal?" I asked him the last time he was at home.

"I just wear their logos, Mama. For me, it's an extension of my overall strategy," he replied.

"How's that, I don't see the connection?"

"If I win this race it will open up the doors to boardrooms to the largest companies in the world. Finances are the way of the world; it takes money to make any meaningful changes so I have to have access to the influence of big dollars."

"I have to trust and believe that you know what you're doing, baby?"

"My trust is in the Lord, Mama, he is my guide."

No matter how many times he told me about his plan it worried me, one thing I know is that the devil and the Lord don't work together.

"Do you want something to eat?" Nelson asked, nudging my shoulder against the armrest.

I looked up at the female attendant and said, "I'll have whatever he's having except for the beer, white wine for me, please."

"Certainly," she responded pleasantly.

"I gazed out the window through the clouds and then it occurred to me. "You and I haven't been on a plane together since our Florida trip. That was nearly 10 years ago."

"Time surely gets away from us. We getting old, Evelyn."

"That's why we have to make the most of everyday. It hurts my heart when I think about the time you've wasted being mad at your own son, it's gone, and you can't ever get it back. Let it go, Nelson."

"I've tried but it ain't easy. When the girls got grown I never expected to have a son, then when Eli was born he never took to me. He was always a mama's boy. Now he doesn't want anything to do with me."

"That's not true, he told you why he wanted to drop his last name, and that's his choice. People change their names all the time. Besides, did you ever hear me complaining about having three 'daddy's girls?' He loves you and that's all that matters."

"I'm too old to change, Evelyn."

"Not too old, just too stubborn is more like it," I said as the female flight attendant brought our meal. Nelson was never one to have much conversation while he ate. So I enjoyed the view from the window eating from real utensils and a glass plate on a plane. It was a first. When we finished the male attendant collected the dishes and served me a delicious cup of coffee. I couldn't help but smile to myself. Who would believe I was 68 years old going to see my 17 year old son run in the Boston Marathon. Life can surely take some unexpected turns.

"Please return to your seats, make sure you are in the upright position, fasten your seatbelts, and turn off all electronic equipment. We will be landing in Boston shortly," one of the female flight attendants directed.

Elise was probably already here to meet us in baggage claim. She was the only other member of the family who could get here.

"I'm not missing this one," Elise said, calling us up as soon as she heard he was registered. "Plus it will give me a chance to visit a few of my old hang-outs."

"Unfortunately Erica and Ebony won't be able to get there, school is still in, but they did get to see him run the marathon in Albany."

"I'm loving it, Mama, Eli is doing his thing. I've missed so much being so far away but now that my little brother is closer I'm getting a front row seat."

"I'm so glad that you can be there for him, it made me feel better that you made it to his debate at Princeton in February, I couldn't make both trips."

"They didn't allow videos or I would have recorded it, Mama, he wore them out. I was so proud. That boy is amazing and he's smooth too."

"I know I wish I could have been there, if only he were a little closer to home."

"Now you can see how I felt all these years being so far from everybody."

"Elise, you know you love the big city life, Nashville is too boring for you."

The plane made a smooth landing and all of the flight attendants wished us well on our way out. Once I stepped my feet off of the plane the excitement of the whole thing hit me. We all disembarked in single-file out of the tunnel into the airport terminal leaving our quiet oasis of the airplane and crossing into the pure chaos of impatient travelers. Nelson took my hand as we waited for an opening between the steady streams of pedestrians pulling their luggage on wheels in every direction.

"The sign says baggage claim is that way," I told Nelson, pointing to the left.

We navigated through the crowd and made our way near the wall on the right where there were less people. Up ahead there was a moving walkway.

"Oh yeah," Nelson said, picking up the pace to get on the walkalator, "No sense in us walking our legs off if we don't have to."

I stepped onto it behind Nelson and we stood to the side, leaving a clear path for those rushing to their various destinations. It gave me a few minutes to observe my fellow travelers. There were couples trying to manage their young children in strollers and backpacks, the solitary persons who sat along the seats reading silently on their kindles, the garbled conversations that served as background music in the eateries without walls, and the crazy looking ones that dashed by with quick long strides talking loud and fast into what I assumed was an invisible phone receiver.

"There's the escalator down to baggage claim," I said as we reached the end of our ride.

Halfway down the escalator I caught sight of Elise waving.

"How's my big girl," Nelson asked, wrapping his arm around her shoulder and kissing her on the cheek.

"I'm good, Daddy. How was the flight?" she answered, giving me a tight hug.

"It spoiled me," I said, "I hope I don't ever have to fly coach again."

"The best part of flying is getting off the plane," Nelson said flatly.

"Come on you guys," Elise said taking us both by the arm, "Let's get your bags and go to the hotel, I'm so excited about the race tomorrow."

Nelson didn't comment as he moved closer to the carousel where the luggage was circling.

"How's Daddy doing?" Elise asked just above a whisper.

"Still mad, but I told him that if he didn't come we were going to have problems."

"He'll get over it, I'm just glad you got him to come. Eli is going to be pumped to see him."

"Where is Eli?"

"He's staying at the Four Seasons where we'll be staying; a lot of the athletes stay there since it's so convenient to the race location. We might be able to get him on his phone if it's turned on but we won't be able to see him until after the race. His coach has him scheduled for a light workout, a massage, a special meal full of carbs and some protein."

"I was hoping we might have dinner together."

"No time, Mama, after he eats he's going straight to bed, he's got to get up early to eat enough carbs to carry him through the race without feeling too full."

"Okay, lead the way," Nelson said, coming over with our two small bags in his hand. "I'm glad at least one of us knows their way around this place."

"Is that all the bags you brought, Mama? You usually pack like Diana Ross."

"Oh yeah, your Daddy left the big fold-over garment bag with most of our clothes in it at home on the bed."

"We don't have to go down that road again, Evelyn. We can stop by a mall on the way to the hotel and get some things to get us by."

"I can't believe it," Elise said, getting a big laugh as we followed her out to the parking garage. "There are some shops in the South End where you can pick up whatever you need and we can get something to eat there too."

"We don't need anything fancy, just something to be clean and covered. Is there a Wal-Mart around here somewhere?" Nelson said.

"Speak for yourself, I'm getting some new outfits courtesy of the man who forgot the bag," I said, climbing in the back of Elise's rental. "I plan to look good while my child runs this race."

"That's exactly why I'll be going to my grave as a poor man."

"It doesn't matter, Daddy," Elise laughed, "You can't take it with you."

"Surrounded by you Winters women for most of my life I haven't been able to save a penny," he complained.

"At least you haven't come up short, honey bear, the ends were always meeting."

Nelson didn't respond, he just grunted and turned his attention to the window. "This must be the place where the folks with all the old money live," he said, taking notice of the architecture.

"The city is in the top three of incomes in the country but there are some having hard times here too," Elise said.

"I bet there are," Nelson said sarcastically, "They always need somebody to wait tables and clean up after them."

"If the market doesn't stop sinking I might move back home to Nashville, the cost of living up here is ridiculous," Elise said, swiping her card at the parking exit.

"You don't even want to come back there, Elise," I interjected, "The job market is pitiful. Almost half the people are looking for a job, the other half is looking for a better job."

"It's like that all over the South," Nelson added, "That's what they get for putting all those Republicans in office. Trying to hurt black people they cut their own throats."

"I guess Calvin is still caught up on that rollercoaster ride," Elise asked.

"Yeah he is, as far as I know he's back in school to get re-trained," I answered.

"How's Ebony doing? I haven't talked to her for a while," Elise asked.

Nelson grunted again.

"She's at a fork in her road," I said. "She's running around with some man who's making her all kinds of promises that he can't keep."

"Is she just having some fun or is she considering a divorce?"

"I don't know but I think she's holding some resentment against Calvin because she's had to carry the load for the family. It's not his fault, it's just been a bad economy for damn near twenty years, but he took his frustrations out on her and that wasn't right. I hope they get it together soon because Amber's hormones are kicking in and it takes two to keep these hot young boys in check."

"I guess that's why I'm still single."

We drove in silence for a few minutes and I took in the sights. The homes were joined in a row, typical for neighborhoods in the northeast. I thought it was a quaint city, not as large as I thought it would be.

"They sure do love their fountains, it seems like they have one on every other block," Nelson said, rejoining the conversation.

"Lots of parks too," I added.

"There is a real unique shop where both of you can find whatever clothes you'll need, it's 'Bobby from Boston's,'" Elise said, pulling into a parking garage on Berkley Street.

"Look at how much the parking is," Nelson said, "We aren't trying to buy the space, we're just parking for an hour."

"That's how it is up here; parking is a small fortune, that's why most people use mass transit," she said, leading us down the three blocks to the store.

"It looks pretty ritzy around here," Nelson said, looking in the shops and eateries.

"Don't worry about it," Elise said leading us through the entrance, "Everything is vintage, Daddy, so it should be easy on your pockets."

"Thank you, baby, I was getting worried," he said, shaking his head and breathing a sigh of relief. "We don't need to spend a fortune on stuff we already have at home."

"I don't see why you're complaining, Eli paid for the flight and the hotel room."

We found some stylish ensembles to my surprise, something casual to wear to the race, something nice to wear for dinner, some jeans and comfortable shirts, and to my surprise Nelson didn't grunt at the total.

"There are some good places to eat up on Tremont Street," Elise said, leading the way, "We can drop the bags off in the car on the way."

"What about that café across the street?" I asked, intrigued. "I love the name, The Garden of Eden; the food has got to be heavenly."

"Not necessarily," Nelson chimed in, "Satan came in and spoiled everything."

"Don't be contrary, I want to eat in there," I insisted.

It turned out that the food wasn't that unusual, we ordered sandwiches and tea.

"If we have time before you go, there's a place called the Butcher Shop you might like," Elise said on the way back to the car.

"Now that sounds interesting too," I said, "It must serve lots of different kinds of meat."

"Evelyn, you don't choose a restaurant just because of the name. It's all about the food," Nelson said condescendingly.

We sat and talked over coffee and listened to the local accents from the other tables. By the time we left the restaurant the evening was settling in.

"We better get to the hotel before more of the streets are blocked off," Elise said.

"Take me on in," I said, "It has been a long day and my age is starting to catch up with me. I am ready to experience all the Four Seasons has to offer."

"Me too, Mama," Elise added.

Nelson grunted and I couldn't have cared less. I had come a long way to see Eli run in the Boston Marathon and there was nothing anybody could do to steal my joy. We had a smooth check-in and caught the elevator up to our floor.

"Hurry up and open the door, Evelyn, my arms are about to fall off," Nelson fussed impatiently.

I scanned the lock with the keycard and a small light flashed green. I pulled down on the door latch, it opened, and lying on the floor was the daily newspaper. The letters spelling out Eli Newman jumped out from the bottom left-hand corner of the page. I picked it up to read it silently. "One of the favorites to watch, Eli Newman, made a phenomenal showing last year in the New York Marathon. He's one of the younger participants and could finish within the top three runners." I folded the newspaper and put it under my arm. No reason to give Nelson a reason to slip back into his funk.

"This room is even nicer than mine," Elise said, looking round.

"Thank God it has two TVs," Nelson added.

"Well, we've got an early start tomorrow so I'll see you in the morning," Elise said, giving me a quick hug and a kiss and then Nelson on her way out.

My eyes roamed around the room taking in a panoramic view. The ample hotel suite was first-class, simply beautiful, and the view of the city was magnificent. If Nelson was thirty years younger I would have kept him up all night making love from one room to the next. Instead, I got a great night's sleep.

18

Room service knocked on the door early in the morning with a breakfast that had everything, cold and hot food. I enjoyed eating all alone and watching the morning news while Nelson showered. I made a mental note that the high temperature would be around 58 degrees. When Nelson came out of the bedroom fully dressed in Dockers and a white button-down shirt I put down my plate to take my turn. I loved to shower in hotel rooms; you never have to worry about the hot water running out. It was the too small towels that spoiled the experience. I paused to admire myself in the mirror after I was dressed in the khaki pants and the polo shirt we bought in the shop yesterday, pink was definitely my color. I was ready for Eli's big day. I slipped on a jacket when I heard a knock on the door.

"We might be able to see Eli when he starts his race since the runners will be staggered," Elise told us after breakfast. "The elite men will start running at 10:00. Hopefully we won't have much trouble getting over to Main Street and Hopkinton."

"How far is that?" Nelson asked as we followed her out the door.

"About 26 miles, Daddy," Elise said, teasing him.

The hotel lobby was full of goodies for the runners. They had all kinds of water and other fluids, energy bars, fruit, and other snacks to give their bodies the fuel to get through the race.

"Do you want to make a poster so Eli can see us, Mama?"

"No, I bought one of his yellow and green t-shirts from the high school track team. I know he can pick it out of the crowd.

They had shuttles to take the participants to the starting line of the race. The buses filled with anxious runners in their colorful shorts and shoes flowed one after the other down the street. The rest of us had to take the subway. In the tunnel of the subway train, with spectators from every description on the earth speaking a host of languages, I grasped how huge this event was for so many people. Nelson hadn't been to any of Eli's marathons and he couldn't believe all the people that had come to support the runners.

Elise pushed and shoved her way through the crowds and security on the street making a path for me and Nelson to follow to the front of the curb. I looked up at the rooftops of the buildings around us that were adorned with policemen. Then my eyes focused on the large digital clock at the gate and it was 9:15. At the front of the starting line there was a line of wheelchairs and behind them a group of competitors in handcycles. Then the gun sounded and the race began. The energy in the air was contagious and my own anticipation was running away with me. My stomach was tightening with my nerves and I felt like I was about to run with the rest of them.

Fifteen minutes later the elite women were crossing the starting line. It was something to see, so many women looking fit and athletic. It made me want to try and get into shape one more time. Elise cheered them on whooping and hollering and pumping her fist in the air as they ran ahead on the course. Once they had cleared the way the elite men took their places at the starting gate. It was like a sea of men flowed into the street from a broken dike.

That's when I saw Eli come to the front with a bib that read Newman pinned across the front of his chest. From a distance I could still see the sheen of perspiration on the side of his face. He was warmed up and ready to go. Even though he was the youngest runner out here today he towered over many of the men standing by him. I watched him shift his legs back and forth while his eyes searched through the crowds of bystanders held back behind the wooden barriers.

"Eli," I yelled at the top of my lungs as I swung his old t-shirt in a circle above my head.

I don't know if he heard my voice above the blaring music and announcements from the PA system but the green and yellow on the t-shirt caught his eye.

"He sees us," Elise screamed, jumping up and down.

I saw a joyful grin spread across his face when he saw his Daddy standing next to me.

"Wave to him, Nelson," I said, nudging him in the side. "That's you son."

Nelson raised up his hand in an unenthusiastic motion. I stood on my toes and raised the shirt up even higher, waving it like a flag. I wanted my boy to win, I wanted him to do all the things that he wanted and needed to do. Suddenly I was free from the fear and worry about his future; all my doubts were gone as I saw him stand tall and confident in the swarm of runners. Then the gun fired. He started running and I was so excited that all I wanted to do was break through security and run with them. Hordes of men poured out of the gate behind him and I lost sight of Eli.

"What do you want to do, Mama?" Elise asked, out of breath as if she had been running. "Do you want to catch the subway and try and meet him at the 13-mile marker?"

"No sweetie, I want to get back downtown where I can see him come across the finish line," I told her as I fought my way through the massive crowd.

"I don't see why we have to fight all these crowds when the whole race is on the TV," Nelson said, irritated. "We could have watched it up close and personal on the couch at the hotel with some snacks."

"Remember the reason we're here is to support Eli," I said, stuffing the t-shirt in my bag and moving more determined through the throngs of people.

"It's going to take a while to get there but we can watch the race live on my phone," Elise said leading us back down into the subway.

The trains were jammed packed and we weren't able to get on the first train. While we waited for the next one Elise found the coverage on CBS.

"Mama and Daddy," she squealed, "Eli is running with the leaders, he's in 3rd place."

"Let me see," I said, grabbing the phone from her hand.

My heart beat faster as I held it to the side where Nelson could see him too. He took a quick glance and then he looked away but I couldn't take my eyes off of the small screen. I was bowled over with pride. When the next train came I led the push to get on it. I gripped the subway pole with one hand and held the phone in the other. All the commotion and noise of the riders and the train were inconsequential to me; I was absorbed by the rhythm of Eli's pace as he ran strong behind the two other men. It had to be less than a couple of seconds between them. The one in the lead was from Kenya, the other was from Ethiopia.

It took us more than an hour to return to Back Bay and my nerves were so raw that I had to give the phone back to Elise. The crowds were already thickly lined along the Boylston Street waiting to see the winner. My eyes were drawn to the large movie screen where we could watch the runners in action. They flashed camera views from the entire race course. "The leaders have passed mile 20 and are now approaching 'Heartbreak Hill,'" the broadcaster announced.

They were all still close with each just one stride behind the other. You could see the effort in each step. It was like a horror movie, it was hard to watch yet I couldn't turn away. My jaw dropped and I felt like I was going to pass out from the anxiety.

"You need to calm yourself down," Nelson said.

"I'm fine," I said, feeling annoyed with his whole attitude. This was our son running his heart out in this race. He could at least show some emotion.

"Mama, drink something," Elise said, handing me a bottle of Gatorade.

I twisted off the cap and drank half of the purple liquid before I took a breath. I decided to take Nelson's advice. I bowed my head and looked down at my feet and said a prayer.

"Dear Lord, help me to be whatever Eli needs me to be today, whether he wins or loses. Please touch Nelson's heart today and let him feel the love he has for his son and let the anger go, in Jesus' name, amen."

I kept my head down for I don't know how long looking at the ground around my feet.

"They're only two miles away," I heard Elise say.

I jerked my head up and my eyes were locked on the large screen.

"Let's move to the front of the finish line," I urged as I kept my eyes on the runners.

I wanted to be as close as I could when Eli ran through the gate. I could barely move, I was shaking from the inside out and from my legs to my hands. When we got near the line two security guards stood at the barrier. Then it happened. Eli lifted his head up to the sky and began to pull away from the other two in a sprint. A loud roar filled with cheers rose from the crowd. He was within our sight moving quickly through the street with a policeman riding a motorcycle riding a few steps behind.

Nelson grabbed my hand and squeezed it hard but I couldn't speak. I could only watch that magnificent young man who I couldn't believe was my flesh and blood run towards the finish. Eli was going to win the race. Cameras came in closer and the ovation reaches a crescendo as he dashed through the tape and the top clock froze at 2 hours, 7 minutes, and 13 seconds.

He stops in his tracks and looks up into the sky and I see his lips moving. I snatch the t-shirt out of my bag and wave it high in the air and he sees it for one moment before a race official pulls him over to the side puts a wreath of olive leaves on his head and wraps a towel around him. In the next minute he is surrounded by a circle of people treating him like a hero, some giving him water, others taking photos, and others asking questions while he is escorted behind a temporary wall. The race continues as more runners cross the finish line but for us it's done.

"I don't care what anybody says my baby brother is the boss," Elise declared, stomping her foot on the ground. "He came up here and did the damn thing."

I wanted to join Elise in her rant but I was so proud of him I was crying. I refused to let the tears show on my face, but they poured from my mind and body like a powerful storm that left me trembling. I was overwhelmed with the position I had to witness the great work that Eli was called to do. It was happening just like he said it would. The sad part was that Nelson didn't have the heart to open up his eyes and see it.

I had forgotten I had my phone until it vibrated in my jacket pocket, "Mama and Daddy thanks for coming," Eli said, elated. "When I saw you all I knew I could do it."

"I'm so happy for you, baby, you ran an incredible race," I said, finally able to speak. "Tell him, Nelson."

I held the phone in front of Nelson and he hesitated until I pinched his side with my free hand.

"Good job," he said, nodding his head.

"I have to take some pictures and some other stuff but I'll meet y'all back at the hotel before the award ceremony," Eli said just before the screen went black.

"Let's go and get some food I'm starved," Elise said, rubbing her belly for emphasis. "I didn't want to eat too heavy that early this morning. My stomach was doing back flips."

"Tell me about it," I said as we walked back towards the Four Seasons.

"I need to freshen up first, my shirt is soaking wet, I'd have everybody thinking that I ran all 26.2 miles," Elise said with her face glowing.

The excitement of the race still spun around in the air. When we reached the entrance of the hotel there were cheers and claps for the runners as they drifted back into the hotel. Food and energy drinks were laid out on tables to refresh them. I wanted to stand in the middle of the floor and shout that my son was the winner of the marathon but I respected his wishes to keep us out of the publicity he generated.

"I could use a nap," Nelson said matter-of-factly when we got on the elevator.

"Don't you want to eat first?" I asked

"Naw, I'll order some room service," he answered.

"Well, the suite is nice but I'm not going to spend my time cooped up in the hotel. I'm feeling great," I said when we reached our floor.

"All right, Mama, I'll be down to get you after I get changed," Elise said, raising her hand to give me a high five.

I slapped her hand and strutted to our room. I couldn't wait to call the other girls even though I was sure they had watched it on the TV. I pressed the screen by Erica's picture.

"Hey Mama," she answered in a low voice, "I can't believe it, I watched it on my notebook during class and could barely stay composed in front of my students."

"I know, sweetie, I forgot that it was Monday and you all had to go to work and to school."

"D.J. tried to pretend he was sick and then Drew called out to stay home too. Ebony called a few minutes ago, she was screaming so loud she's probably fired."

"I feel so good; it was surely something to see. These are the times that I really miss Macey, I wish I could call her."

"Just pick up the phone and call her, I bet she would be glad to hear from you."

"I doubt it; she hasn't taken my calls for years," I said, reminiscing.

"I've got to go, Mama, I'll call you later," she said, ending the call.

Elise and I had a wonderful late lunch at the Bristol Lounge located on the second floor of the hotel. We ordered the New England lobster cake and champagne and toasted to Eli's win of the race. He called again while we were eating to tell us that he was still giving interviews and would meet us at the Fairmount in the Grand Ballroom at 5:00 for the awards ceremony.

Back in the suite I showered and changed into a kelly green sheath dress that had a matching cardigan. Nelson was pretending to sleep and I let him. I didn't want to take a chance that he might spoil this evening for Eli. Elise said the Fairmount Copeland Plaza wasn't that far away and we could walk.

It turned out to be a twenty minute walk but I didn't mind. Elise spent the hold time talking on her phone and I got a chance to hear myself think. I looked at all the exquisite architecture of the hotels and restaurants in this exclusive area. I was seeing things I had never expected to see and I was here for an experience that I had never imagined. I shook my head as I marveled at a young woman on a bike as she maneuvered through the traffic. That's what we all learn to do along the twists that life always has for us.

I trailed Elise when she turned under the ruby colored awning at the entrance of the hotel guarded by bronze lions on either side and walked along the red carpet like any other celebrity.

The ceremony in the ballroom was open to the public but Eli had reserved us a table. We watched as they called up the winners in the different categories before they called Eli Newman as the first place winner and handed him a humongous trophy. The flashes from the cameras had me seeing white dots as applause broke up and spread around the room.

My smile refused to be concealed when Eli joined us at the table. Elise and I both stood up to give him tight hugs.

"Where's Dad," he asked, confused.

"He wore himself out at the race and wasn't feeling good after we ate," I said quickly. "We are all so proud of you."

"I don't know what's next little brother after this but I can't wait," Elise said, "I needed this lift in my life."

"I don't know if I'll run any more marathons," he replied, "I think I've accomplished what I needed to."

"You mean winning all of the money?" Elise asked.

"No, it's not about the money for me, it's the connections that I have made," he answered.

"The money doesn't hurt, Eli," I added.

"Tell me what you want Mama and you'll have it," he said with a sincerity that touched me.

"Baby, with you and your sisters I've been richly blessed. What I want most is for you to be happy."

"I am happy, Mama," he said, smiling.

"The ladies are going to be all over you for real now, Eli. Are you ready for that?"

He smiled and said, "Not right now, I have been tempted by some real hotties but I can't allow myself to be distracted from what I have to do. We can be friends but not my girlfriend."

"Eli, you are allowed to have fun and enjoy yourself," Elise urged, "You only have one more year left in school and then what. You just won the Boston Marathon, slow down; you're already ahead of the pack."

"Leave him alone, the girls will always be there when he's ready."

"It's about time for me to make my next move anyway," he said.

"What's on your mind, baby?" I asked curiously.

"I'm going international. I applied for the Rhodes Scholarship at the University of Oxford and I've been accepted. I'm going to England in the fall to study public policy and international relations."

Silently I thanked God that Nelson hadn't come to the award ceremony; I know he would have made a scene for the entire world to see. It was hard enough that Eli had dropped his name, now he planned to leave the country.

"Maybe you are moving too fast, Eli, you can't come back and be a teenager again," I said.

"There's no time to waste, Mama. The world is in crisis right now and it could break down into chaos and devastation at any moment. Most of the wealth on the entire globe belongs to less than 100 people. Greed and selfishness have thrown off the balance of nature. Evil forces are more alive now than ever. We have to work fast if there's any chance to prevent mass destruction."

I was speechless.

"Shouldn't you finish your degree at CMU before you go?" Elise asked.

"I'm going to take a full load this summer and I can finish the rest on-line."

"I'm behind you 100 percent, it's just that I loved having you closer to me for a change," Elise said regretfully.

"Don't worry, if things go according to my plan I'm going to be moving to New York in a couple of years and I might need to stay with you," he said.

I changed the subject and he told us about the race and how good it felt to win and that Coach Templeton had called to congratulate him. I told him about what was going on in Nashville with his nieces and asked him to call D.J. more often since he was hanging with some thugs. After another ten minutes he got a message on his phone.

He balled up his fist and pounded the air, "Yes, that's what I'm talking about."

"What is it?" I asked, interested.

"I've been invited to the White House for a reception on Wednesday," he said, "I'll be flying to D.C. tomorrow afternoon."

I hadn't even begun to process any of these new developments when a man who looked like he might be his trainer and a woman in a business suit came over to usher him back to the fray of sponsors, politicians, and the media.

"I'll call you when I get a chance," he said. Then he mouthed the words "I love you, Mama."

I waved and then he was gone again. I didn't know when I would see him again.

19

The peace in the house is deafening and disarming for me at times. I thought this was the ultimate goal, to have a quiet home to myself so I could work on my writing again. Ebony had moved out to a condominium in Green Hills despite my many efforts to convince her to stay a little longer. The girls were teenagers, Amber was fifteen and Azura was thirteen, and they were too cute and trying to be too sexy for their own good. It's a different day and one parent can't watch out for this generation A thru Z, they have far too many means of communication that most adults can't keep up with. Nevertheless, Ebony is a grown woman and can't stand living in her mama and daddy's house with us minding all of her business on a daily basis. I can't say I blame her but to me it was all about the timing.

I was surprised when Calvin called me last week; I hadn't seen or spoken to him in over a year. He and Ebony were still married but they hadn't lived together in three years.

"Hello, Miss Evelyn," he said hesitantly, "I'm just around the corner and I was wondering if I could stop by and talk to you for a minute."

"Sure, Calvin, you're always welcome here, you're still my family."

"Is Mr. Winters around?" he asked, "I don't want to cause any problems."

"He's out in the yard as usual, son, come on in the front door."

I always liked Calvin, he was a good guy, he wanted to be a hero for his family but every time he got things running smoothly somebody pulled the power plug out on him. Then he always felt like he had to compete with Drew. I wasn't sure what this was about but some green tea might help to keep it mellow.

I had just put the tea bags in the mugs and covered them with honey when I heard the tap on the front door.

"Hey, Calvin, you look good," I said, opening the door wide to welcome him in.

"Thanks, Miss Evelyn, I'm doing a lot better."

"We can relax and talk in the den unless you want something to eat."

"No, thank you, I'm not hungry."

"All right, have a seat and I'll bring us a cup of tea."

He went in the den to sit down and I went to the kitchen. I filled the cups with hot water from the fridge and that still amazed me, hot water coming out of a refrigerator. There are truly some geniuses walking the earth who never stop thinking.

I sat down, placed the mugs on the coffee table, and pulled my feet out of my house slippers. I smiled to put him at ease, he smiled too, and I was reminded of how much Amber favored her daddy.

"How have you been, son? I know things were rough for a while, but you're looking good."

"It was real tough not knowing how I was going to keep a roof over our heads and feed my kids every time I got laid-off. I didn't mean to be tripping but I was just so mad at myself for not finishing my degree and having a secure career."

"There's no reason to blame yourself, there's no such thing as a secure career, the recession hit everybody, and it didn't matter if you had a big time degree or not."

"I went through it, Miss Evelyn, I'm not gonna lie, I lived on the street for eight months. I hustled doing day labor while I went to school at night. I graduated a year ago and I got a good job programming security cameras."

"You should be proud of yourself, Calvin. It's not easy to keep fighting when you're down."

"Maybe Ebony and I wouldn't have had to struggle so hard if I had prepared better. I took my anger out on her because I thought she rushed me to get married but I was wrong. I was the one who rushed to marry her because I didn't want to lose her to somebody else and then I ended up losing her anyway."

"It takes two to get together and two to hold it together. Marriage is not easy and Ebony may not have understood that. I'm partially to blame for that, I never let them know how hard it is to make a marriage work. It takes a lot more forgiveness than anything else."

"Well, I wanted to get your opinion or advice on some things, basically my relationship with Ebony. She has always been decent as far as me seeing the girls and when I came to pick them up about a month ago they weren't there and some things went down between us. It happened again last week. I love her and would love to have my family back; I can take care of them now. I want more than a physical thing but she doesn't talk about us getting back together. Do you know if she's serious about somebody else?"

"I'm not sure what's going on with Ebony," I answered, even though I had my suspicions. "She moved out and keeps her private life to herself. If I were you I wouldn't let anything else happen again unless she wants to go into counseling and repair the marriage. You have more to offer her than that as the girls' daddy. Then she'll have some decisions to make."

"Thanks, Miss Evelyn," he said, reaching for his mug of tea.

"I was wondering how you made it all those months on the street. How were you able to clean up and study for school? Did your family help out?"

"Most of my family was in the same shape as me. I registered with Human Services as an indigent citizen and they gave me vouchers for one meal a day at the State Kitchens. You wouldn't believe how many hungry people are out there on the street. They have State Resource facilities all over town where you wash your clothes and shower. I studied in the public library after work. Everything I owned fit in a backpack."

"I wish you would have come and let us help you."

"I knew you were helping Ebony and the girls and that was more than I had a right to ask?"

"Thank the Lord that's behind you now."

"Yes ma'am. I don't want to take all of your time; Azura told me there's a party this evening for D.J.'s graduation," he said, standing up to leave.

I slid my feet back in my house shoes and stood up to see him out. "You're welcome to come as my guest, I mean it, and we're family even if you and Ebony don't work things out."

"Not today, I don't want to cause any drama," he said, walking to the front door.

"Okay, but keep in touch," I said, patting him on the back.

"I will," he said, turning around with his hands in his pockets.

***

"Come on in, Nelson," I shouted impatiently out of the back door, "We only have an hour to meet Erica at the front of the Ivy Center."

It had gotten so Nelson spent most of his waking hours and a few napping ones out in the backyard. I don't know if he was diligently avoiding my company or doing some serious communing with nature. Most of the time when I peeped out at him, he was just gazing up into the clouds at nothing. All my life I've heard that women had emotional problems with aging but that opinion was obviously put out there by an old man in denial.

"I'll take a quick shower and be ready in no time," he said, dragging his feet as he walked through the kitchen.

"Just put on a clean shirt, you haven't done anything out there to break a sweat."

I sat down and signed the graduation card for D.J. from

"Grandmom and Grandpop with love." I slid in a gift card for $500. Nelson would have a fit if he knew how much I was giving him. He was pinching every dime like it was his last. Sure we live on a fixed income but we weren't hurting for anything. Eli had given me half of the winnings he received from the marathon two years ago to use for whatever I saw fit and this was one of those occasions. I wanted to show D.J. that we were proud of him and ready to support him in whatever he wanted to do with his life. We didn't attend the graduation ceremony, students were given only four tickets, and Erica asked if we didn't mind if Drew's parents used the tickets. Nelson was so contrary lately that I told her it was no problem.

"I don't see why Erica is going through all of this expense," Nelson complained, hesitating on each step as he made his way down the stairs into the living room. "It don't make sense, blowing good money as hard as times are."

"It's for her only child graduating from high school, she wants to celebrate. It's her money; she can spend it any way she likes. Besides she doesn't have to pay rental for the center because she's an AKA."

"The truth is the boy barely got out of high school. It's a wonder we're not going to visit him in the jailhouse."

"Leave all that negative talk right here at the door, Nelson. I don't want you to go over there and spoil this for him or Erica. You need to encourage the boy sometimes not just criticize."

"I'll drive," Nelson said, exasperated.

I pushed the button to set the house alarm, opened the car door and dropped down into the seat on the passenger side. I turned on the radio to fill the silence while he drove. Lately you could tell when it was Saturday by the number of yard sales that peppered the neighborhood selling everything from furniture and clothes to food homegrown in gardens and selling dinners. Folks without jobs had learned creative ways to keep food on the table.

Nelson pulled up into a handicapped space up in the front.

"You know we don't have handicapped tags," I said, feeling annoyed.

"What difference does it make? We're going to be the oldest ones here anyway."

"Don't say anything if you get a ticket," I said, getting out of the car. Nelson had gotten so stubborn I knew better than to waste my time arguing with him.

The accelerated Chinese water torture that these young people refer to as music met us at the front of the gathering room. Erica was already busy laying out the food on three long tables in the back while Drew was busy taking pictures. I recognized his parents sitting at a table near a movie screen across the room.

"Why don't you go and sit with Drew's folks and I'll see if Erica needs any help," I told Nelson, giving him my handbag.

"Hey, ladybug," I said, hugging her around the waist, "What do you need me to do?"

"Just relax and enjoy yourself, Mama, everything is done."

"Where's D.J.?" I asked, looking around the room.

"He's not here yet and he's not answering my calls or texts."

"Don't you still have GPS on his phone; we can go and get him if we need to."

"I don't want to have to drag my child to his own graduation party, Mama," she said, and I could hear the worry she was feeling in every word.

"I'll get Amber to call him, he'll answer her. Where is Ebony sitting?"

"Over there in the corner with her man."

I looked in the direction where Erica nodded and saw Ebony and a man sitting close at the table with Amber and Azura standing by the wall behind them. I squinted, requesting my eyes to give me a better look, and that's when I realized why Ebony had hidden him away.

"He looks like he's damn near your daddy's age, how old is he?" I asked Erica.

"I don't know, I've only met him a couple of times."

I sauntered across the room making a few stops to greet some students that were already at Holland High School before I retired. I caught Ebony's eye before I reached her table.

"Well hello, baby girl," I said, smiling, "I haven't had the pleasure of meeting your friend."

"Hey, Mama," she answered, standing up to give me a kiss on the cheek. "This is Maurice Sanders. Maurice, this is my mother, Evelyn Winters."

"Pleased to meet you, Mrs. Winters," he said, standing up to shake my hand.

"My pleasure also," I said, "Ebony mentioned you on several occasions, I'm glad we finally got a chance to meet. I'm sure we'll get to talk more later, right now I need Amber to make a call for me."

"I look forward to it," he said, smiling.

The girls were a few feet away bouncing to the monotonous beat with their phones in their hands taking pictures of each other.

"Amber, I need you to get D.J. on the phone for me real quick." She didn't respond, she just pushed a couple of buttons and his face popped up. Then she hand me her phone. "D. J. where are you?" I asked, trying to hold my temper.

"Whatsup, Grandma?" he answered with at toothy grin.

"Did you forget that your mama and daddy are having a party for you today?"

"Naw, I'll be there in a while."

"Look here, boy, if you're not here in ten minutes you won't get what I put in this envelope, and that's a promise."

When the smirk on his face straightened I handed the phone back to Amber and joined Nelson at the table with Drew's family.

"Hello Sandra and Marshall," I said, sitting across from them at the table. "It's been too long since we've gotten together. How have you been?"

"We're hanging in there," Marshall answered while Sandra smiled.

Less than ten minutes had passed when D.J. walked in the room with three of his less-than desirable friends. I could see Erica's face light up with relief from across the room. Then Drew went to the front and grabbed a wireless microphone and motioned for the volume of the music to be lowered.

"The man of the hour has finally arrived so let's get this party started," Drew said, "D.J. would you join me up here for a minute.

Erica took him by the arm and they strolled up to the front.

"We want to take this time to congratulate our son and let him know that we support and believe in him and the best is yet to come," Drew announced.

Applause spread across the room and Erica struggled to hold in her emotions when she added, "Everybody eat, drink, and shake your booty."

The room of mostly teens flooded the floor with a gush towards the tables of food. Drew's parents excused themselves and went to the front and gave D.J. a hug, handed him a card, and made a straight line to the exit. When Nelson saw that he seized the opportunity to follow right behind them.

"Evelyn, this music is giving me a headache, I'm going home. Erica or Ebony can drop you later if you want to stay."

"Yes I'm going to stay and celebrate my first grandchild's graduation from high school," I said with as much sarcasm as I could muster.

He was unfazed by my comment and ambled on out the door, stopping for only a second to say goodbye to Amber and Azura in the food line. Erica came and sat down beside me and I could see the fatigue in her rounded shoulders.

"What's the matter, honey?" I asked, rubbing her back.

"Everything is all right now that he's here. Relax and enjoy yourself."

"He's high, Mama, I can see it in his eyes."

"I don't know what to tell you, baby, you can't control these kids today. I'm thrilled that you got him out of high school with all the bad influences they have to deal with."

"That's not going to get him anywhere. He doesn't want to go to college or get any type of training; he keeps telling us he doesn't know what he wants to do with his life. Maybe if you hadn't pushed Eli so fast he might have been around to pull D.J. up with him."

"Eli is so different, I can't take credit for anything that boy has done, he came out of the womb knowing what he wanted to do. It's not over for D.J., he's only 18 years old. He's got plenty of time to get his shit together."

"He's experimenting with all kinds of drugs. I did everything I was supposed to, it doesn't make sense to me, and he is still not trying. He's just so lazy."

"It's because they're used to everything being instant. Food, phone, traveling, and money. I remember when you had to wait for water to boil."

"I know that but I can't help worrying about him."

"More than half of them don't want to work and they expect to get something for nothing. You must have forgotten that I worked with young people his age for 30 years. I've seen them change with the culture and that hip-hop mess makes them think they are going to accomplish great things just by looking good. You're not alone in this battle, all parents are worried, and I'm still worrying about you girls."

"There's so much more danger around than it was when we were coming up. Half the time when he leaves the house I don't know if I'll see him again. He's messing with those painkillers and they'll take you out of here quick, Mama."

"Has Drew talked to him?"

"Over and over and it hasn't even phased him. I wish that Eli could come home for a while, I think it would really give him another perspective. Isn't he finished with his studies in England? He's been there so long he'll probably come back with an accent."

"He's completed his work at Oxford and will be home in a few weeks. He has more job offers than he can count. I'll call him tonight and see if he can take some time off and come check on his nephew."

Erica smiled for the first time all evening and I knew what she was feeling as I watched Ebony walk over to the table to join us. It's hard to watch your children struggle and reject any help you try to give them.

"Go ahead, Mama," Ebony said, sitting across from me, "I know you have something to say."

"I'm not saying anything, I'm just surprised. I didn't know you liked older men."

"Age is just a number," she said defensively, "He's well established and he's very good to me and the girls."

"You mean you like his money," Erica chimed in.

"Calvin came to see me about a week ago," I said casually.

"So, what does that have to do with anything?" she asked, trying to appear indifferent, but the table quivering from her knee tapping against it told the real story.

"It's simply that I've seen a lot of things in my years but I hadn't heard of a woman cheating on her older boyfriend with her younger husband."

Erica laughed loud and hard, needing to release some of her own tension.

"That shouldn't have happened but I'll always have some feelings for Calvin, he was my first love and the girl's father."

"Maybe it happened because money ain't everything, sister," Erica teased.

"I'm not even going to discuss that with y'all," Ebony said, getting irritated. "I'm happy so be happy for me. I came over here to give you congrats on getting D.J. out of school."

"I'm sorry, lil sis," Erica said, "Don't be so sensitive. Nobody is judging you. Do what you have to do to get through these days."

"I intend to," Ebony said, slightly annoyed. "Anyway Maurice is ready to go and the girls want to stay longer, would you mind dropping them home when you leave?" she asked Erica.

"No problem, sis," Erica answered.

"In that case, I'm riding with you, Ebony, I want to get home and call Eli before it gets too late, they're six hours ahead of us."

***

"Hey, Mama, how was D.J.'s party. I wish I could have been there."

"The party was good, except he came late and Erica thought he was high."

"I haven't talked to him in a while, I'll ring him tonight."

"It's more serious than that, Erica thinks it would help if you came home and spent some time with him this summer."

"I don't know, Mama, I've narrowed down my options and I'm seriously considering accepting the offer at the United Nations. There is a network there where I can begin to institute philosophical changes instead of slapping band-aids on critical problems."

"I understand all that, Eli, but we haven't seen you in two years, we're your family. We love you and miss you, and we need you too."

"I need to get working as soon as I can. There are so many people who are hungry and out of work all around the world. It's reaching a breaking point. You can see on the news that governments are setting up emergency operations to deal with it as national disasters. If some provisions aren't made soon it could start revolutions all over the globe."

"I don't want to sound selfish, your commitment is something that I have always admired about you, son, and the passion that you have for helping people is important but it can't be at the expense of your own family."

"It's not just a passion of mine; it's my path, the purpose of my life. I didn't choose it, it was chosen for me. I have to follow it."

Eli has always been so headstrong in all of his decisions, not allowing anything or anyone to distract him from fulfilling his destiny, and I respected that. I knew the only way I could persuade him was to show him that it was not my wishes but based on the word of God. I was prepared for this argument.

"The bible says in first Timothy 5:8, "But if anyone does not provide for his own, and especially for those of his household, he has denied the faith and is worse than an unbeliever."

I could see the effect the words had on him as his facial expression changed and the squareness in his shoulders rounded.

"I've already talked to Elise about moving to New York and staying with her for a while until I get my own place. I need some time to get things wrapped up here and ship my stuff to Manhattan but I'll be there in less than two weeks."

"I don't mean to pressure you, baby, but it's important."

"No stress, Mama, you're right, my bad. I get caught up sometimes. I want to see everybody. I just don't know if Dad wants to see me. He might not even want me to stay there."

"This is your home too, you'll always be welcome here. Your Daddy is fine, he barks but he doesn't bite, you know that."

"I know, it's just that I didn't want things to go this way."

"It's an important lesson that you have to learn and accept, Eli, you can't control other people's reactions to what you're doing no matter how good your intentions are."

"I'm learning that, believe me, I just want some extra consideration from those who love me."

"We're only human too, baby, salt and sugar like everybody else."

"Okay, Mama, I got to finish up some papers to submit tomorrow."

"All right, I'll see you soon."

I looked in the den and Nelson was asleep on the couch. He seemed to be sleeping a lot more lately. I can't blame him though; it's one way to escape the confusion and continual problems of living life. "It's not fair," I muttered, turning to go upstairs to put my tired body to bed. "Daddy gets to clock out when his day is done, for Mama it's never done."

20

"What's up, Mama?" a voice asked behind me.

I turned around from the window where I was watching Nelson watch whatever he was watching.

"Eli, what in the world, why didn't you call me to pick you up?" I said, wrapping my arms around the child I had not seen for more than two years.

"Not necessary, I just rode the underground, it's quicker."

"You look good, baby," I said, stepping back to admire this young man in front of me, "I'm loving the mustache, it really becomes you."

"It makes me look a little older and I need a few years with the crowd I'm moving in."

"Well, I'll buy whatever you selling, my dear."

"How's Dad doing?" he asked looking out of the kitchen window.

"He's fine, that's still his favorite pastime, sitting in the yard watching the grass grow. Come on," I said, grabbing his arm, "Say hello to him."

Eli had grown another inch or two and put on about 15 or 20 pounds since I had last seen him. He had been grown-up mentally from about twelve years old and now he looked it. I felt the strength in his arm as he walked beside me across the lawn. When Nelson noticed us he shifted his weight and put his hands on the arms of the chair but he didn't stand.

"Well, well, well," Nelson said, nodding his head up and down, "I should have checked the morning news, I didn't know you were coming to town."

"Hey Dad, how's it going?" Eli asked, squatting down in the grass beside him.

"I don't have any complaints," Nelson answered.

"It's good to be home," Eli said, putting his hand on top of his on the arm of the chair, "I've missed everybody. I hadn't realized that until my plane landed."

"I know you're real busy, son, it's nice of you to stop by and see us," Nelson said, edgily.

"We would have planned something if we had known the day you were coming," I added, reaching out for Eli to take my hand, "Let's go take a ride over to your sisters' houses. Are you coming, Nelson?"

"You two go ahead, I'll be here when you get back."

Eli clenched his fists and bumped them against each other in frustration. I took his right hand in mine and swung it while we walked inside to get my handbag.

"Don't let him get to you, Eli. He loves you, he just doesn't know how to show it, and believe me he's proud of you but he's too stubborn to admit that he overreacted to the name thing."

"I understand that but we can't get the time back that we've lost and I want to get past it. I feel like it was wasted without a reason."

"Not really, son, God has given you everything you've needed to do what you have to do. Your obligations are not to your mama and daddy specifically, they're bigger than just us, and you're in a position to make a difference for millions of people in the world."

I got my bag from the end table in the living room and rummaged through it until I found my keys.

"I love you, Mama, you make all the difference for me," he said as we were walking outside to the car.

"Don't make me start crying, boy, or I won't be able to see where I'm going," I said with my emotions rising.

"Don't sweat it, I'll do the driving. You get in the passenger side, seeing as you have always been my 'ride or die' lady," he teased.

"You know what time it is," I laughed, enjoying the moment.

I was sorry that Nelson was missing out on the company of our son, but nothing I had said over the years had changed his attitude. Nelson wouldn't admit when he was wrong back when we first met and that has yet to change. When we got on the interstate I leaned back and let the window down to feel the air on my face.

"Let's go by Erica's first," he said over the old-school music on the radio, "I texted D.J. when my plane landed and said I was stopping by."

"All right, we can stop at the store near them and get some food," I added. Then I pushed the phone in the car to call Ebony.

"Hello, Mama, what's up?" Ebony asked, sounding exasperated, as if I was going to start in on her about Maurice.

"Your brother is here, we're on our way over to Erica's, we going to pick up something to eat before we get there. Why don't you come by and join the party."

"Why didn't you give me some notice, I made some plans for this evening."

"Excuse me; I didn't know that was required. Do what you want; I wouldn't want to inconvenience you, I thought the girls might want to see their uncle while he's in town."

"Stop being extra, Mama, I hear you, we'll be there," she said, giving in.

"What's that about?" Eli asked, sensing some tension.

"Some older guy with a little money has been turning Ebony's head for a while right now and it seems like she's getting serious about him."

"What about Calvin, is he ready to move on too?"

"No, I talked to him a few weeks ago and he wants them to get back together."

"I know that they had a rough time but that was the regular, half the city was looking for a decent paying job, it wasn't his fault, I like Calvin."

"She still has feelings for him too, but it's so crazy out here with most folks struggling to eat and she's scared. She wants the security that she thinks this Maurice has. Only thing, you pay a high price to live with somebody just for the finances."

"It's all over the world, Mama, people are doing desperate things to survive, and it has to change soon before we reach a state of global lawlessness. Nobody wants to go there."

"Now you're talking over my head again, I can't think past my own family's issues, much less the world. Get off at the next exit, there's a Publix store where we can make a quick stop."

"That's the point, all of our problems are the same now," he said, parking close to the front of the store, "Do you see how empty this parking lot is, the prices are too high because the environment is out of balance, perpetuated by a global economy that is out of balance."

"Eli, now I'm really worried. Is this how you talk when you take a young lady out?"

"Not all the time," he answered laughing, "Maybe that's why they don't answer when I call them back."

"Probably so," I laughed, leading the way into the store.

The situation inside reiterated what Eli had said in the car, most stores were poorly stocked because the food went bad sitting on the shelves with price tags way above what most folks can pay. It's the unemployment that's the culprit. There aren't enough jobs to go around. As soon as they can find a machine to do your job they point you to the door.

"Let's get some stuff to make tacos, I can't remember the last time I had one," Eli said.

"That's because you been in England eating all those fish and chips," I joked

He rolled the cart and I got some lettuce and tomatoes, lemons for lemonade, and then the ground beef, $8.99 a pound, it's beyond ridiculous.

"I remember when it was less than $2.00 a pound, and I was making the same money I am now."

"Don't get me started again, Mama, I'm trying to hold back."

"Okay," I said as we got the taco shells, cheese, sour cream, and picante sauce.

We scanned the groceries and the total was $58.29 for a meal of tacos. "You're right, son, the world has gone off the deep end."

He grabbed the bags in one hand and put his arm around me and said, "Don't worry, Mama, I got you covered."

***

"D.J., what up, brother," Eli hollered as soon as we got out of the car.

From the perspiration on his shirt and the smell of fresh-cut grass, Erica must have insisted he mow the lawn.

"Uh-oh, all hell must be breaking loose if you're in town," he yelled back, turning around with a big grin on his face.

"Don't play, I might be here to check your situation," Eli joked.

"Hey, baby brother," Erica said, coming out of the house and giving Eli a hug, "Glad to see you still know your way home."

"Come on, Erica, give me a pass," Eli said, smiling.

"One more since you didn't come empty-handed," she said, taking the bags out of his hands. "Sit down and catch your breath while I make something to snack on, you too, Mama."

I walked past the guys and stretched out on the chaise lounge, it was my favorite place to sit at Erica's house. It was shady in her backyard and the sound of the rushing water from the creek that ran behind it always relaxed me. I close my eyes, and when the boys thought I was asleep the conversation changed.

"I hear you're messing up D., taking pills and on the grind," Eli said, confronting him about the drugs, "What's going on with you, man?"

"You got your hustle and I got mine," D.J. answered.

"I do what I do for a reason, D. What's your reason for what you do?"

"It's the only thing I can do, I'm not like you."

"That's bullshit; you've got to up your game if you want better, D., you're just lazy as hell, that's the only difference between us."

"I'm not as smart as you, Eli."

"It's not about being smart, it's about working your ass off. Nobody's going to give you anything out here."

"I'm not asking for anything. I'm smooth right now."

"Yeah, I know, right up until they lock your ass in jail to make a slave out of you. There's nothing this country likes better than free labor, and all the knuckleheads like you who think they're going to get over give them a steady supply."

"What other options do we have?" D.J. asked, sarcastically.

"You can go to college and get your head on straight, I'll pay for it."

"That's not my thing, that's you, man."

"How do you know if you haven't been? What's so great about what you're doing?"

"I'm happy, ain't nothing worrying me but my folks."

"Don't act like you don't know why, we don't want to watch you throw your life away. You're young and strong, how about getting a job; it'll make your mama happy."

"No it won't, she expects too much. Hell, you can't even make granddad happy and your shit is straight. Let it go, uncle, I got to live my own life, right or wrong."

"I can accept that, but if you won't let anybody help you, then you need to get your own place. Don't put the bullshit in their faces."

"How about I come up to New York City with you?"

"You have to prove you can handle your business here before you go anyplace else. I can't hold your hand, you talking like you a grown man, so that's what you have to be."

"That's what I thought," D.J. said angrily.

It was taking more self-control than I thought I had to lay there with my mouth shut but this conversation was between them. I can sympathize with young people who don't have any support, but this jackass grandson of mine has help. His problem is he doesn't have a backbone. It's probably all of our faults; we barely let his feet touch the ground carrying him from the time he was born until now and we're wondering why he can't figure out how to get his shit together.

"Chow time folks," Erica called out from the back door, "Build your own tacos."

"Right on time, I'm hungry as hell," D.J. said, moving towards the door.

I opened my eyes and saw Eli sitting with his head in his hands. I leaned up and put my feet on the ground and pushed my weight onto my sore knees to stand.

"It's not your fight, Eli. D.J. is right; he's got to find his own way."

"You're the one who reminded me that I have a responsibility to my family."

"I know, son, but there are limits to what you can do. Let's eat," I said, leading the way into the house, "Your tacos are waiting for you."

Right as I was filling up my tortilla shells the room was suddenly overflowing. Drew had come down from napping and Ebony, Amber, and Azura had come in from the front.

"Elijah, what's up, big business," Drew said, welcoming Eli home with a bear hug and a pat on the back, "How you been?"

"Never better, brother," Eli answered with a smile that shone with love and respect.

When I think about it for a moment, Drew has probably been more of a father to Eli than Nelson has been. Somehow common blood complicates the relationship instead of simplifying it.

"Hey, baby brother," Ebony said, kissing him on the cheek, "We miss you around here."

"I miss you all too," Eli said, grinning.

"I see you brought your appetite home with you," Drew said, taking notice of his heaping plate of tacos.

"I can't help myself; you don't get homemade food unless you're at home, man. I need you to fire up that grill before I go back to New York," Eli replied.

"Just say when, you're the one flying all over the place like you have wings on your feet."

"I'll be around a few days, and are these two gorgeous ladies my little nieces?" he joked, putting down his food to give Amber and Azura both side hugs. "I might need to move back and help Calvin keep all the dogs off of the doorstep."

"Don't worry, I've got it under control," Ebony said. "The only contact they have with the young dudes around here is verbal; my girls are strictly college material."

Both the girls roll their eyes with no comment. Ebony should know better than anybody that mamas don't have the control they think they have.

"Where's Maurice?" I asked, squeezing into the space beside her while she spooned up the seasoned ground beef. "Did he decide not to come with you?"

"Do you want Drew to call Calvin?" Erica asked, teasing her.

"You all need to stop with the drama," Ebony fussed, getting annoyed.

"We're all family here," D.J. added, "They put me on blast already. Why don't we go around the room and let everybody get a chance before the firing squad, ain't no babies in here."

"I don't mind," Erica said, "As long as we keep it PG13 for Azura."

"I'm game," Amber said, "And since I'm not going to hold back I volunteer to be next."

"All right, Amber," I said, "I'll start. You are a pretty girl, smart, and confident, so I don't understand why you have to wear all those "hoochie-come-and-get-me" outfits that show everything you got and so much make-up?"

"Oh yeah, right on time, Mama," Erica said, co-signing the point.

"I've got a nice body, why shouldn't I flaunt it, anyway it's the style. I'm not the only one dressing like this. All my friends wear the same stuff."

"From a man's point-of-view, I think you are selling yourself short. With all you have to offer you don't have to show your behind," Drew said. "That's for the chickenheads."

"I'm next," Azura said, standing up.

"You can watch your outfits too, young lady," I said.

"You can also exist without headphones in your ears 24/7," Erica said, "You can't hear what's going on around you listening to music or talking on the phone every minute."

"Excuse me,"Azura remarked, getting in a huff, "It's not like you all talk to me anyway, nobody pays me any attention."

"You have to give some to get some," Ebony added.

"Even from my mama?" Azura asked, returning the jab to Ebony as she sat down.

"Who's next," D.J. asked, rubbing his hands together, "We should have played this a long time ago.

"I'm next," Drew said, volunteering.

"Oh yeah," Erica cheered, "I'm ready for you."

"Bring it on, baby," he grinned.

"Okay, you are an easy-going guy and I like that about you but I don't think you can be that way raising a son," Erica said, "I think you have been way too easy on D.J."

"That's not it, Mama," D.J. objected, "You might as well stand up too. Neither of you ever bothered to ask me what I wanted to do nor what I'm interested in. Just because you both are teachers doesn't mean I want to be a teacher."

"Why don't you stand up and tell us what you want to do," I interjected, "I'm sure we are all interested."

"As a matter of fact I want to work outside in the air where I can breathe, I wouldn't mind being in construction or something like that."

"Well, thanks for the revelation," Erica said, throwing her hands in the air, "Now can you handle that Drew?"

"Not a problem," Drew answered, "I got you D.J."

"Now who's next," Amber yelled out, "How about you Grandmama?"

"I don't mind," I said, standing on my feet.

"The only thing I have to say to you, Mama, is that you didn't make Daddy get up off of his behind and come over here with you," Erica said. "He acts like a kid whose mama told him he can't go out of the yard."

"That is right," Ebony added, "Y'all acted like your lives were on hold for us, that you were making that sacrifice for us, now that both of you are retired y'all don't do anything but hang around the house or get in other folks business."

"I gave up trying to tell your daddy what to do before any of you were born, that's the reason I don't have high blood pressure and sleep well at night," I told them. "As for me, I'm ready to do my thing and I plan on spending some time in New York with Elise later in the year."

"Your time is up on the hot seat, Mama, I'll take your place," Eli said, "Most of Dad's mood is because of me and my decisions."

"Oh yeah, Uncle E, it's about time you got blasted," D.J. urged, "We are tired of always having to hear about you and what you're doing, how good your grades were, and how you're going to make a difference. Do you realize how much pressure you put on us?"

"Say it again, D.J.," Amber cheered, "We can't all be the chosen one."

Then Ebony stood up for emphasis and complained, "My thing

is that your concern is always on the condition of the rest of the world. Who's suffering out there, who doesn't have an opportunity, and who's struggling over there? In the meantime, your own family was struggling. Why haven't you used your power and influence to make our lives better?"

"I feel bad about what went down between you and Calvin but my focus is not my own, I have to do what I am led to do," Eli said in his defense.

"I respect that but things got so bad for us that I couldn't even put food on the table for your nieces. Why couldn't you have worked some of your magic and at least gotten Calvin a decent job," Ebony said, venting her frustrations on him.

I had heard enough. "Now that you've purged your soul of any responsibility for your own circumstances I think it's your turn, Ebony."

"Bring it on, I'm at peace with my shit, my conscience is clear," Ebony huffed.

"Yours maybe, but somebody else's isn't," Azura added, implying some impropriety.

"What's that supposed to mean?" Ebony asked irately.

"She means Maurice is not right," Amber insisted. "You tell us how to act and dress and then you bring some shady guy in our house to gawk at us every chance he gets."

"Oh hell no," Erica shouted.

"That's not true," Ebony said, beyond furious.

"Trust and know, Mama," Amber said, "We knew you were going to react like this, that's why we didn't tell you."

"You need to squash that immediately, Ebony, before I end up in jail over some bullshit," Drew threatened, "It's not going to work."

"The girls are probably saying that because they don't like him," Ebony protested.

"It doesn't even matter, baby, we can't take a chance that any of it is true," I told her.

"Who do you think you're fooling, Ebony?" Erica said, "You

know you don't even want that man. While you're trying to get his money, he's got a plan too."

"Old Maurice likes them young, auntie," D.J. joked, "You're younger but not young enough."

"That's enough for me, I'm done with this frigging game," Ebony said, worn out. "I'm leaving; I shouldn't have even come over here."

Ebony threw her plate of half-eaten tacos in the kitchen sink and the clang of the glass against stainless steel stunned us all into silence. The next sound we heard was the back door slamming behind her, then the car speeding away with Amber and Azura still sitting at the table. I felt the anguish of her dilemma but I had no regrets for what happened. I hoped she knew that any intentions of her tying herself to Maurice's wallet were out of the question.

"I didn't know y'all were going to take it there," D.J. said, shaking his head. "That was deep. I thought we were having a nice family get-together."

"Obviously we had some issues we needed to address," Drew said.

Erica started clearing the table without a word. I was sure she wanted the smoke to clear before Drew got more heated.

"She needs some time and space to cool off," I said to smooth over the upset. "You girls can come home with me for a while."

"That means I get a chance to take my nieces to a movie," Eli said, smiling.

I sat in the back seat thinking about my children and grandchildren. From what we experienced today I can only say there is no such thing as a steady state. Whenever you have the nerve to think that you have solved a pressing problem, trust and believe that there is another one moving in to take its place.

***

"Are you sure I can't drive you to the airport, baby?" I asked Eli, "I want to see you off."

"No, Mama, I only have one bag. I'll take the Metroline, it

goes right inside the airport. Besides security won't allow you to go further," he answered as he typed something into his hand-held personal assistant.

"Well, anyway, it was good to have you home for a while; I'm going to miss you."

"I'm going to miss you too but I'll see you in a few months when you come up to New York," he said, giving me a tight hug.

"I'm so excited for you starting your new post, Eli. I can't believe my son was appointed as Assistant Secretary General of the Program Planning, Budget and Finance, and Controller Committee of the United Nations."

"I'm eager to get working, Mama. Finally I'm in the position where I can truly make a difference. It won't be easy by any means, yet, there are no other options."

"If anybody can make it work, it's you, baby, I have every confidence in you. The word failure is not in the language we speak."

"It never has and never will be," he said confidently.

"I don't want to start bawling so let's get you on the road. Did you tell your Daddy goodbye?"

"Not yet, I was going to do it on my way out."

Nelson was in his usual spot in the yard. Once again he had made no effort to spend any quality time with Eli. At dinner, he came to the table and ate in silence. When Eli tried to make conversation he gave him short answers that bordered on rude. I couldn't help but wonder if he even recollected why he was acting in that manner. I trailed Eli over near the weeping willow where Nelson regularly camped.

"Dad, I'm on my way to the airport, I wanted to say goodbye and that I love you," Eli said, standing in front of his chair.

"All right, son, take care of yourself and keep in touch with your mama."

"Definitely, Dad, I promise you that."

There was a lull and then all of a sudden Eli knelt down and put his arms around his daddy and leaned his head against his chest. When Nelson wrapped his arms around him and kissed him on the top of his head, I felt a sense of vertigo. I reached in the air around me for something to support me but there was nothing there. I moved my feet apart to regain my balance. I was overwhelmed; blissful is the only word that can describe what I felt to see them embrace. It was a beautiful and meaningful moment. More than a minute passed and when Eli stood up I could see the wet spot that the release of his tears had left on Nelson's shirt. I ordered my feet to get closer and took his hand in mine.

We had turned to leave and were walking away when Nelson called out, "I love you too, Elijah," using the full length of his first name. "Remember, son, we're here for you. You're not alone even though sometimes it might seem that way."

We both stopped in our tracks, I was overjoyed but at the same time bowled over with the whole scene. What had brought this on?

Eli turned back around and said, "I know that, Dad, as well as I know my own name, Elijah Newman Winters."

21

Things were getting back to a steady state level as the heat of the summer gave way to the fall. The family venting session had been a huge success. In less than ninety days, Maurice had been given his walking papers, Drew had helped D.J. find a job working with a construction company as an apprentice, and Nelson and I were on better terms than we had been on in decades. Every now and then I couldn't help but sit across from him at the dining table and wonder what had brought about the abrupt change; then again it wasn't important, I was just grateful he had finally come to his senses.

Things were in fast-forward mode for Eli for the next five years. He had taken off running in his new position. Water had become a valuable commodity and competition for unpolluted areas had created a rift between farmers and fisherman. The fish population had to be protected but farmers needed more water for the growing demand of crops. Eli used his international influence through a forum of nations and private businesses to broker a compromise between the two entities. After that achievement he was given more authority and he went on to implement a program of geoengineering to reverse the damaging effects of carbon emissions around the world. It included artificial trees and fertilization of the ocean to foster cooler temperatures in the ocean and reverse the melting of glaciers on the ends of the earth. It was an enormous accomplishment to be able to unite the scientific community, international corporations, and world leaders in the fight for global preservation.

His skills as a negotiator didn't go unnoticed and had led to his nomination for the vacant post as Secretary-General of the United Nations by the United Nations Security council. There were many objections because his age and limited experience but his ability to obtain results was undeniable. The last of the baby boomers were dying out and the young people were running things we had to wait a lifetime to take charge over. I wasn't hating though, I hope they can do a better job than the old folks did. At least they have youth on their side to climb the mountains of bad decisions and mistakes that have been made.

I refused to move after I heard the announcement on the news; I knew Eli would be calling.

"Mama, where's Dad? I have fantastic news," Eli said elatedly, speaking from the TV screen in the den where I sat after dinner.

"You know he's in his spot out in the yard. I saw the news on the web," I responded to his smiling face on the screen. "You've earned all the success, congratulations, baby."

"This is where the hard work begins. If my confirmation goes unchallenged I will begin my term on January 1st. In the acceptance speech I'm going to announce policy changes that are going to be unpopular among the powers brokers so don't be alarmed by the firestorm."

"I'm not worried about that, when you're unpopular that pretty much means you're doing something right. Besides I plan to be there to hear you speak."

"It will be all that if you and dad could come to New York."

"That's the plan, baby. I'll tell him you called. I'll make the arrangements with Elise."

"Let me know if you need any money for the tickets."

"We're fine, Eli. You just concentrate on what you have in front of you."

"Thanks, Mama, I love you."

I was in awe of all the things that Eli was able to achieve in such a short time. He had followed the map he had drawn out for me when he was a young boy and even though I knew his life was pre-ordained it was amazing to see the events unfold. Why was I so blessed to observe this miracle so closely, I hadn't done anything to deserve it? I grabbed my sweater from the back of the sofa and went out to tell Nelson the news.

"Have you been listening to the news," I asked loudly, seeing Nelson had earphones connected to wrist phone.

He nodded yes with a strange expression on his face. I used my hand to shield my eyes from the bright sun setting behind him so I could look at him closer.

"Eli called, he wanted to give you the news about his nomination," I said, looking for some type of reaction. He just nodded again.

I wasn't about to let him spoil my mood. I tightened my sweater around me against the chilled air and went back inside. I dug my journal out of the end table where I kept it and started to write. I wrote about how no matter how much I had been determined to live my own life it had been centered on my children and my husband. My life had been restricted. I hadn't explored the planet as an astronaut; I hadn't delved deep near the oceans floor as a marine geologist. I hadn't climbed Mount Everest; I hadn't crossed the desert or sky-dived from a plane. I had lived more than the three-score-and-ten years and even with some things beyond my scope I knew there was more of this life for me to live.

Thunder rolled over the house and I turned to see the first drops of rain hit the patio door. Through the blinds I shook my head at Nelson's stubbornness, he hadn't moved. What was he trying to prove? I watched him sit in the twilight with the rain falling around him until I couldn't take it anymore. This didn't make any sense. I went to the foyer closet, put on my raincoat, picked up an umbrella, and snatched down his London Fog coat.

"If you refuse to come in out of the rain, at least have the sense to cover yourself," I said, thrusting the coat and umbrella towards him.

"Thank you, Evelyn," he responded nonchalantly, taking the coat and umbrella, "I'm fine, the rain doesn't bother me."

"It's not the rain you need to worry about, Nelson, its freezing out here. I'm not going to be nursing you when you catch a cold."

"I'm on my way in," he said.

I stood there in front of him waiting but he kept sitting there looking past me like it wasn't even raining. I bent my knees slightly in an effort to make eye contact but he had dismissed my presence. I went in the house, hung up my raincoat, made myself a cup of tea, and went upstairs to watch TV in bed. I couldn't make any sense of what was going on in my own house so I might as well tune in to someone else's.

Nelson woke me up when he eased into the bed; I must have fallen asleep with the TV on. I pressed the info button on the remote and the time was 3:04. The bed rapidly turned cold as the length of his chilled body absorbed the heat from mine.

"Nelson, you feel like ice. Why don't you take a quick hot shower to warm up?" I suggested, tightening the blankets around me.

"It'll get me wide awake and I won't be able to sleep," he commented.

I lay in there in the quiet beside him and I can feel the small tremors in the bed as his body shivered trying to generate its own body heat.

"I don't think either of us will get any sleep like this," I complained, reaching for my robe at the foot of the bed, "I'll make you some hot chocolate."

In the kitchen my mind drifts as I wait for the bubbles to appear around the edges of the milk in the small pan. There is always some tension underneath my life and I can feel it rising to the surface just like the heat under this pot. Where is it going to pop up this time? I talked to Elise a few days ago and she was doing great, practically running the firm. Erica and Drew are fine since D.J. got a job; Ebony finally got rid of Maurice and the girls are happy, so the family should all be good. Maybe it's Eli who has me feeling on edge. I know he's going to come into some strong opposition; the last thing that the most powerful people of the world want is change.

The sound of the milk searing in the pan brought my attention back to the task at hand. I poured the milk in a mug and added the chocolate syrup. Swirling the mixtures together and watching them merge and disappear bothers me for some reason and I can't imagine why. It must be time to get away and take a vacation, I'm stressing out over nothing.

I sit down on Nelson's side of the bed and watch him slurp down the hot chocolate.

"That did the trick, Evelyn, thank you, honey," he said as he pulled the comforter around his shoulders and drew his legs up into a mound.

I slid in close to him to share my warmth but every now and then I could feel him shudder when a chill ran through him. He woke me up the next morning with a loud sneeze.

"I told you to come in out of the rain," I said, throwing over the blanket to get up, "I don't know why you have to be so hard-headed about everything, Nelson."

"You're right, honey, but I wasn't trying to ignore you. I was just mad at myself."

"Mad about what?" I asked, confused, totally in dark about what he was talking about.

"Mad about getting old I guess, the choices I've made, and the things I've done."

"That doesn't make any sense, name me one person who's not getting old or wishing they would have done something different. Remember that old song by Phoebe Snow, "No Regrets," sing that and keep moving."

"That's not what I mean, Evelyn. I got old without doing something meaningful with my life. I don't have a legacy."

"Now you're just talking stupid, you've successfully raised four children during some rough years. That is a legacy, and it's as meaningful as it gets, my darling."

"What would I do without you, honey," he said looking at me with puppy dog eyes.

"You are about to find out, my love, because I'm not staying in here with you. I have no intentions of catching whatever germs you brought in here with you last night."

"Okay, sweetheart," he said with a chuckle that turned into a cough.

I made Nelson some thin oatmeal and a soft boiled egg for breakfast. Oddly, I didn't have an appetite; I ate a piece of toast and jelly with a cup of milk. It was days like this that I missed the structure and predictability of going to work. I didn't want to hear anything negative so I refused to turn on the TV. Being at loose ends was unnerving. I had to get out of the house. I went upstairs to check on Nelson before I left and I could hear his snoring from the top of the stairs.

Inside the car, I pushed Erica's name on the touch screen.

"Hey Mama," she answered, "What's going on?"

"I'm on my way to the store, your daddy sat out in the rain last night and caught a cold, I'm going to Walgreens to get him some Nyquil or something."

"That's what he gets, maybe now he'll stop sitting out there like he's homeless."

"Leave him alone, he's going through some things. I think he's feeling sorry for how he acted about Eli and the name thing."

"Well, it took him long enough."

"He's stubborn but he means well."

"That trait skipped me and I'm not mad, but Ebony is Dad made over. She's been acting funny towards me ever since

Amber and Azura 'outed' Maurice. I thought she would have been glad to find out the truth about his perverted ass but I think she's still feeling some kind of way behind it."

"She'll come around, she had pinned her hopes on that man."

"I'll call and talk to her when I get home."

"Okay, Mama, let me know if y'all need anything."

It was a pretty day; the sun was shining high after the rain last night even though the temperature hovered just about 50 degrees. After my stop at the store I felt like driving by the school. I didn't want to go in, I didn't know what I was longing for, I just wanted to be there for a few minutes and reminisce. I thought about all the advice and direction I had given my students over the years. Sitting in the car watching the movement through the windows I knew it wasn't near enough to prepare them as they went on with their lives. There's nothing that can prepare you for the challenges of this life, not even for me at seventy-seven years old.

The light flashes on the dashboard, its Nelson calling.

"What do you need?" I answered half-joking.

"I'm aching all over," he said between hacking coughs, "I'm still cold."

"I'll bet you're running a fever. I got you something to take. I'll be home in a minute."

Nelson had a temperature of 103 degrees when I got home. I gave him a dose of Nyquil and a cough drop to soothe his throat.

"Thanks, honey," he said hoarsely.

"I'm going downstairs to make you a bowl of soup," I said.

"I don't feel much like eating," he said, turning over.

"You're going to need something in your system to fight this cold," I said, feeling his head and rubbing him on his back.

***

Thirty minutes later I came back carrying a tray with chicken soup, tea with lemon, and saltine crackers. Nelson lay there sprawled across the bed with the covers thrown back; his pajamas and the sheets were soaked with perspiration.

He looked over at the tray with steam rising from the bowl and the cup and said, "I don't want anything hot, I'm burning up."

"The fever must have broken, I'll take your temperature," I said, setting the tray down on the dresser. His temperature was close to normal, just above 99 degrees. "Sit over in the chair while I change the sheets and then I'll get you some clean pajamas."

I got a sheet set out of the linen closet and proceeded to change the bed.

"Thanks for putting up with me and taking care of me, Evelyn honey," he said sweetly, "I know I can be a pain in the ass sometimes."

"Don't start getting sentimental on me at this late stage," I said, throwing the folded sheet in the air to straighten it. "You are the salt and pepper in my life, without you everything would be bland and boring, you're my flavor, baby."

"Then I have to say you're my sugar, it's been my treat to share my life with you."

"Stop talking like you're going to die, Nelson, you just have a cold."

"Well, hurry up with the bed; I'm catching another chill sitting over here."

"Now that's more like it," I said, fluffing up the last of the pillows. "Get back in the bed and stop all that complaining."

With Nelson comfortable and back in bed I turned on the TV. I needed something else to focus my attention on. The change in his demeanor and disposition since Eli had left was worrisome at times. Most of it was probably him thinking about his own mortality as he got older, still, I hated it. I think it's morbid to dwell on the past as if you don't have a future. I was about to make something for dinner when I realized that I hadn't called Ebony.

I grabbed the remote, pressed phone, and then the number three for her number.

"Hey Mama," she answered and her face appeared on the screen.

"Hello, baby girl, how are things going?"

"I'm living my life, what's up?"

"I haven't talked to you in a while and I wanted to check on you and the girls."

"We're fine, no worries," she said offhandedly.

"That's good, but you could show some concern about somebody other than yourself sometime. You could check on me and your daddy too."

"You look all right to me. Where's Daddy, outside guarding the house as usual?"

"No, he isn't. He's upstairs in bed with a bad cold. Maybe you should come by and see about him. You act like you live in another state."

"Okay, enough said, I'll be there tomorrow," she said before her face blinked out.

I put some fish in the oven to bake and made some mashed potatoes and peas. It wouldn't take much chewing and it would be more substantial than soup to eat. I poured him a glass of orange juice for extra vitamin C. I loaded up the tray and climbed the stairs. From the doorway I could only see the top of his head from the mass of twisted blankets.

"I brought you some dinner," I called out, "How are you feeling?"

"My stomach is upset, I don't think I can eat," he answered from beneath the pile.

"Your fever may be back, it's time to take another dose of medicine," I said, setting down the tray and reaching for the thermometer.

The reading was 105 degrees. I filled the small medicine cup up with a full dose. I sat down in his lay-z-boy and picked over the food. I had lost my appetite but I figured I better take care of myself so I could take care of him.

We spent the rest of the evening and the night repeating the scene, the fever breaking, changing into dry clothes, the fever rising, and more medicine. By the time the sun rose the next morning I was worn out and I didn't think I could continue on my own anymore, and the persistent fever was troubling me. This was more than a cold, it was probably the flu.

I sat on the edge of the bed beside Nelson and asked, "How are feeling?"

"Not one of my best days," he answered slowly.

"Here, drink some water; with all of this sweating you need plenty of fluids in you."

He leaned forward on his side and took two small sips. He paused and I patiently waited for him to drink a bit more. Then the water gushed up from his throat as if he had choked on it.

"I can't keep it down, my stomach is too upset," he muttered as he collapsed back on the bed.

"You can't lay here and get dehydrated; I think we need to get you to emergency where they can give you some fluids, Nelson. You might have the flu."

"Let's give it another day, honey, I just need some rest."

"Uh-uh, I can't take another night of watching you with this fever; we are going out of here," I told him forcefully. "Now do you have enough strength to get in the car or do I need to call an ambulance to come pick you up?"

"I can make it," he replied halfheartedly.

I got his thick forest green velour robe out of the closet that Elise gave him for Christmas last year to wear to the hospital; it still had the Ralph Lauren tag hanging from the sleeve. He hadn't even worn it yet. Once he was wrapped up warm I slid his fleece-lined slippers on his feet. It took us practically ten minutes to get downstairs. He was so light-headed that he had to lean against the wall after each step.

"Sit here in the living room, I'll pull the car around to the front," I said, easing him down into a chair.

I put on a heavy jacket, pushed my phone into my bra, threw my handbag over my shoulder, and locked the backdoor on my way out. I drove the car onto the grass to get as close to the door as possible. When Nelson didn't make an ugly comment about the lawn on the way out I knew he was really sick. I could feel his weight more heavily as the effort to get out of bed, down the steps, and into the car had drained whatever energy he had.

I clicked on my emergency signals but I kept a slow and steady pace, drifting through stop signs and pushing through traffic lights as they turned red. Once I got on to 28th Avenue it was a straight shot to Centennial Medical. One eye was fixed on the road and the other was on Nelson. I had never seen him look so powerless in all the years I had known him. His back, always broad and straight seemed small and curved. In his discomfort I could see the age in his face. It almost made me want to break down and cry.

Finally we were outside the emergency room. I parked in a handicap space right outside the entrance door.

"Wait here, honey bear; I'm going to get a wheel chair."

The hysteria that I had been holding in for the whole car ride jumped out the moment I was inside and out of Nelson's presence.

"Please, somebody, I need some help, my husband is outside sick," I yelled frantically from the middle of the floor in the waiting area.

A young man in light blue scrubs and rubber shoes behind a glass door stood up and said something to another man beside him. He pushed a wheel chair in front of him and came out to speak with me.

"He's out here," I said, leading the way.

Nelson was barely conscious when we got to him. His eyes rolled up into his head and then back down again.

"What's been going on with him," the young man asked as he lifted Nelson into the chair.

I closed the car door and said, "It started out like a cold on the day before yesterday, then it got worse, he's been running a fever and he can't keep anything down on his stomach."

The young man wheeled him back into a large room where the beds were separated by curtains. A woman wearing a white jacket helped him lift Nelson onto the bed. They begin to talk to him as they took all of his vitals. One of them starting to pull the curtain around the bed, then a heavyset woman tugged at my elbow.

"I need to get some information from you," she said as she pulled a small keyboard and monitor on wheels.

We set down in the row of chairs against other rooms with glass walls. She asked me my husband's name, his age, his insurance company, his health history, and what brought us to the emergency. I listened to my voice like a bystander as I gave her all of the information.

"They'll be right with you," she said, smiling. "You can sit here."

"Thank you," I replied as she rolled away with her computer on wheels.

I took a deep breath to clear my head. I reached into my shirt to get my phone. It was moist with sweat. Then I remembered that I hadn't showered since yesterday morning and I was wearing the same clothes from then also. I hadn't even gone to bed last night. I pushed the number two, the code for Erica.

"Good morning, Mama, what's the word?" she asked, knowing I rarely called her at work unless it was important.

"I didn't want to bother you at work but your daddy kept running that fever and he was getting dehydrated so I brought him to the hospital this morning."

"O Lord, why didn't you call me last night or before you left," she said, getting upset, "I would have come and gone with you."

Chapter Twenty-One

"It seemed like just a cold at first but then it got too much."

"Are you at Centennial?"

"Yes we are."

"I'm on my way," she said.

I decided to wait until after I talked to the doctor before I called Ebony, Elise, or Eli. It shouldn't be that serious. I'm probably on edge because I didn't get any sleep last night. I rest my head against the glass wall behind me. I needed to close my eyes for a second.

"Mrs. Winters," a voice called out.

"Yes," I answered, rising to my feet.

It was a man wearing a long white coat over a shirt and tie. He was around my height when I stood in front of him. His hair was combed over to one side to cover the thinning top. I stared through his thick glasses to see his eyes.

"I'm Dr. Sherman," he said with his hand out to greet me. "Your husband is very ill; we are transferring him up into the Respiratory Intensive Care Unit."

While he's talking the curtain around Nelson is opened and I can see he's connected to an IV drip and has an oxygen mask on.

"Does he have the flu?" I asked, stepping aside of Dr. Sherman.

"No, Mrs. Winters, he has pneumonia. We've already started administering antibiotics and we're increasing the flow of oxygen in his blood."

"I'm going with him," I said when I saw the bed Nelson lay in begin to roll.

On the elevator Nelson's eyes are closed so I grasp his hand to let him know I'm there. I can feel his fingers curl around mine. When the elevator door opens his hand slips away as the patient transporters pull ahead of me. They move through double doors that say 'Do Not Enter.'

I grappled against my first instinct to ignore the sign and proceed right behind them. There was an information desk just on my left.

"Pardon me," I said, approaching a woman sitting there, "My husband was brought up here from the emergency room. Where's the door where I can go in and see him?"

"May I have his name?" she asked politely.

"His name is Nelson Winters."

She touched the screen in front of her four times before she responded.

"You can enter the RICU on the other side of the corridor. Visiting hours in the critical unit are from 11:00 am to 1:00 pm and from 3:00 to 7:00 in the evening. There is a waiting area for family straight ahead; you're welcome to stay in there at any time of the day or night."

I looked at my watch and it was close to 10:00, more than an hour before visiting time.

"I need to speak with my husband for just a minute; I promise I won't stay for long," I said, pleading with her.

"Let me check if Mr. Winters is situated in his room first. You can go in for a minute if the doctor is not with him," she said, standing and moving to the 'Do Not Enter' door.

"Thank you so much," I said, stretching my neck to get a glimpse inside before the door closed silently behind her.

She came back out shortly. "You can go in for a little while, he's in room 1004," she whispered, "Make sure that your cell phone is turned off."

I eased through the doors quietly; moving slow and trying to be invisible as I pushed open the door that had Nelson Winters written in black marker on a white board. It occurred to me that he had never been in the hospital as a patient since we had been together. The sight of him laying there in the bed was traumatic, suddenly I felt like I needed an oxygen mask for myself.

I touched the side of his face with the back of my hand. "Nelson," I said in a low voice, "How do you feel?"

He opened his eyes and lifted his arm to remove the oxygen mask from his face. "I'm fine, Evelyn. I don't want you worrying about me," he answered, straining to speak.

"The doctors say you have pneumonia, it's more serious than we thought."

He nodded his head and said, "It's all right."

"This is scaring me, honey bear. I'm going to call Eli; he can take care of you."

"I don't want you to call him. Let it be," he uttered weakly.

"Don't be stubborn, man, he can fix everything, let him do that for you."

"I'm an old man, Evelyn, there's nothing else for me in this life."

"That's not true, I need you, Nelson."

"You'll be fine, honey, I need some peace right now."

"The children need you."

"Let me rest, baby. When it's your time, I'll be back to get you."

Nelson started breathing fast as if he was struggling for air and one of the monitors began to beep. Two people burst into the door, it was Dr. Sherman and a nurse.

"Would you wait outside, Mrs. Winters," the nurse said, guiding me out of the door.

What is going on with Nelson? How did we get here? Two days ago everything was fine. I started to feel dizzy standing there with my world turning upside down.

"Mama, where's Daddy?" I heard Erica call out urgently as she hurried towards me. "Why didn't you answer your phone, I've been trying to call you."

"He's in there, he's having trouble breathing," I answered, pointing as his door.

"What's going on, what have the doctors told you?"

"They say he has pneumonia. I don't think he wants to get

better. He told me he's tired," I said, feeling like I was about to faint.

"Mama, you're not making sense, come and sit down in the waiting area," she said, pulling me by the arm. "I'll find out what's going on. What's his doctor's name?"

"Dr. Sherman," I said, falling into a chair.

Erica left the room like it was on fire. I bowed my head to pray but I was disorientated. I couldn't find the words to speak my heart. Nelson's words kept echoing in my mind. Silently I repeated the Lord's Prayer over and over to myself until Erica came back.

"I talked to the doctor and he said Daddy is unconscious and his condition is critical. Have you called Ebony yet?" she asked softly.

I shook my head no.

"I'll call her and then I'll call Elise and Eli, they all need to be here."

I nodded my head yes.

I sat there on her left side and watched Erica bury her panic and calmly call Ebony. This child had been my right hand more times than I could count. I could hear Ebony cry out with fear as her sister urged her to pull herself together and get Azura out of school and Amber from her class at TSU and hurry to the hospital. Elise was at work but she promised to be on the next plane. Eli's phone went to voicemail; he was probably in a meeting. Erica left a message holding her phone so he could see the both of us. I know I looked pitiful, Erica did it to put the fear of God in him and emphasize that this was a family emergency. Then she called Drew at his school and told him what was going on, that she needed him to be there, and to try and bring D.J. with him. Her last call was to Calvin.

"Mama, do you need anything, are you hungry?" she asked, putting her arm around me.

"No, I'm fine," I answered. "I'm just wondering why you're

acting like your daddy is about to die?"

"I'm just trying to get everybody here; we have to be here to support Daddy. The doctor said that so far he's not responding that well to the antibiotics, they feel like he isn't fighting. If we can all rally around him I know he'll pull through this."

"I'm sorry, I didn't mean to lash out at you, I'm flustered right now. This is all so unexpected."

"I know, Mama. Don't worry."

I listened to her call Drew back and tell him to bring me some food and coffee. Then she called Ebony back and told her to bring me some clean clothes. I didn't know how to tell her thank you or how much that meant to me. I leaned my head down on her shoulder and hoped she could hear my thoughts. Her legs started to bounce with nervousness as we waited impatiently for visiting hours to begin. Finally it was 11:00 and the green light by the sign on the door lit up.

I led the way to Nelson's room, 1004, with Erica close behind. She opened the door and I went in first. The oxygen mask was gone; there were tubes in his nose. I stood on one side of the bed closest to the door and she walked around to the other.

"Hey there, honey bear," I said, rubbing the thin spot of hair on the top of his head.

"Wake up, Daddy," Erica said firmly as she shook his arm without the IV in it.

He moved at the sound of our voices and slowly his eyes opened slightly. "Hey, sweetie," he said with a weak smile, looking at Erica.

"Daddy what are you doing laying up here in the hospital working my nerves, my class is probably out of control by now," she said, smiling back at him.

"I'm okay," he said, not taking his eyes off of her.

"You better be," she said, "I've called Ebony, Elise, and Eli. I know you don't want all of us to gang up on you."

He kept looking at her and shook his head slightly to say no. I didn't hear the door open but I saw the extra light fill the room for a moment. It was Ebony. She came beside me, took my hand, and squeezed it tight in her fist while she talked.

"Daddy, are you feeling better?" she said, leaning close to him, "I was so scared I almost killed myself trying to get here."

"You didn't have to rush here, I'm all right, baby girl," he said softly.

"Yes, I did," she said, starting to cry. "I want you to know how much I love you and how much I need you so you won't leave me."

Nelson closed his eyes and drifted off to sleep. Ebony covered her mouth to contain her emotions but her tears flowed freely.

"He's doing better, Ebony," I said, trying to console her. "He's breathing a lot easier than he was before."

Erica could sense that Ebony was a few seconds from getting hysterical. She came around the bed and gave her a hug. "Are Amber and Azura here too?" she asked quietly.

Ebony nodded yes.

"Let's go out and check on them."

Inside the waiting room, there was another emotional scene, Calvin was there sitting between the girls, and they were all in tears.

22

Erica forced me to wash my face, change my clothes, and put some food on my stomach during the break between visiting hours. I was glad Calvin came, and I could see Ebony was just as happy as the girls were to see him. Drew and D.J. had gotten there too, but they left to pick up Elise and Eli from the airport. Dr. Sherman had explained Nelson's condition to us, he said they were doing everything they can, and we would have to wait while Nelson fought the infection. If Eli wasn't on his way here I would have been sick enough with worry that I probably would have been admitted as a patient myself.

My hope walked towards me when Eli got off the elevator with Elise, Drew, and D.J. We held hands in a circle and I said a prayer. As the visiting time got closer we decided that only two of us would go in at a time. Elise and Drew went in first. We all sat in silence for the whole fifteen minutes they were in there. I held my breath when they walked out of the ICU.

"Was he conscious?" Erica asked hesitantly.

"Yeah, he was," Elise answered. "He was glad to see me, except he didn't want to talk about getting well; he only wanted to reminisce about when we were little."

"He knows I'm not having that, I want him to concentrate on getting out of here," Erica said, "Come on D.J., it's our turn."

Erica walked through the door and like she was the Chief of Staff and D.J. trailed her. After a few minutes D.J. came out with his eyes bigger than saucers.

"I ain't never seen Grandpop looking like that," he said, sitting beside Drew. "He don't look like he just got here. He looks like he's been sick for a long time."

"This came down on him like a ton of bricks," I said, "He's strong though and he'll bounce back once the antibiotics take hold."

When Erica came out she didn't have much to say. Ebony and Amber went in and they weren't in there for five minutes. I'm sure Ebony didn't want Amber to see her lose it. I saw Azura telling Calvin she didn't want to go in when she saw Amber's face but he whispered something in her ear and she went in leaning on his right side. Watching them all go in and come out despondent was weakening my resolve and chipping away at the hope that came with Eli. I dried the stubborn tear that had forced its way out of my eye and down my cheek.

"Dad's going to be fine, Mama," Eli assured me, rubbing on my bad knee.

"That's what I'm praying for, baby."

Calvin and Azura were in there longer than I thought they would be. Ebony looked at him with questions written all over her face.

"We had a good talk," he said, sitting next to her.

"It's time for us now, Mama," Eli said, pulling me up to my feet.

"I was wondering when I was going to see you, Eli," Nelson said as we approached his bed.

"I got here as fast as I could, Dad."

"Where have you been all day, Evelyn?" he asked me.

"Everybody wanted to make sure you're doing okay so we had to take turns," I answered. "Have we tired you out too much?"

"No, honey, I'm glad they all are here. The family should be together."

"That means you too, Dad," Eli added, laying his hand on top of Nelson's.

"I don't want you here to work any miracle on me, Elijah Winters," Nelson said, snatching his hand away, "I've made my peace with my maker and this is in his hands."

"Don't lay here and give up, honey bear, your life isn't over. There's a lot more for us to do together," I begged him.

"Dad, you can walk out of here if you want. Let me touch you."

"No, son. When you were fifteen years old you asked me to allow you to live your life in the way that you were compelled, I wasn't as understanding as I should have been, I ask your forgiveness on that, and now you have to allow me that same courtesy."

"No, Nelson, your family is out there in pain, hurting over you being in here. Don't leave them like that. Don't leave me like that," I pleaded.

"Evelyn, you are the love of my life, but I can't live forever. None of us can. I couldn't live without you but you can live without me. There is more left for you here."

"That's not for you to say, it's not just your life," I said with anger mixing in my sadness.

"Why don't you take some more time to think about it?" Eli asked as if they were having a rational conversation."

"I know I fell short sometimes but I always loved you, Eli, and I believe that you are the best part of me and I'm satisfied with that."

"Don't listen to him, baby. Do something, don't let him die," I said in a hushed scream.

Eli stood there torn between us, not knowing what to do, and then Nelson pushed the button for help that hung on a cord inside the bed. A nurse rushed into the room after only a few seconds had passed.

"Do you need something, Mr. Winters?" she asked attentively.

"I'm tired now," he told her, "I've had enough visitors for

today."

"All right, sir" she said as she turned to guide us out. "I'm sorry but he needs to rest right now."

Eli rushed out of Nelson's room; I lingered there searching for a way to reverse the course of this day. I had to get Nelson to snap out of his 'right to die' funk and decide that he wants to live but how could I do that if he kept me out of his room. This isn't how we do things. He is as much of a fighter as I am; I know that because we had some confrontations over the years where both of us had balled fists we barely held back from throwing.

Something inside me said "don't leave," as I walked with slow small steps toward the door out of the ICU. I glanced at Eli who stood at the door waiting for me. His chest heaved as he gasped for air as if he had just finished a race and his face was sad and covered with tears.

"I'm sorry, Mama," he said, opening the door.

"Don't be," I said.

We crossed the hallway back over to the waiting room.

"How did it go?" Ebony asked anxiously, rushing over to me and Eli.

"Not so good," I replied, "Your daddy said he was tired and wanted to rest, then the nurse ushered us out."

"Eli needs to go back in there and handle his business, this has gone on long enough, my nerves are shot to hell and back," she insisted.

"It's not that simple, Ebony. You daddy doesn't want to be bothered," I said helplessly.

"He's sick; he doesn't know what he wants, Mama. Why didn't you do something, Eli? I know you could have healed him, you just didn't want to. You're punishing him for not loving you," Ebony screamed.

"Hush up that mess, child, Eli isn't God, it's not his decision to make," I scolded.

"You need to calm down, babe," Calvin said, coming over to console Ebony. "You're getting loud; there are other people up here going through their own problems."

"I'm sorry for them but my daddy is in there and he doesn't have to be. Eli can go in there and take care of him and then we can all go home."

Elise rushed over to us, "Stop it, Ebony," she said, "That's not fair."

Then Erica joined us, "Let's go sit down," she said sternly, "You're upsetting everybody in here including your girls."

At that point Ebony caved in from the onslaught of fear, hurt, anger, and frustration that we were all battling against and collapsed. Calvin carried her over to the section of the waiting room that we had taken possession of. Amber and Azura tried to comfort her with the touch of their hands. Amber rubbed her across her back and Azura held one hand. Ebony's head knocked alongside Calvin's arm as if she were delirious. Drew and D.J. sat in the row of chairs that turned on the other side of the corner in the room with the same posture; both of them leaned over clasped hands looking at the floor. Elise had her arm around Eli speaking so softly to him that I couldn't hear, and Erica sat at my right hand with her back straight as an arrow ready to take on whatever adversary that came in our way.

That's the way we were when Dr. Sherman walked into the waiting area. I saw him coming towards me and it was if he moved in slow motion. He kneeled down in front of me, put his hand on my bad knee, and started to speak.

"Mrs. Winters, Mr. Winters went into respiratory arrest, we did everything we could short of artificial ventilation which he requested not be used if he were to stop breathing. I'm very sorry but we weren't able to resuscitate him."

The only response I could muster was to nod my head.

Erica stepped in and asked, "When did he make this request,

Dr. Sherman?"

"He made the request and signed the forms when he was brought into the emergency room," he answered gently as he stood. "Is there anything I can do for you?"

"No, thank you," I said.

Eli jumped up and ran out of the room and Drew and D.J. went after him.

"He's never been here when we needed him," Ebony said bitterly.

"Eli wasn't born to serve us or to be genie to grant all of our wishes. He was a blessing to our family. He has never asked anything of us, and you have never given him anything. Why do you think you have the right to expect so much from him?" I said, rising to my feet. "Dr. Sherman, I would like to see my husband."

"Certainly," he said, leading the way into the RICU.

Erica was close behind but at the entrance I stopped and told her, "I'll be all right, baby, I want some time with him by myself."

"Okay, Mama," she said, backing away.

Dr. Sherman opened the door of room 1004 for me and closed it behind me. I stood at the side of the bed for a minute before I lowered the rail and climbed in with Nelson. The warmth from his body had been captured under the blankets. I kissed his lips and then his cheek, but they didn't feel the same. The life in him was gone. His face was different too, all the tension and stress that had been there for so many years was gone. He had finally relaxed. He was at peace.

I laid there for another ten minutes wondering how I could I make myself accept this, and how could I continue to live my life without the man I had spent more than fifty years with, more than two-thirds of all my days. If only it was my grief I could manage, except I had to deal with the grief of my children. "Lord, please help me," I prayed as I slid out of the bed.

***

Erica was with me through all the arrangements at the funeral home and she and Elise prepared the program for the service. Sitting on the second row of the pew felt like an out-of-body experience. Ebony cried through the whole thing like a baby, it was expected and fitting because she had always been Nelson's baby. I thanked God for Calvin; he was the only thing standing between her and the brink of a breakdown. She had chosen this moment to purge herself of all the hurt, pain, and disappointment she had suffered in her life.

I walked up the aisle behind Nelson's casket as it rolled to the back of the church hiding my emotions behind the dark glasses from the rows of well-wishers standing on both sides. I sat up front with the driver of the limousine so I could be closer to Nelson, Elise and Eli sat behind me in silence. I watched the faces inside of the cars when we passed, some showing sympathy and some agitation as we slowly navigated through the traffic. At the cemetery we marched in single-file up into the tent. I took a seat. My mind flashed back to the first time I met Nelson.

He looked too good with his fresh trimmed big afro and sideburns. I liked his style in the high-waist bell bottoms and platform shoes. When he told me his name and asked what was mine it was all over. The fact that he loved to spend money on me was the icing on the cake. On that day I just wanted to have some fun, I would never have guessed that we would have ended up getting married, and I surely never envisioned that I would be sitting at his gravesite. The years had gone by so quickly.

Our children took turns dropping a flower down in the plot after he was lowered. Then it was time to leave. Elise and Eli both pulled on my arms to lift me from my chair.

"You both go on ahead, I'll be there in a minute," I said, resisting their tugging.

I sat there wondering how to finish it, how to close this chapter. I wanted the happy ending and this wasn't it. How could it all be over so abruptly? I couldn't stand the site of the open hole before me so I close my eyes. I felt someone sit beside me but I kept my eyes closed. A smooth breeze blew and I smelled the familiar perfume of my friend.

"I couldn't stay away, Evie, not anymore," Macey said.

"I've missed you," I said without opening my eyes.

"I'm so sorry Evie, please forgive me. I was wrong."

"There's nothing to forgive. I knew that under the circumstances you couldn't understand my position. What I didn't understand is how you let it come between our friendship," I said, taking off my glasses to see her face.

"I was under so much pressure. When we got through the rough patch, I wanted to clear the air with you but you never reached out."

"I thought you were still mad at me."

"No, Evie, I was ashamed of the way I acted. You didn't owe me anything. I didn't know how to make it right."

"You're my sister, Macey, I understood why you asked and I didn't hold it against you."

"What can I do? I feel so bad."

"You can stay with me."

"I'm here and I won't leave until you tell me to."

"Where's Richard?"

"I lost him four years ago."

"I didn't know, Macey, I would have come."

"I know you would have. We were living with Martin in Dallas. I didn't put an announcement in the Nashville paper. I've been back in our house for a year now."

"Let's go, I'm sure they're all tired and ready to eat."

"Okay, old woman, take my arm and lean on me," she said, sticking out her elbow.

***

Even though Nelson spent the majority of his time sitting out in the yard, the house seemed so empty without him. I was driving myself crazy staring out at his spot under the tree, so much so that there were days when I actually conjured up his image and he sat out there all day. If it weren't for Macey getting me out of the house every Saturday I probably would have lost touch with reality. Life had gone back to its normal rhythm for the rest of the family.

"I need to do something with myself, Macey. I'm stuck in the moment and I don't know how to move forward. Yesterday I spent the whole day without speaking a word. I didn't go anywhere, no one called me, and I didn't call anyone. I wasn't expected anywhere and nobody missed me. At least if I were still working I would serve some purpose."

"You're in transition, Evie, it's a process and it takes time."

"I don't want to live like that. It makes me feel like I died too."

"Don't get yourself worked up, that will only make you feel worse. You're alive, it's just a different life than the one you had before. I took a long cruise after Richard passed. When I came home I had adapted to being alone."

"Do I need to remind you that my parents went on a cruise and I never saw or heard from them again?"

"I didn't know that. It must have been after Richard first got sick. I'm sorry. Still, it would do you some good to get away for a while. You can work on the book you always said you were going to write."

"We had planned to go to New York after Christmas to see Eli sworn in as Secretary-General of the United Nations."

"You don't have to wait for that, go now. You can visit with Elise and see what it's like to spend Thanksgiving and Christmas in the big city. Take the AirTrain so you can see something on the way."

"That's a good idea. I'm going to call Elise, I'm not tied to Nashville, I'm leaving as soon as I can get packed."

23

The AirTrain ran above the tracks at 120 miles per hour held by a magnetic field. I stared out of the window ignoring the strain on my eyes as I tried to focus. I wanted to see all I could see on this trip, from the empty fields of grass to the traffic logged towns all along the way. I knew from experience that the years fly by when you're not looking. Who would have thought that ten years had gone by since I had been out of Nashville? The last time was when Eli ran in the Boston Marathon in 2019. I was determined that for the rest of my years I was going to pay close attention to each day. Elise was going to pick me up at the station in Manhattan. Nelson had tried to convince her to move to New Jersey and commute, it would save a ton of money, but she's stuck in ways just like he was.

The depot was packed with people bustling in every direction. When I stepped off the train I felt like I was taken up by a human tsunami. I moved sideways against the surge trying to get nearer to the shops that lined the station. I made it to the refuge of an inner door when I felt my wrist phone vibrate. It was Elise.

"There's a Jamaican coffee shop at gate C. I'll be waiting for you there," she said, smiling.

I nodded and rejoined the flow of people to the next gate.

"Hello sweetheart," I said as she grabbed my elbow and moved me through the coffee shop to the other exit."

"Hey Mama, I'm glad you're here."

"I'm happy to be here," I said as she steered me into a waiting taxi.

I stared out the right passenger window the whole time

fascinated by the controlled chaos that was New York City.

"Somebody's living the life," I murmured on the elevator of her posh building as it rose higher.

"They should be after working thirty years," she replied as we got off.

"Are you that old, child?" I asked, teasing her.

"If I am, what about my mama?" she laughed.

Elise showed me to the guestroom and I unpacked while she stir-fried some vegetables with chicken. We took our plates to her great room and sat down on the sofa to relax. She turned on CNN and to my surprise they were running a segment about Eli on the program.

"That boy did everything he set out to do," I said in amazement.

"He's all that and some extra. Eli is a heavyweight, Mama, not just in the U.S but around the world. A lot of people are counting on him to be a peace broker and a champion for the under-classes. The United Nations has been given expanded power and influence to produce results through a unified effort around the globe, and Eli will soon be the head-nigga-in-charge."

"I wonder if we can get there to hear his speech when he is inaugurated," I asked.

"There's so much security around the United Nations Headquarters that you couldn't get near him if you tried."

"When's the last time you talked to him?" I asked when his segment ended.

"About a week ago, he was busy preparing his speech."

"I texted him on his private line that I was coming before I left, I didn't get a response."

"You'll probably hear from him tomorrow, he's got a lot on his plate," she said, taking our dishes into the kitchen.

The next day Elise took me on a tour of New York. I hadn't been in the city for years and it was like visiting some place I had never been. She treated me to some much needed retail therapy; a woman never loses her taste for quality shoes and designer bags. One thing I couldn't get over was how many newspapers and magazines had pictures of Elijah Newman on the front.

Elise picked up some Chinese take-out for me since she was going out for the evening with friends. I was tired from being on my feet all day and I wanted to go to bed early. The next morning my son would be the fourteenth Secretary General of the United Nations.

***

With my cup of coffee in one hand and the TV remote in the other I sat in front of the TV fully dressed as if I were seated in attendance among the other dignitaries to witness the inauguration. The anchor of the pre-swearing-in-ceremony commentary concluded his program alluding to numerous threats that had been received to prevent Elijah Newman from taking office. I was stunned and starting to feel alarmed when the screen broke away to Eli, suited-up with more poise than Sidney Poitier, moving with the swag of Barack Obama through the parted sea of security in the auditorium into the circled room. Interpreters filled the room speaking quietly into small microphones poised at their lips.

"Hurry up, Elise," I yelled, "Its beginning."

Flashing lights of a thousand cameras created a glare on the TV screen as I strained to see him. When he approached the podium he placed his hand over a book laying there, Elise snatched the remote and turned the volume up.

A woman walks over to the podium and with a thick accent said, "I would like you, Mr. Elijah Newman to repeat after me the oath of office."

He answered her prompts saying, *"I solemnly swear to exercise in all loyalty, discretion and conscience the functions entrusted to me as Secretary-General of the United Nations, to discharge these functions and regulate my conduct with the interests of the United Nations only in view, and not to seek or accept instructions in regard to the performance of my duties from any Government or other authority external to the Organization."*

When he finishes the room explodes with applause that falls into a dignified silence while he shook the hands of all the persons seated on the stage. He returned to the podium for his address.

"Good morning, Mr. President of the General Assembly, Distinguished Heads of State, Excellencies, Honorable Ministers, Colleagues, and Ladies and Gentlemen. This is the 75th anniversary of the UN General Assembly; it is time for the advent of fundamental changes. The reform agenda with unity of purpose being the following mission will mark a new epoch in peace and resolution for the world. Twenty-five years ago Secretary-General Kofi Annan in his resignation speech spoke of three major issues confronting the world today, "an unjust economy, world disorder, and widespread contempt for human rights and the rule of law," which he concluded had worsened during his tenure in office. I stand before you today with the same assessment as I take this office but I vow that it will not conclude with those circumstances.

We will work harmoniously with a revival of Kofi Annan's Grand Strategy in a combination of diplomatic, economic, military and political factors. We are now officially and technically the United Nations acting on behalf of all constituents in a democratic forum. Today, I issue a Call to Action to address inequalities and unemployment. We have made great strides in technology and have created robots and machines to perform countless skills, but we must remain cognizant that in this progress we have eliminated the means of which millions earn a living. Now we must ask ourselves where our loyalties lie and where is our sense of obligation to mankind. The Global Compact initiative will be altered to promote corporate social responsibility. The consumers of global resources will become the protectors of the world's reserves and assets.

Violence is intolerance in its purest form! History has taught us that it only leads us down a path to our own destruction. The UN Security Council will be enlarged to include thirty-one members for a diverse union to maintain international peace and security. Military action will be the last option for the resolution of aggression and any threats to world peace. I thank the UN Security Council for their vote of confidence and I will do everything within my power to accomplish all the objectives that have been set forth in the overall purpose for the United Nations, to bring all nations of the world together to work for peace and development, based on the principles of justice, human dignity and the well-being of all people.

Applause fills the room and the CNN anchors return to their commentary. Elise turns down the volume and throws her hands up in the air.

"Wow, Mama, that's all I can say. Eli is the baddest thing out there. Go on, baby brother, do your thing."

"It was truly impressive, but he was talking about serious changes, the people who hold all the cards like everything the way it is. They didn't get where they are doing the right thing. Eli is a sheep among wolves."

"I wouldn't worry about him. He knows what he's doing. He told you he was going to be right where he is twenty years ago."

I spent the rest of the day watching replays of the inauguration. The next day after Elise went to work they announced that Eli had been nominated for the Nobel Prize in Economic Sciences. I was thrilled to my bones. I called Elise at work to give her the news.

"Guess what the latest is?" I said, trying to appear calm.

"No, Mama, you guess," she answered, appearing pissed off.

"What is it, what happened?" I asked with growing concern.

I was in a conference today and during the course of the discussion the blame for the uncertainty in the markets was put on Eli Newman and his radical policies. They were ragging on him so bad I was about to tell them that he was my brother and start knocking in some heads."

"Oh no, Elise. That's what Eli warned us about."

"I was cool, I stopped short, but I did say that I support the measures he proposed to bring about equity and fairness in compensation for more workers."

"I'm sure that went over well in a room full of investment bankers making damn near seven figures or higher."

"The hell it did, I hadn't been back in my office for an hour when the vice president of the firm came in and asked for my resignation. I couldn't believe it. I've been at this firm more than twenty-five years."

"Are you going to fight it?"

"No, Mama, I'm going out and start my own company. If they don't think any more of me and the years I've put into this firm, not to mention the money I've made for them, then it's time for me to go."

"I'm sorry about that, sweetheart. Eli said connections to him would be a problem."

"I know that, but I never thought it would cost me my job. Anyway, don't tell him, I'm just venting. This forces me to do something I should have done a long time ago."

***

I spent six weeks in New York, half of the time I was a captive of the round-the-clock news network, doing what I always fussed at Nelson about, and the other half I was writing in my journal. Elise was busy working around the clock on her new venture and I was ready to go back home to Nashville. I really wanted to have some quality time with Eli before I left but it didn't look like that was going to happen, we had spoken for only brief moments over my notebook. I was packing my suitcase when the song for Eli played on my phone.

"Hello, baby," I said, staring into the screen searching for any uncertainty in his eyes.

"Hello, Mama, there's a car downstairs waiting to pick you and Elise up for dinner," he said.

"Elise is having a late meeting with her new staff but I'm available."

"Well, come on, I can catch Elise another day. I can't let my mama leave town without breaking bread one time," he said, smiling.

I pulled a sweater dress and a pair of boots back out of the suitcase to change into, hurried into the bathroom and freshened up the best I could in three minutes. In record time I stood at the elevator pushing the down button nonstop with my hat pulled over my head and my coat half buttoned. I hadn't even left Elise a note. I would have to call her later. The speculations on the news had me on edge, I felt like I was losing Eli to the world and I might never see him again.

There was a tall, slim, attractive woman dressed in a dark pantsuit waiting by a limousine when I exited the building.

"Hello," she said pleasantly as she opened the car door.

I climbed in and the luxury of it reminded me of the time we were in Boston and Eli won the marathon. There was no small talk inside from the driver or the attractive woman, the windows were darkly tinted, and we rode to our destination in silence. When the limo came to a stop I half expected them to throw a bag over my head to keep me from knowing the location where my own son was living.

We walked through the lobby back to a private elevator. The woman entered in a code and a few seconds later the door open. I stepped inside but she remained outside. When the door opened, Eli was standing there.

"Mama," he said, wrapping his arms around me, "I'm very sorry that I haven't been able to get over there and see you earlier.

You wouldn't believe the challenges I'm having right now and I don't want your safety or security compromised in any way."

"I understand that, son," I said, holding his arm and following him into a dining room.

On the table there was a platter of salmon, wild rice, and asparagus. I sat down and Eli picked up a plate and served me. He poured me a tall glass of ice water and a hot cup of tea. He remembered I liked to have both during the winter.

"I'm not here to add to your load," I said, taking a sip of water. "Of course I wanted to see you sworn in but more than that I needed to distance myself from my own life so I could learn to be a single woman at this point in the game."

"I feel bad that I can't be there for you in Nashville. I didn't want you to be alone but Dad insisted I let him go."

"I took care of you, boy. I can take care of myself. It's you I'm worried about; I don't want you to put yourself in any danger pressing for things to change too fast."

"The problems are urgent, Mama, how long can a starving man wait to eat?"

"You may need to slow your roll; fundamental change isn't easy or fast. You're a long distance runner, pace yourself."

"Not in this race, it's got to be a sprint to get past the ones who intend to stand in the way of progress. They only want to keep filling their pockets. The philosophy of giving to those who have so they can create opportunities has been nothing but a swindle to rob governments, and people are the government."

"If money is power, what can you do?"

"We have a lot to learn from the past, the great structures of the world like the Pyramids and the Taj Mahal were built on strong foundations below them and they are still standing. You can't build anything from the top down; it has to be from the bottom up. I have a plan I've worked on and it will be announced next week."

"Do you ever put down your work for a while and enjoy

yourself?" I asked sincerely. "There is such a thing as fun. I want you to have a life of your own and be happy, maybe even settle down and have a family."

"I knew what my mission was for as long as I can remember and I have to fulfill my purpose on this earth."

"I wish there was more balance in your life, not only living from one battle to another."

"Mama, the world will fight the messengers for years to come, there will be others."

"You're my baby and I want to protect you from the madness."

"I'm doing what I want to do, what I need to do, and I'm happy doing it. I want you to know that you were a great mother to me and I'm thankful for that."

My anxiety ebbed with those words and I let my spine relax against the back of my chair while Eli took our plates into the kitchen to re-warm them in the microwave oven. When he came back to the table the serious talk was over. We laughed and reminisced about the family vacations we had taken. After we ate, he took me out on his terrace and we enjoyed the spectacular view of Manhattan until the cold filtered its way through the soft cashmere of my new coat. I could feel that time for our visit was growing short and I didn't want to leave him. There was no way he could ever come back home and be my child again. Even when the girls grew up and left, I never felt like the connection was going to be lost.

I hesitated at the door and said, "I hear so many things and I can't help worrying about you and thinking that somebody will try to hurt you."

"Don't worry about me, Mama, because I won't die, I promise you that."

We walked through the apartment to the elevator. I hugged my son and kissed his face as if it was my last opportunity. He pushed a code and the door opened. I held his hand until the closing door approached it and then our visit was over. The woman was waiting for me when the elevator opened and she led me back out to the waiting limo. We rode back to Elise's in silence just like before. When the car stopped she opened the door and I stepped out.

I was glad I had beaten Elise back home; I didn't feel like discussing the events of my evening. When she got in I had resumed packing my things for my early flight.

24

Being back home was strange but consoling, there were moments when I expected Nelson to walk in the door and ask me for a beer. The silver lining in his passing was that it brought Ebony and Calvin back together. They planned to renew their vows on Friday evening, Valentine's Day, at the church where the children were all baptized. Amber and Azura were going to be her bridesmaids. We're having a small reception back here at the house with family and a few friends. Eli is out of the country and won't be able to make it. He sent them tickets to go back to the Bahamas for their thirtieth anniversary in September.

Macey sat next to me at the church before the ceremony while soft music played in the background. Looking at the flowers, I reflected back on their first wedding day when Nelson was by my side, the pure blue sky, the fresh salt air, and the crystal clear water that rolled up on the beach. I could almost hear his voice speaking to me when the music abruptly changed and "Here comes the Bride" began to play. The pastor moved to the center of the aisle and motioned for us to stand. We all faced the rear and then the double doors opened.

The girls wore rose colored dresses. Amber and Drew walked up the aisle first, next it was Azura and D.J., and then it was Ebony and Calvin. She looked radiant in an elegant form fitting gown colored in the palest of pinks.

"Ain't love a beautiful thing, Evie," Macey said, admiring Calvin and Ebony as they strolled passed us.

"It sure is," I answered, taking in the sight of my family assembled there in front of me.

We had lived so much life together over the years and now my grandbabies were all grown up and on their own. The pastor motioned for the congregation to take our seats as he started the ceremony. Hearing the vows and those two professing their love pulled the top off my contained emotions and I made no effort to hold back my tears of joy. When my eyes burned I suspected there were tears of sadness flowing with the others.

Erica had organized the reception at the house; the decorations and the food were all on point as usual. Macey and I didn't have to lift a finger and everybody had a great time. The newly re-weds left early to spend the rest of the weekend at the Ritz-Carlton downtown. D.J. eased away with his girlfriend and I would bet my last two dollars that he would be the next one in the family to jump the broom. Elise was running with Amber and Azura, they were going to take their aunt out for a night of clubbing.

"Are you sure you can hang?" Drew joked as they grabbed their coats.

"Don't worry about me, brother," Elise laughed, "I've been hanging a lot longer than they have. Trust and believe I'll be the last one standing. While they're throwing back shots of tequila I'll be downing Monster energy drinks."

"If you all need a designated driver I'm available," Macey teased, "I'm ready to prowl too."

"Uh-uh," I said, "They'd check her ID and turn you all away. I'm sure there's a law against old women her age trying to get hooked up."

We sat there talking some more while Erica cleaned up.

"Have you talked to Eli lately?" Drew asked. "I caught the press conference about his announcement in England. It blew my mind."

I knew what he was talking about and it had me stressed out completely. I knew there were going to be repercussions.

"What did he propose, I missed it," Macey said, interested.

"He initiated a plan for worldwide economic redevelopment that proposes changes to the distribution of wealth. It advocates a one-time 33 percent tax on personal assets above $100 million. It passed unanimously in the United Nations Assembly and several countries are adopting the measure."

"That's deep and over-the-top," Macey exclaimed. "I like it, every nation represented in the world needs resources to better the quality of life for the working class."

"My concern is that several powerful leaders are jealous of his influence, and the global business community wants to condemn him. I wish I had a dollar for every time they have called him a communist and socialist," I said.

"Don't sweat it, Mom," Drew said confidently, "Eli has a sixth sense that's out of this world. He'll always be one step ahead of them."

"I have to believe that, otherwise I would have to go armed and sit in front of his door."

"Okay, Mama, your kitchen has been restored to its original condition," Erica said, coming into the den to join us. "Now I'm going to take my husband home and maybe he can refresh my memory about the day we got married."

"I'd be happy to," Drew said, standing up wrapping her arm inside of his."

"Do you need anything else before I go?" Erica asked.

"No sweetheart, I've got my running buddy here," I said, as she leaned over to give me a hug.

When I heard the door shut and Erica lock the bolt I reached on the end table to write in my journal and Macey starting surfing channels on the TV.

"There's nothing worth watching on this thing," she said, disgusted. "What are you working on in that fat book so intently?"

"It's the journal you suggested I start to write in thirty years ago."

"Oh my goodness, Evie, that's got to have some interesting stuff in it."

"It's my family bible," I said, flipping through the pages.

"Let me take a look at that," she said, reaching out her hands.

I handed it to her and watched with apprehension as she read page after page.

"I love it, girlfriend, it's real, from the heart. I think you should publish it. I can be your editor and we can have this done in no time," Macey said. "Now I'm going to bed, I'm so tired I can't even see straight."

"Go on and get your rest, old woman, but you probably won't be able to see any straighter in the morning," I joked.

"Have mercy, Lord, I know that's the truth," she said, leaving the room.

I ruffled through the pages of my journal thinking about how I could form it into a book, but Eli was still on my mind and I needed to talk to him. I punched in the number on my remote that he said I could use in emergencies and as far as I was concerned this was an emergency. Dots and dashes ran across the TV screen and then he answered.

"Hey, Mama, what's going on?" he said, looking animated.

"I called to see what's going on with you," I said. "You look like you just won the Nobel Prize again. Tell me."

"I do have great news as a matter of fact; my proposal has been approved by seventy-two sovereign nations, including the largest economies, China, US, India, Japan, and Brazil. The codicil for elimination of impure energy sources was a boon. I'm walking in the clouds right now. Progress is really being made. Finally the needs of those who have less will be addressed."

"I'm happy for you, Eli, but Drew was telling me that there have been some serious threats against members of the Assembly."

"Anytime you try to accomplish anything meaningful there

are going to be angry people. I don't give that any consideration or I couldn't do my job."

"Promise me you'll be careful and cautious at all times."

"Mama, I've already promised you that I won't die."

I blew him a kiss with both hands and he blew one back to me.

***

One month after Ebony's re-wedding, Macey and I were sitting in the Jamaican coffee shop working on the book when a news bulletin flashed up on the screen. There had been an assassination attempt on the United Nations General Assembly members in route to a conference in Russia from Japan by a ground to air missal over North Korea. The plane caught fire but made an emergency landing in China. It was undoubtedly a miracle that the plane did not explode and there were only 57 casualties among the 293 passengers.

My mouth hung open as wide as my eyes, Eli was on that flight. The victims' names were not going to be released until their next of kin had been notified.

"Come on, let's get you home," Macey said, pulling me up from the chair by my arm.

My legs felt like lead as I labored on every step out of the coffee shop and into the car. Macey opened the rear door of the driver's side to help me in. My body collapsed against the cushion upholstery and rolled down until I was lying in the crease between the back support and the seat. I lie there in a daze not different from the day when the doctors informed me I was pregnant with Eli. Similar questions from that day flooded my thoughts. What was the fate of this life God had blessed me with?

"Are you all right back there, sister?" Macey asked as she adjusted the rearview mirror to keep an eye on me.

"He said he wouldn't die," I told her.

"You believed the other things he said to you and you can

believe that," she said without any hesitation.

Macey drove slowly as if I was a vase of fresh flowers she didn't want to spill over. She sat with me all night as I scoured every news channel like a hungry mother bear searching for food. When daylight came I wanted to make her go home and get a break but I need her there to field the phone calls from the kids. I couldn't talk to them; I didn't have any answers for myself.

It was torture over the next week, we never received a word, and Eli never listed us as his next of kin. As far as anyone knew he was an orphan. I did learn from the news that he was not listed among the casualties. The puzzling thing was that he was also not listed among the survivors and no one could remember if he had boarded the plane in Japan or not. To further add to my present state of purgatory he wasn't answering the private number he had given to me to use for emergencies and they were referring to him as missing. Not knowing where he was or if he was safe was unadulterated agony. Each day I held onto my sanity gripping the microphone as I dictated my book into the computer for Macey to edit.

My suspense ended on Easter Sunday morning after a bouquet of lilies was delivered to the house. I couldn't find a note as I placed the flowers carefully in the living room. Then the phone rang. I walked into the den and saw Eli's face in the corner of the TV screen. I pushed the phone button on the remote.

"Eli, where are you," I cried out, "I've been on pins and needles worrying about you."

"I'm fine, Mama, I wanted you to know that I kept my promise to you."

"When can you come home, I want to see you in person."

"I don't know about that, it might be a very long time."

"What about your job, do they know where you are?"

"That's not important. The objectives I was sent here to achieve have been put into action and they can't be undone."

"Since it's all done, you can home, leave all the danger and threats behind and live your life. Find a wife, have some children, and become an old stubborn man like your daddy."

"It doesn't matter to me whether I will become an old man or not. My purpose has been fulfilled, so don't grieve for the rest. Be sure you know that I will never leave you."

"Okay, baby, that's good enough. I love you Eli."

"I love you too, Mama, and it's Elijah Newman Winters. Till we meet again."

The picture of my son on the screen collapsed to the center into a tiny small silver dot like a star far off in the night sky. The heaviness of anguish had been lifted. On this morning I found out my child was alive. It was time to rejoice.

Erica picked me up for church at 9:45 and if she would have looked close into my face she would have seen pure happiness oozing from my pores. Once we were seated in our regular pew, I gave up trying to "hold my mule" as my grandmother would say as I swayed to my own rhythm. The choir hadn't started to sing yet but I didn't need any music to make me dance. When the pastor opened the service for us to give praise for the resurrection, I jumped to my feet and shouted. I swung my arms in praise, thanking God for not only Jesus' resurrection, but for all the resurrections in my life. I tapped my feet and clapped my hands because joy had come in the morning, Hallelujah.

Final Chapter

I got up every morning ready to sit in front of my laptop. When I was writing I could feel my blood flowing, I was alive again. My novel was an unexpected success, both popular and critically acclaimed even though it was all non-fiction. Macey and I traveled all across the country for book signings and speaking engagements on the talk-circuit. There was even a feeler out from one motion picture studio interested in purchasing the movie rights. I wouldn't have bet two nickels I would be sitting where I am today.

"For the Pulitzer Prize in fiction, *Caught up in Elijah's Whirlwind* by Evelyn Winters is our winner. It's a story of a personal and professional journey of a young man who feels he's called to lead a revival of the Poor Peoples Campaign. Mrs. Winters Please come up."

I hear the applause and I love the feeling. It's the confirmation that maybe I did something right in my life. Macey helps me to my feet, these knees of mine are crying out loud, and I make my way up to the podium to accept my award. I smile for the camera, praying that my partials are straight and in place. I graciously accept the award and there is a standing ovation. I'm humbled but I smile and soak it all in.

Finding my way back to my seat is tricky with the glare from the camera flash blocking my vision.

"I'm so happy for you, Evie," Macey says, guiding me back down in the chair.

"Not bad for an eighty year old woman, emphasis on old," I say.

"Now what are you going to do with yourself?" she asks.

I look up at the ceiling and say, "Something, who knows, girlfriend, it's not over yet."

www.ingramcontent.com/pod-product-compliance
Lightning Source LLC
Chambersburg PA
CBHW070428120726
47910CB00003B/695